Emily [barcode obscured] Cheryl Arguile. She is th[obscured] [obscured]er mystery series, and [obscured] s as Sarah Temple and Yo[obscured] Cheryl Lanham. She lives in Southern California.

[obscured] Brightwell's website at
RO[obscured] ybrightwell.com

En[obscured]
www.ro[obscured]

Mrs Jeffries on the Ball

Emily Brightwell

Constable • London

CONSTABLE

First published in the US in 1994 by The Berkley Publishing Group,
an imprint of Penguin Group (USA) Inc.

This edition published in Great Britain in 2014 by Constable

Text copyright © Cheryl Arguile, 1996

The moral right of the author has been asserted.

A CIP catalogue record for this book
is available from the British Library.

ISBN 978-1-47210-887-6 (paperback)
ISBN 978-1-47210-899-9 (ebook)

Typeset in Bembo by TW Typesetting, Plymouth, Devon
Printed and bound by CPI Group (UK) Ltd, Croydon, CR0 4YY

Constable
is an imprint of
Constable & Robinson Ltd
100 Victoria Embankment
London EC4Y 0DY

An Hachette UK Company
www.hachette.co.uk

www.constablerobinson.com

CHAPTER ONE

THE WOMAN WAS no better than a common streetwalker!

Hannah Greenwood glared at the tall blonde following the butler through the double doors. Her lip curled in disgust as she watched the odious creature make her way toward the centre of activity. Rowena Stanwick. The cow. With her head held high and her long, slender back ramrod straight, she entered the Marlow drawing room as though she were the queen herself.

Hannah snorted derisively, ignoring the startled expression on the face of Mrs Putnam, who was sitting in the chair next to her, as she glared at the Stanwick woman. The tart might have the rest of them fooled, she thought, but she doesn't pull the wool over my eyes. All of her pretentious airs and fancy clothes won't protect her one whit, not when I'm through with her. I'll make her pay for what she's done. Really pay.

'I'm so dreadfully sorry to be late,' Rowena apologized to the group at large. Dressed in a dark red afternoon gown that contrasted beautifully with her colouring, she moved gracefully to the velvet settee in the middle of a semicircle of chairs placed in front of the marble fireplace. 'Exciting as Her Majesty's Jubilee celebration might be, it does make for an extraordinary amount of traffic. It took us ages to get down Regent Street. The streets were mobbed, absolutely mobbed.'

'That's quite all right,' Dr Oxton Sloan assured her. 'We've only just started. Do sit down and catch your breath.'

Sloan, the president of the Hyde Park Literary Circle, waited until the latecomer settled next to Shelby Locke. He cleared his throat and called for attention. 'The Hyde Park Literary Circle will now come to order,' he announced. Wiping his high, balding forehead, he asked Mr Warburton, the secretary, to call the roll.

Sloan sat down behind the table, turning his back slightly so he had a good view of the membership. As the first names were called, his eyes narrowed assessingly.

'Mr and Mrs Horace Putnam.'

Sloan glanced at the middle-aged couple seated to his left. Mrs Putnam, grey-haired and round as a barrel, was listening intently to the roll call. Her husband, on the other hand, appeared to be asleep. He immediately discounted them. They weren't serious about literature. They were only here for social reasons. Neither of them would know a decent verse from doggerel.

'Miss Lucinda Marlow.'

He studied her with more interest. She certainly was a fetching creature with all that lovely dark brown hair and those big hazel eyes. Sloan frowned. He was forgetting himself; Lucinda Marlow could be a danger to him, and he'd best remember that. She was the one who'd started the group. Unlike many females of his acquaintance, she actually read books. Worse, the poem she had written and read to the circle at their last meeting hadn't been half-bad. Not up to his standards, of course, but acceptable, nonetheless.

'Mr Shelby Locke.'

Sloan gritted his teeth as he stared at the tall, auburn-haired man sitting beside Rowena Stanwick. Blast. Now, there was real trouble. Locke actually had brains. Even worse, he was well read. The man could spout Shakespeare at the drop of a hat. He watched as Locke turned to gaze adoringly at Mrs Stanwick. A slow, crafty smile crossed Sloan's thin face. Perhaps Mr Locke wouldn't be much of a competitor after all, he told himself. The fool was so besotted with the fair Rowena, he probably couldn't write a decent verse if his life depended on it. No doubt they'd all be treated to some ridiculous maudlin romantic drivel about the Queen and Prince Albert's courtship. If the fool managed to turn in anything at all.

'Mrs Hannah Greenwood.'

He glanced at the widow Greenwood, and his heart almost stopped. She was looking straight at him. Sloan shifted uneasily. The expression on her face was strange. He didn't like it one whit. Her thin

3

mouth curved upward in a sly, mirthless smile, and her eyes gleamed with cold malevolence. He suddenly remembered her cryptic comments from their last meeting, and panic, like bile, rose in his throat. Surely she didn't know. She couldn't know. It was impossible. He'd been far too careful. Sloan immediately pushed the troublesome Mrs Greenwood from his mind.

'Mrs Lester Hiatt, Miss Cecilia Mansfield, and Lady Cannonberry.' Warburton's voice droned on as he called the rest of the roll.

Sloan didn't even bother to glance at these people as their names were called. None of them were important. But he did watch the secretary carefully. Edgar Warburton was an unknown. He'd been a member of their group for only a little over a month. The man was such a dreadful snob it had been difficult for Sloan to ascertain precisely how much he actually knew about literature. Warburton seemed to deem it a favour even to speak to you. He'd bear watching as well. Sloan didn't like surprises.

'As you know,' Sloan began when the roll call was finished, 'we agreed at our last meeting to honour our sovereign's Jubilee in our own unique fashion. I am, of course, referring to our poetry contest. I trust that you are all working diligently.'

Lucinda Marlow knew what was coming next, so she ignored their esteemed president and turned her attention toward the centre of the circle, where Rowena Stanwick was sitting far closer than propriety dictated to Shelby Locke.

Lucinda's fingers curled into fists beneath the fold

4

of her simple yellow day dress. She wished she'd worn her lavender gown. Leave it to Rowena to overdress for the occasion, she thought hastily, as she saw Shelby flash a warm smile in the widow's direction. Men are such fools; they didn't have the intelligence to see a sow's ear dressed like a silk purse even when it was sitting right beside them.

'I take it all of you have, by now, allowed the muse free rein of your creative endeavours,' Sloan said. 'As I promised at our last meeting, I did, indeed, arrange for the esteemed poet, Mr Richard Venerable, to act as the judge in our own modest but most exciting contest. Mr Venerable will announce the winner of the poetry contest at a ball to be given here, at Miss Marlow's residence, in two weeks' time.'

Edgar Warburton, who was sitting next to Miss Cecilia Mansfield at the end of the circle of chairs, slanted the widow Stanwick a hate-filled glance. The bitch. Who did she think she was? With one long, skinny finger Warburton stroked the rim of his muttonchop whiskers and then smoothed a lock of mousy brown hair off his high forehead. He kept his gaze on her for several minutes, willing her to look in his direction so he could have the pleasure of snubbing her. But Rowena Stanwick only had eyes for Shelby Locke. She kept giving him coy, secretive smiles and little pats on the hand.

Warburton forced his attention away from the couple. He glanced around the overly furnished drawing room, and his lips curled in a faint sneer. The walls were covered with a ghastly emerald-green embossed wallpaper. Every table was cluttered with china figurines and ugly vases of flowers sitting on cream-coloured silk table coverings. The settees and chairs, though of good quality mahogany and done in fine fabric, were the same hideous green as the wall, and the most awful gold and brown Brussels carpet covered the floor. The house and its contents were opulent, expensive and in horribly bad taste. But that was only to be expected. The Marlow wealth, extensive as it was, came from trade. He looked at the owner of the house, Lucinda Marlow, and felt a tinge of shame. Poor woman; of course her home was furnished with no regard to art or beauty. How could it be any different? Tradespeople, really! Regardless of how much money they spent or how many paintings they purchased, they were hopelessly lost.

Warburton wished he could be attracted to Lucinda. God knows, though he was by no means poor, a fortune of that size could always come in handy. But there was something decidedly odd about her. Despite the Marlow family wealth, he'd heard she'd never had a proper Season. And of course, the way she lived here all alone, with only her servants to look after her. Scandalous, really. You'd think she'd have the decency to find some old relative to hang about and act as chaperon.

He saw Lucinda turn her head and frown at Locke and Rowena, and he immediately forgot what he'd been thinking about as another shaft of anger flooded his thin body.

Dr Oxton Sloan droned on about the silly poetry contest and Warburton continued to ignore him while he fed his rage about Rowena Stanwick.

Damn the woman. She'd brought him low. He'd only joined this ridiculous group to be near her, and she treated him like dirt. That upstart of an adventuress. That nobody. His mouth flattened into a cruel, thin line as he glared at her. She'd taken one look at Locke and tossed him aside like an old pair of gloves. But he wouldn't stand for it. Not anymore.

We'll just see who has the last laugh here, he thought bitterly. He'd make the bitch sorry she ever laid eyes on Shelby Locke.

'Of course, the form of the poem is entirely up to you,' Sloan said enthusiastically, 'and as you know, the topic of the poem can celebrate any aspect of Her Majesty's life, reign or achievements.' As he spoke, Sloan felt his confidence return. Even with those few who might actually know how to write a poem, he didn't think there was much reason for worry. Not a lot of competition here, he thought. Most of them wouldn't know good poetry if it walked up and bit them on the arse.

They were such fools. Richard Venerable, their judge, hadn't written anything worthwhile in years. He'd hardly read anything more than labels on a whisky bottle! Sloan hoped the man wouldn't be so drunk he couldn't give out the prize medallion at the ball. He was looking forward to that particular ceremony. He intended to win.

Shelby Locke tried to concentrate on Dr Sloan's instructions for the contest, but really, how was one expected to concentrate when the love of one's life breezed into the room and sat down next to one? He stole another quick look at Rowena and his heart fluttered. She was so beautiful. So sweet. And she was in love with him. His fingers tightened around the bound leather notebook in his lap.

'Are there any questions?' Sloan asked.

Locke looked down at the notebook. He'd dozens of poems written, of course. But he couldn't conjure up a whit of enthusiasm for the contest. Who cared about the Queen's silly Jubilee? His poems were about life. About love and feelings and that exquisite torment of two souls overcoming obstacles so they could come together.

Shelby Locke only wrote about those things which had meaning to him. He poured his heart and his spirit into his words. Why, only this morning he'd written the most eloquent poem about Rowena. About their wonderful night together. Shelby smiled secretly. Perhaps the poem was too bold. Perhaps she would be offended when he presented it to her tonight at dinner. But surely, she'd understand what he was trying to express. Physical love was to be celebrated as much as spiritual love. It wasn't as if anyone else would ever see the poem. No, he thought, glancing again at his beloved, Rowena wouldn't be in the least offended.

An hour later the meeting concluded and Miss Marlow led the way into the dining room for refreshments. The group milled around the buffet table.

Lucinda Marlow circled the room, making sure her guests had food and drink. Mrs Stanwick and Mr Locke stood close together in one of the far corners, talking in low voices. Mrs Greenwood had cornered Dr Sloan and was speaking to him with a set, earnest expression on her face. Mr Warburton picked up a glass of sherry and walked over to the window to stare morosely out into the summer night.

Lady Cannonberry smiled politely as Mrs Putnam prattled on, but she wasn't really listening. Her mind was fully occupied, thinking about the ball. She would so like an escort. Yet there were so few gentlemen that a genteel, middle-aged woman could prevail upon. Of course, there was her neighbour, that nice Inspector Witherspoon. But he was so dreadfully shy. Lady Cannonberry sighed softly.

'Are you all right?' Mrs Putnam asked briskly. 'Oh, I know, you're probably anxious about your poem. But you mustn't worry so, I'm sure you'll do fine. Why, Horace and I have already done ours. It's really quite easy. But you must make sure you end each line with a simple word. A nice word, one that has many other words that rhyme with it. You know, like moon and June or two and who or queen and mean. There are any number of good words to choose from, just be sure not to use a difficult one like . . . oh, pianoforte. There aren't many words that rhyme with pianoforte. I know – Horace ended one of his lines with that word. Took him ages to think up another one. I tell you, Lady Cannonberry, if you keep it simple, writing good poetry is as easy as writing a supper menu.'

'I'll keep that in mind,' she replied quickly. She wasn't in the least worried about her poem. She was worried about being the only woman at the ball without an escort.

If only Inspector Witherspoon weren't so very

reticent. The few times they'd spoken, while they were walking their dogs in the park, she'd found him a most congenial man. Perhaps she could have a word with his housekeeper, Mrs Jeffries. Mrs Jeffries was the most understanding of women. One could really talk to her. Yes, Lady Cannonberry thought, that's precisely what she would do. She'd have a word with Mrs Jeffries and see if there wasn't some very delicate way to best let the inspector know she was in dire need of an escort.

Across the room Cecilia Mansfield stared enviously at Rowena Stanwick's slim figure. The opulent gown stood out like a bright crimson poppy in a field of weeds. The pleated overskirt and the curve of the bustle emphasized Mrs Stanwick's tiny waist. The touch of lace on the cuffs showed off her remarkably slim wrists and hands to perfection, and the dainty buttons around the high neck of the dress lent a graceful air to her already perfect carriage. Cecilia sighed. She'd spent a fortune at the dressmakers and still never managed to look as wonderful as Mrs Stanwick. It wasn't fair. Mrs Stanwick had already had a husband; she didn't need to find another one. 'I wonder what she'll be wearing to the ball,' she murmured to Mrs Hiatt.

'Who?'

'Rowena Stanwick,' Cecilia replied. 'I wonder what she'll wear to the ball. I hear she's got her dressmaker copying princess Beatrice's gowns.'

'Half the women in London are copying the princess's gowns,' Mrs Hiatt replied as she studied the table in search of a tidbit she hadn't tasted yet. 'More important, I wonder what they'll serve for supper?' She put an apple turnover on her plate and picked up her fork. 'Do you think it'll be hot or cold?'

'What?'

'The supper at the ball,' Mrs Hiatt said impatiently.

'Miss Marlow always does things correctly,' Cecilia replied, turning to stare at their hostess. 'I expect she'll have both a hot and cold buffet. Goodness, look at that. She's squinting again, the poor thing. I say, I do think she ought to wear her spectacles. Everyone knows she doesn't see all that well without them.'

Mrs Hiatt smiled cynically. 'I do believe Miss Marlow is more concerned with her appearance than she is with seeing clearly,' she stated. 'You can't blame her for wanting to took her best, especially with Mr Locke here. With all the mourning she's done, she hasn't had much chance for young men to pay court to her.'

Cecilia frowned. She hadn't had all that many men paying court to her, either, and she hadn't noticed any sympathy for her from Mrs Hiatt. But it would be uncharitable to say such a thing. 'That's true, I suppose,' she said grudgingly.

Mrs Hiatt looked up from her plate. 'Indeed it is.'

Thinking she might be considered less than kind, Cecilia forced herself to smile benevolently. 'Poor Lucinda. She has had a rather bad time of it. But I've had it on good authority that she and Mr Locke will be announcing their engagement at the ball.'

Mrs Hiatt, who was not a romantic, having seen enough of human nature to disabuse her of foolish notions, shook her head. Her gaze shifted to Rowena Stanwick, who was standing indecently close to Shelby Locke and talking to him with an earnest, entreating expression on her face. 'Really?'

Cecilia gave her a puzzled stare. 'Yes, really. You're the one who implied Mr Locke was paying court to Miss Marlow.'

'You're quite mistaken, Miss Mansfield,' Mrs Hiatt said slowly, her gaze still on the couple across the room. 'I implied that Miss Marlow was interested in Mr Locke. And at one time he was certainly interested in her, but I do believe things have changed.'

Cecilia snorted. She was getting rather annoyed with Mrs Hiatt. Honestly, the woman thought she knew everything. 'Well, I know for a fact that Miss Marlow has ordered a whole new wardrobe. We have the same dressmaker, you know. Madam Deloffre told me specifically, and, of course, in the strictest confidence, that it's her trousseau.'

Mrs Hiatt merely smiled. 'She may have ordered a trousseau, my dear. But that doesn't mean she's getting married.'

Bright June sunshine poured through the windows of the kitchen in Upper Edmonton Gardens, home of Inspector Gerald Witherspoon. The shafts of light danced against the copper utensils lining the walls, the air filled with the scent of peppermint and lemon. On the long oak table a pink-flowered teapot sat next to a tray of mouthwatering gooseberry tarts.

Five people were sitting in a semicircle at the far

end of the table. They were Inspector Witherspoon's loyal servants.

Mrs Goodge, the cook, banged her fist against the tabletop. 'When's that horrible woman goin' to leave so we can have a bit of peace!' she cried. Her considerable bulk shook with fury, and a lock of grey hair dislodged itself from her bun and dangled across her ear. From behind a pair of spectacles her eyes narrowed in anger.

Mrs Jeffries, the housekeeper, sighed inwardly. She was a kind, motherly looking woman who always listened to the servants' grievances. She was good at listening. It was one of her foremost abilities. Her hair was a dark auburn, liberally sprinkled with white at the temples, her eyes a deep, understanding brown. Though small of stature and rather plump, she had the air of one used to the rigorous demands of leadership.

She wasn't in the least surprised by the cook's outburst. Edwina Livingston-Graves, the inspector's cousin and houseguest, had a rather unfortunate effect on the staff. Truth to tell, Mrs Livingston-Graves had a rather unfortunate effect on everyone. She wasn't a particularly nice person. 'I'm afraid Mrs Livingston-Graves will be here until after the Jubilee,' Mrs Jeffries said cautiously.

'After the Jubilee!' the cook yelped. 'But that's not for another two weeks! I swear, Mrs Jeffries, if I have to put up with her for a fortnight, I'll not be responsible for my actions. Do you know what she had the effrontery to say to me today after lunch? She claimed the rabbit was tough. She actually had the nerve to ask if we had any Cockle's Antibilious Pills! Claimed she had indigestion. Did you ever hear the like? My stewed rabbit and onions . . . one of my best dishes . . .'

'At least she didn't stand over your shoulder and natter in your ear while you was cooking it,' Betsy interrupted. The pretty blonde maid was as furious as the cook. Her ivory complexion was rosy with anger and her slender frame stiff with indignation. 'That's what I had to put up with this mornin' while I was polishin' the furniture in the drawin' room. Half an hour, it was, too,' she continued, her blue eyes widening. 'And on and on she went about how I was goin' to ruin the shine if I didn't stop usin' the wrong polish. And it was Adam's Furniture Polish I was usin' as well, the kind we've used for years. It's bad enough we haven't had a decent murder in weeks . . .'

'Well, if I catch that woman kickin' Fred again,' Wiggins, the footman, chimed in, 'we will 'ave us a murder right 'ere.'

Mrs Jeffries didn't take the footman's threats all that seriously. Wiggins was only just past his twentieth birthday, a slightly pudgy brown-haired lad with apple cheeks and a generally affable nature. He didn't look very affable at the moment, though.

'Kicking Fred?' Smythe's heavy brows drew together. 'You didn't tell me the old girl 'ad a go at Fred.'

Fred, a shaggy mixture of black, brown, and white fur, raised his pointed nose in the air as he heard the coachman mention his name. Wagging his tail, he rose to his feet from his spot in the sunlight by the door and wandered toward the table. He looked hopefully toward the tray of tarts.

Wiggins shook his head. 'I saw it with me own eyes. She give 'im a right 'ard kick in his ribs, she did. And all because poor Fred were just defendin' 'imself against that wretched cat of hers.' He paused and took a breath.

'Maybe I should take the dog down to the stables until she's gone,' Smythe mused. Tall and strong, with a headful of thick black hair, olive complexion, and full mouth, he would have been a brutal-looking sort to be sitting in a cozy kitchen save for a pair of twinkling, kind brown eyes. 'I'm afraid that won't do at all,' Mrs Jeffries said quickly. 'You know how devoted the inspector is to Fred. He'd miss him terribly.'

'Then what are we goin' to do?' Smythe asked. 'Mrs Livingston-Graves and her ruddy cat show up on our doorstep just a few days ago and already she's actin' like she owns the place. Her and that silly animal is enough to drive a man bonkers. Cor, it's a good thing we ain't investigatin' one of the inspector's murders! Be hard to keep things to ourselves with that old harridan snoopin' around.'

'At least you can escape to the pubs of the evening,' Betsy said, making it sound like an accusation. 'We've got to put up with her twenty-four hours a day. She's always sneakin' about and eavesdroppin'! I caught her listenin' at the door this morning when Mrs Goodge was havin' a word with the man from the gas works.'

15

'She were eavesdroppin' on me and Albert?' Mrs Goodge was truly outraged. Her relations with the various people who trouped through her kitchen were her own private domain. In all their investigations for the inspector, she'd used her sources to provide many important facts and clues. How dare that woman snoop!

Mrs Jeffries held up her hand. 'Please,' she began, 'I know you're all upset. Mrs Livingston-Graves is a trial, but we all have our crosses in life to bear.'

'And she's a mighty heavy one,' the coachman muttered. He crossed his arms over his massively muscled chest.

'But she won't be here forever,' the housekeeper continued. She fervently hoped that was true. But she wasn't certain. Of late, Mrs Jeffries was beginning to suspect that Cousin Edwina was angling to be invited to stay on a permanent basis. However, she wasn't going to mention her suspicions to the rest of the staff. They were upset enough. 'And the Jubilee Thanksgiving procession isn't that far away. So why don't we all go about our business and try to ignore the lady?'

'But what if we gets us a murder?' Wiggins asked. 'What'll we do then?'

Mrs Jeffries looked thoughtful. The lad had a point. If their inspector did get involved in another murder, of course they'd have to step in. The dear man had no idea his devoted staff actually investigated his cases, of course. That would never do. They were most careful to keep their inquiries discreet. None of them would ever want the inspector to feel that he couldn't solve a murder on his own. That, of course, wasn't quite true. But they would have a problem if the inspector were to get another case. Thanks to their prodigious efforts, the inspector now had a reputation to uphold. His superiors at the Yard were amazed at the 'unsolvable' cases the man solved. She shook herself slightly. It was pointless to fret over something that hadn't happened yet. She had other matters involving the inspector on her mind. 'We'll cross that bridge when we come to it,' she said firmly. 'As it is, we don't have a murder to investigate at the present, and if we're very lucky Mrs Livingston-Graves will be gone by the time we do. Right now our only concern is to get through the next two weeks with a minimum of disruption to our normal routines.'

From the stairwell they heard the sound of rapidly descending footsteps. Knowing who it was, Smythe pushed back his chair and leapt to his feet, but he wasn't quick enough.

Mrs Livingston-Graves sailed into the kitchen. Thin, medium height and possessed of a raw-boned face and mousy brown hair that she wore pulled back in a severe bun, she frowned at them. 'I say, Mrs Jeffries,' she said in a nasal whine, 'how many tea breaks do the servants take in this household? Every time I come into the kitchen someone's sitting here sipping tea. That's not what my cousin pays your wages for, surely.'

Mrs Jeffries forced a polite smile to her lips. 'Was there something you wanted?'

The woman's lips flattened to a disapproving line

as she realized the housekeeper was not going to answer her question. 'I'm looking for Alphonse.'

Fred scurried under the table.

'I'd best get down to Howard's,' Smythe announced as he edged toward the back door. 'The carriage needs a good clean.'

Wiggins got up. 'I'll finish up oiling them hinges on the back gate, Mrs Jeffries,' the footman muttered as he, too, hurried from the room.

'Better finish dustin' the landing,' Betsy said as she leapt to her feet. Mrs Goodge fixed Mrs Livingston-Graves with a cold stare. 'I'd better see to them berries,' she said slowly as she heaved her bulk out of her chair and made her way down the hall toward the wet larder.

From outside the kitchen window there was the sound of a hansom drawing up. Mrs Jeffries cocked her head to one side and listened intently.

'I asked if you'd seen my cat,' Mrs Livingston-Graves said loudly.

The footsteps crossing the pavement were as familiar to Mrs Jeffries as her own. She glanced at Mrs Livingston-Graves. 'I do believe that Alphonse is out in the garden,' she said calmly.

'Out in the garden!' Mrs Livingston-Graves screeched. She turned on her heel and flew down the hall. 'Oh, my gracious. The poor baby's probably terrified. He's not allowed outside without me!' she cried.

Mrs Jeffries nodded in satisfaction as the woman disappeared. She needed to speak privately to the inspector.

★ ★ ★

Inspector Gerald Witherspoon peered around the corner of the drawing room door. 'I say,' he said to Mrs Jeffries, 'where is Mrs Livingston-Graves? Up in her room?'

Tall and robust, with a fine-boned angular face, a neatly trimmed moustache, a sharp, pointed nose, clear blue-grey eyes, and thinning brown hair, the inspector crept quietly into the room and headed for his favourite armchair.

'Your cousin is out in the gardens, looking for her cat.'

He sighed in relief. 'Excellent. The fresh air will do her good. Where's Fred?'

'Hiding under the kitchen table,' she replied as she poured out two glasses of fine sherry. She gave one to her employer and sat down opposite him.

'Why ever is he hiding?'

'I'm afraid that poor Fred has been rather cowed by Mrs Livingston-Graves and her cat. Presumably he feels that discretion is the better part of valour.'

'Oh, dear.' Witherspoon frowned. 'That is awkward. I mean, she is, after all, my relation. I don't like the idea that she's been less than kind to the poor dog, but then again, what can one say?'

'I shouldn't worry about it if I were you,' Mrs Jeffries said firmly. 'You can always take Fred for a nice long walk yourself this evening. That'll make him feel better. How was your day, sir?'

'The usual,' he replied, sipping his sherry. 'There's an enormous amount of planning, what with the Jubilee celebrations and all. Thank goodness, I've no other pressing cases or murders to investigate. Most of my time is tied up in planning traffic routes.'

'Oh, yes, the Jubilee.' She sighed dramatically.

Concerned, Witherspoon leaned forward. 'Why, Mrs Jeffries, is something wrong?'

'Nothing's really wrong, sir,' she said carefully. 'It's just that I feel so very sorry for our neighbour, Lady Cannonberry. She's been invited to a Jubilee Ball and she hasn't an escort. It's a rather embarrassing situation for the poor lady. You see, the ball is being given by a young woman who is a member of the same literary circle as Lady Cannonberry. It's really for the members of the circle. They're having a contest to see who can write the best poem celebrating Her Majesty's Jubilee. So it's not as if Lady Cannonberry can in good conscience decline the invitation. She is a very supportive member of the circle.'

Witherspoon gulped his sherry. 'Oh, dear.'

'You can see her difficulty, sir,' Mrs Jeffries said, 'You know sir, I was wondering . . .'

'Now, Mrs Jeffries,' the inspector protested, 'surely you're not going to suggest that I offer to escort Lady Cannonberry. That would never do. She's a member of the nobility and I'm merely a humble policeman.'

'That's not true, sir. You are a fine, honourable gentleman. You have a beautiful home, excellent employment and your prospects are superb.'

As the inspector had inherited his fine home and most of his servants from his late aunt Euphemia, he didn't really feel he could take all that much credit. 'Yes, but—'

'There's no buts about it, sir,' his housekeeper continued doggedly. 'You've not only persevered in a very difficult and important occupation, you've become famous for your brilliance at solving the most heinous of crimes. Why, just look at all the cases you've had – those horrible Kensington High Street murders, that terribly difficult one involving that fake medium, that dreadful one where that poor girl was brutally stabbed and buried in the bottom of an abandoned house. If it hadn't been for you, none of those murders would have been solved. You've every right to be proud of yourself, sir. You're much too modest.'

Witherspoon smiled shyly. 'Well, yes, I suppose I have been fortunate when it comes to homicide,' he began modestly. 'But escorting Lady Cannonberry would be an entirely different matter.' Panic fluttered in his stomach. Solving murders was one thing; spending an entire evening in the company of a woman was something else entirely.

'Furthermore,' Mrs Jeffries said firmly, 'Lady Cannonberry was a simple country doctor's daughter before she married her late husband. And he wouldn't have inherited his title if his two elder brothers hadn't taken it into their heads to sail to South America and both been lost at sea.'

The sharp, clicking heels of Mrs Livingston-Graves pounded down the hallway. The inspector visibly cringed. Mrs Jeffries hid a smile behind her glass of sherry.

'Good evening, Gerald,' Mrs Livingston-Graves barked as she charged into the room. She held a

21

rather dirty and bedraggled Siamese cat in her arms. 'Will you just look at this,' she complained, shoving the animal under the inspector's nose. 'Alphonse is absolutely filthy. I found the poor dear outside, cowering under a bush, trembling with fear.'

Alphonse snarled and swiped at Witherspoon's nose with his paw.

'Er, is something wrong?' The inspector shrank back from the hissing cat.

'Of course something's wrong,' Mrs Livingston-Graves snapped. She pushed the cat's paw down and dumped the animal directly in Witherspoon's lap. 'Dear Alphonse has been attacked. Go on, have a look at him.'

Witherspoon forced himself to examine the animal closely. All he saw was dirt and mud, no sign of injury. 'I don't see any blood,' he murmured finally.

Alphonse stared up at him from a pair of cold blue eyes and hissed.

'Don't be absurd, Gerald. Of course he's injured. You just can't see it. His poor nerves will probably never be the same. He's very delicate, you know.' Mrs Livingston-Graves snatched her precious darling to her bosom and began stroking the animal's back.

'How do you know Alphonse has been attacked? Did you see it?' Witherspoon asked, wanting to placate his angry cousin.

'No, I didn't see it, but it's obvious.' She glared pointedly at the housekeeper. 'Someone deliberately left the back door open so poor Alphonse could wander off. Your entire staff hates my cat. By the time I found him, he was dreadfully upset. And I saw that wretched spaniel again. I know the horrid creature attacked my darling.'

'Spaniel?' the inspector mumbled. 'I'm sure you must be mistaken. The only spaniel that I know of out in the gardens belongs to Lady Cannonberry. She's a very nice little dog, quite a harmless animal. Why, she and Fred often go tumbling about together having a jolly good time.'

'Speaking of Fred' – Mrs Jeffries glanced at the carriage clock on the mantelpiece – 'I do believe you'll have time to take him for a walk, Inspector. He does so love a brisk perambulation in Holland Park. Dinner won't be served for another hour, so you've plenty of time.'

'But what about my poor Alphonse?' Mrs Livingston-Graves sputtered. 'Something really must be done. I won't have him being mistreated.'

'Why don't you take Alphonse upstairs and give him a saucer of milk,' Mrs Jeffries suggested.

Witherspoon, knowing a good escape when he saw one, leapt from his chair and hurried toward the door. 'I'm sure Alphonse will be fine as soon as he's had his milk,' he called.

'But, Gerald . . .' Mrs Livingston-Graves protested. She scurried after him, her dark skirts swishing angrily.

Mrs Jeffries leaned back in her chair and smiled. If everything went as she planned, her dear employer should be running into Lady Cannonberry in less than ten minutes.

CHAPTER TWO

O<small>N THE NIGHT</small> of the Hyde Park Literary Circle's Jubilee Ball, the weather was perfect: warm, dry, and with a light wind from the north that blew the worst of London's noxious odours well away from the Marlow home. The front of the tall redbrick house blazed with welcoming light. Hansom cabs clip-clopped up and down the length of Redcliffe Square, dropping off guests. Inside the house, ladies in opulent gowns and gentlemen in formal black evening wear danced, drank, and ate with great enthusiasm.

The festivities spilled out into the garden. Enclosed by high brick walls, the guests at the ball were assured of privacy as they enjoyed themselves. Couples strolled through the open French doors, the music spilling onto the terrace. Giant torches flamed from the first-floor balcony, casting dancing shadows on the people milling about below. Above the first floor only an occasional light could be seen, leaving most of the rear of the imposing structure in darkness, a stark contrast to the brilliance illuminating the garden.

Lucinda Marlow had spared no expense for her

guests' enjoyment. Japanese lanterns, limelights, and additional torches had been strategically placed around the huge garden. The scent of summer roses filled the air. A maze of paths meandered through the heavy shrubbery and leafy trees, beckoning those young people who were of a mind to slip away from the eagle eyes of their chaperons.

Cecilia Mansfield shook her head and glanced at the clusters of people scattered across the terrace. 'Everyone's acting most peculiar this evening,' she commented to Mrs Hiatt, who was sitting on a bench holding a plate of pastries.

'Really? How so?'

'No one from our circle seems to be having a good time at all,' Cecila said slowly. She smoothed a wrinkle out of the overskirt of her pink tulle dress. 'I saw Dr Sloan and Mrs Greenwood a few minutes ago. I think they were exchanging words.'

Mrs Hiatt shot her companion a sharp glance. 'Did you actually hear them quarrelling?' she asked. 'Or are you only guessing?' She was annoyed that Miss Mansfield always seemed to know everything.

'Well,' Cecilia replied, 'I didn't actually hear what they were saying, but you could tell by their expressions they were arguing. Dr Sloan's face was as red as a radish and Mrs Greenwood looked positively livid.'

'I shouldn't take any notice, if I were you.' Mrs Hiatt shrugged. She eyed her plate carefully, trying to decide whether to eat the lemon tart or the napoleon next. 'Mrs Greenwood's never in good spirits. I don't know why she even bothered to come tonight. It's not as if she likes our company overly much. Besides, she's been in a snit all evening: She took one look at Rowena Stanwick's dress and flounced off in a rage. Not that it was Mrs Stanwick's fault, of course. Half the women here are wearing blue gowns. It's become a very popular colour this Season. Princess Beatrice favours it.'

Cecilia giggled. 'Mrs Greenwood's not the only one who's in a tizzy. I was standing by the door when Mrs Stanwick arrived. You should have seen Miss Marlow's face, and Miss Gordon didn't look all that pleased, either. Half the women in the room were shooting daggers at poor Mrs Stanwick. Of course, her gown is a bit grander than the others. I must say, I think the bustle is just a tad overdone.'

'Her bustle isn't any larger than Mrs Greenwood's,' Mrs Hiatt said. 'But I daresay I think you're right about our circle. I've seen more than one long face this evening. None of them seem to be enjoying themselves very much.'

Cecilia was visibly startled. 'You've noticed it as well, have you?'

'Naturally, when one gets to be my age, one doesn't have much else to do but eat and observe. Mr Warburton's been walking around with a dog-in-the-manger expression all night,' Mrs Hiatt continued, taking satisfaction in seeing the look of surprise on her companion's face. She pressed her advantage. 'He's spent most of his time glaring at Mrs Stanwick's back. Miss Marlow looks as though her smile is beginning to crack, and Mr Locke is still moaning about his notebook.'

'He hasn't found it?'

Mrs Hiatt shook her head. 'I actually overheard him implying to Dr Sloan that his notebook had been stolen. He claimed he had it here at our last meeting, and when he went to leave, it was gone.'

Cecilia snorted delicately. 'That's ridiculous. Who'd steal it?'

Mrs Hiatt chuckled. 'He didn't exactly come right out and say so, but from what I heard, I think he suspects Miss Marlow.'

'But that's absurd. Why should she care about his silly poems?'

'I think it's this contest. Everyone's nerves are on edge. Gracious, the way Mr Locke was haranguing poor Miss Marlow, you'd think the prize for winning the ruddy contest was a chest of gold and not just a silly medallion.'

Cecilia's eyes widened. 'You overheard him speaking to Miss Marlow?'

'Oh, yes, didn't I mention that?' Mrs Hiatt smiled smugly. From the corner of her eye she saw Lady Cannonberry and her escort come out of the French doors and onto the terrace. 'I wonder who that gentleman escorting Lady Cannonberry is.'

Now it was Cecilia's turn to look smug. 'That's Inspector Gerald Witherspoon. He's with the police.'

'Lady Cannonberry's with a policeman?'

'He's not just any policeman,' Cecilia said quickly. She liked Lady Cannonberry very much and she'd rather liked the shy gentleman she'd met earlier in the evening. 'He's actually quite famous. He's the one who solved those horrible Kensington High Street murders last year and the murder of that American man they found in the Thames a few months ago. They say he's quite brilliant.'

Inspector Witherspoon wasn't feeling in the least brilliant. Dressed in the most uncomfortable set of formal black clothes and a pair of tight shoes, he hoped the evening would progress quickly so he could go home. He still hadn't a clue how he happened to be here. One moment he was walking Fred in Holland Park and the next he was walking with Lady Cannonberry. Before he could snap his fingers, he'd found himself asking if he might escort her to the Jubilee Ball.

'I do so hope you're enjoying yourself, Inspector,' Lady Cannonberry said politely. She lifted the hem of her heavy sapphire-blue gown as they approached the stairs leading to the garden.

'Very much,' Witherspoon replied. He tried desperately to think of what to say next. Drat. Talking with ladies was such a chore. Gracious, how on earth did some men manage it? 'Er, did you get your poem finished in time for the contest?' he asked.

'Yes.' Lady Cannonberry frowned slightly. 'But I wasn't very pleased with the verse. I don't think I've a chance at winning. But then again, winning isn't all that important to me. Everyone expects that Dr Sloan will take the prize. He's the only one in the group who's actually published, you see.'

'What did you write about, if I may ask?' Witherspoon began to relax. Perhaps the trick to talking to ladies was to ask them questions about those topics which interested them.

'Oh, nothing terribly exciting, I'm afraid. I . . . uh, well . . .' She hesitated and took a breath. 'I wrote about trains.'

Witherspoon stopped and turned to stare at her. 'Trains?'

'Yes,' Lady Cannonberry replied enthusiastically, 'I'm quite fond of them, you see. The rules of the contest said we could write about any aspect of Her Majesty's reign. The railroads have expanded enormously and Her Majesty is such a supporter . . . well, I do so love steam engines . . .' Her voice faltered.

'How wonderful!' the inspector cried. He took her arm and continued down the terrace steps. 'I quite like steam engines and trains as well. Tell me, Lady Cannonberry, have you seen the new engine on the Great Northern?'

'But of course,' she replied, smiling radiantly. 'It's wonderful. However, I still believe it's not really all that much of an improvement on the classic British four-four-oh. I saw the North British Railway's number two-twenty-four on her first trip out. She was magnificent. Four coupled wheels, inside cylinders, and a leading bogie.'

Witherspoon laughed. His nervousness was somehow completely gone. 'I'm familiar with the four-four-ohs. You're right, they are wonderful trains.' He paused. 'Number two-twenty-four? I'm sure I know that train. I know most of them, you see. Train spotting is rather a hobby of mine. I say, isn't she the one that had to be fished out of the Firth of Tay?'

'Well, yes, but it wasn't the train's fault the bridge collapsed. Besides, she was rebuilt.'

Mrs Horace Putnam was frantic. She sighed in relief as she spotted two members of the Hyde Park Literary Circle and rushed across the terrace toward them. 'Have you seen anyone?' she cried.

'We've seen quite a few people,' Mrs Hiatt replied. 'The house is full of them.'

'I'm not looking for people,' Mrs Putnam retorted. 'I'm looking for members of our group. It's almost time to make the announcement and I can't find, anyone.'

'Lady Cannonberry's just over there,' Cecilia said helpfully as she pointed in the direction of the couple hovering near the steps.

'Oh, good. But where is Dr Sloan or Mrs Stanwick or Mr Locke? Merciful heavens! Everyone's disappeared. Miss Marlow and Mr Warburton are nowhere about, and Mrs Greenwood seems to have vanished into thin air as well.'

'I saw Mrs Greenwood about fifteen minutes ago,' Cecilia said. 'She was in the drawing room, talking with Dr Sloan.'

'They aren't in the drawing room now,' Mrs Putnam snapped 'They aren't anywhere that I can find, and neither is anyone else. I've looked everywhere. It's almost ten-thirty. We're supposed to announce the winner of the contest.'

'Do calm yourself, Mrs Putnam,' Mrs Hiatt said briskly. 'I don't think it will matter if the announcement's a few moments late.'

'But of course it will matter. It must be done as soon as possible or it won't be done at all. Our judge,

Mr Venerable, seems well on his way to being incapacitated. One doesn't like to tell tales, but I think he's in his cups.'

'You mean he's drunk,' said Mrs Hiatt bluntly. She loathed euphemisms.

Suddenly there was a loud scream. Everyone on the terrace froze.

A body plummeted through the air and landed with a sickening thud on the stone pavement two feet away from where the ladies stood.

Cecilia screamed, Mrs Putnam gasped, and Mrs Hiatt leapt to her feet. She hurried over to the unmoving form and knelt down. 'Oh, my God, there's a knife sticking out of the back!' she cried. Her face grim, she gently reached down and brushed a stray lock of blonde hair off the side of the woman's face. Mrs Hiatt looked up at Mrs Putnam. 'I do believe we've found Mrs Greenwood.'

Witherspoon, who'd been engrossed in discussing steam engines with Lady Cannonberry, broke off in midsentence as he heard the scream. Not believing his eyes, he blinked as the body landed on the terrace. For a moment he was so surprised he couldn't move. Then, remembering his duty, he hurried over to where Mrs Hiatt was kneeling beside the body.

'Excuse me, madam,' he said politely, 'I'm a police officer. Perhaps I'd better just have a look here.'

Having a look was the last thing the inspector wanted to do. He was quite squeamish.

He knelt down beside the woman and took a deep

breath. The body lay on its side. Witherspoon shuddered as he saw the knife protruding obscenely from the poor lady's back. The first thing he had to do was establish if she was dead or merely injured.

Witherspoon swallowed and felt for a pulse. There was none. He continued looking for signs of life, finally giving up when he realized that not only had the victim been stabbed; the side of her skull was crushed from the fall.

The inspector stood up. 'I'm afraid I'll have to ask all of you to please go into the ballroom.'

'What's happened?' Lucinda Marlow's frantic voice cut through the crowd that had gathered. 'Has there been an accident?' She broke through the ring of people and stopped dead, her eyes widening as she saw the figure lying on her terrace. 'Oh, my—'

'Miss Marlow,' the inspector said softly. 'Please send someone for the police. One of your guests has been murdered.'

An hour later the inspector and the uniformed branch had things well under control. The police surgeon had examined the body and taken it away. The murder weapon, or at least the knife taken out of Mrs Greenwood's back that Witherspoon would assume was the murder weapon until the autopsy was completed, was identified as belonging to the Marlow house. More precisely, the butler had verified it had last been seen slicing roast beef at the cold buffet table.

Witherspoon had allowed those guests who could verify they were in the ballroom or in the garden at the time of the murder to leave. The rest were waiting for him in the drawing room.

Smythe had driven Lady Cannonberry home. Witherspoon sighed as he entered the now almost deserted ballroom. He spotted Constable Barnes, a robust grey-haired man with a craggy face and hazel-green eyes, coming toward him from the other end of the room.

'Evening, sir,' Barnes said. 'I got here as soon as I could. The report is there's been a murder.'

'Unfortunately, yes. The victim was one of the guests, Mrs Hannah Greenwood. Someone stabbed her and pushed her off the third-floor balcony.'

Barnes clucked his tongue. 'That's horrible, sir. Sounds like the killer wanted to make doubly sure she were dead. Good thing you were here, isn't it, sir?'

'It certainly seems that way,' Witherspoon replied. Actually, he thought it rather appalling that he'd been 'on the scene', so to speak. Oddly, he felt guilty, as though he should have stopped the murder. Of course, he knew that was nonsense. One doesn't go to a Jubilee Ball and expect a fellow guest to be stabbed and tossed off a balcony. It just wasn't done.

Cecilia Mansfield rushed across the floor and hurried toward the inspector. 'Excuse me,' she said firmly. She was a bit annoyed. Every time she tried to speak to any of the policemen, they ignored her. 'But I must speak with you, Inspector.'

Witherspoon stared at the plump young woman with the light-blue eyes and pale skin. 'Yes, Miss Mansfield. What can I do for you?'

'I've got some rather important information, and none of your policemen seems in the least interested in listening to me.'

'We'll be happy to take your statement, Miss,' Barnes said politely, 'Now, what have you got to tell us?'

'To begin with, I don't think you ought to bother questioning anyone who isn't a member of the Hyde Park Literary Circle. None of the other ball guests had anything to do with Mrs Greenwood,' Miss Mansfield stated.

'How do you know that?' the inspector asked curiously.

She gave him a superior smile. 'Because Mrs Greenwood herself mentioned it to me when she first arrived tonight. She wasn't an overly sociable person, you know. She took one look at the mob hanging about the punch bowl and told me that, except for the members of our group, she didn't know a soul here and didn't want to, either.'

'Thank you, Miss Mansfield,' Witherspoon said. 'I'm sure that information will be very useful to us.' He wasn't merely being polite to her, either. Knowing that the victim had no connection to any of the other ball guests could drastically reduce the amount of time it would take to solve this murder.

'But that's not all I've got to say,' Cecilia protested. 'I saw Mrs Greenwood having an argument with Dr Sloan earlier this evening. Don't you think that's important?'

'Yes, of course it is,' Barnes said smoothly. 'We'll speak with Dr Sloan about it right away.'

Cecilia shook her head. 'But you can't. He's left and so have most of the others.'

'Left?' The inspector frowned. 'Oh, dear. I specifically wanted to question the members of your group.'

'Then you knew that Mrs Greenwood wasn't acquainted with anyone outside the group, sir?' Barnes asked. He gazed in admiration at his superior. The inspector felt his confidence increase just a tad.

'I can't say that I actually knew, Constable,' he admitted honestly. 'But I suspected that might be the case.'

'I do hope you catch the murderer soon,' Cecilia said earnestly. 'I daresay we probably won't find out who won the poetry contest until this matter is cleared up.'

The inspector didn't know how to respond to this outrageous statement. Really, people amazed him. Here a perfectly innocent woman had been murdered, and all Miss Mansfield was concerned about was who won the contest. 'Er, yes, I suppose that might be true,' he murmured. 'Is there anything else?'

Cecilia cocked her head to one side, her plain face creased in thought. 'I don't think so. Now, if you don't mind, I must get home. Mama and Papa will be dreadfully put out when they find out what's happened.'

She flounced away, her bright pink skirts swishing with every step she took.

Barnes turned to the inspector. 'What do you think, sir?'

'I think, Constable,' Witherspoon replied glumly,

'that this case is going to be very nasty. Very nasty, indeed.'

'Not to worry, sir,' Barnes replied cheerfully. 'You're good with the nasty ones. Brings out the best in you, so to speak.'

The inspector suppressed a shudder. He knew he was going to get stuck with this murder. He just knew it. And Inspector Nigel Nivens would no doubt raise a terrible fuss. Nivens seemed to think that Witherspoon was 'hogging all the homicides', when, really, it was hardly his fault that he got them. And certainly being here tonight wasn't his fault, either. He hadn't even wanted to come.

'Thank you, Constable,' he replied. 'Let's have a word with Miss Marlow, the owner of the house. Then let's get up to the balcony and have a look round. Perhaps we'll get lucky and find that our killer has made a mistake and left some valuable evidence lying about.'

'Right, sir. Was the victim a good-size woman?'

'A bit taller than average, I'd say. She wasn't fat, but she wasn't slender, either, if you understand what I mean.'

Barnes nodded. 'Then even with a knife in her, I'll warrant she didn't go over the edge without puttin' up a bit of a struggle.'

They made their way to the drawing room. Lucinda Marlow, looking pale and frightened, sat huddled on the settee. The inspector cleared his throat. 'Miss Marlow,' he said softly.

'Inspector Witherspoon,' she said, her voice shaky. 'I expect you want to ask me a few questions.'

'Only a few, Miss Marlow, I assure you,' he said kindly. 'I realize this must be most upsetting for you.'

'It's awful.' Her lovely hazel eyes filled with tears. 'But please, ask me whatever you like.'

The inspector's mind went blank.

They stood there for a moment and the silence grew. Finally Barnes cleared his throat. The inspector blurted out the first thought that sprang into his head. 'Er, how well did you know Mrs Greenwood?'

'Not very well at all,' Miss Marlow replied. 'She joined our circle a few months ago, but she's not very friendly. Frankly, I was surprised when she came tonight. I quite expected her to stay away.'

'But I thought the winner of your poetry contest was going to be announced tonight. Surely Mrs Greenwood would have been interested in that,' Witherspoon said.

Miss Marlow gave a dainty shrug. 'Perhaps she was.'

'Did you see anything unusual tonight, Miss Marlow?' Barnes asked. 'Anyone following Mrs Greenwood. Anyone acting in a strange manner toward the lady?'

'No, I can't say that I did.'

The inspector stifled a sigh. This was going to be a complicated case. He could feel it in his bones. It was going to be one of those terrible murders where no one saw or heard a ruddy thing of any use at all to the police. Drat. And he did so want justice to be done. Even if the victim hadn't been a very friendly person, she certainly hadn't deserved to be murdered. 'Do you know if she had any enemies?'

Lucinda Marlow looked down at the carpet. 'Actually, Inspector, I can't say that she had any enemies, but I do know that she didn't like Mrs Stanwick. She's also one of the members of our group. There were several occasions that I can remember when Mrs Greenwood went out of her way to be rude to Mrs Stanwick.'

'How about Dr Sloan?' Barnes asked. 'Did she dislike him as well?'

Miss Marlow glanced up in surprise. 'Dr Sloan? No. As far as I know Mrs Greenwood had no feelings about Dr Sloan one way or the other. I certainly wasn't aware of any animosity between them.'

'Miss Marlow, is Mrs Stanwick still here?' Witherspoon asked hopefully.

She bit her lip and blushed. 'No, I told everyone they could leave,' she stammered. 'I'm sorry, I hope that was all right. But that young policeman took down everyone's name and address, and, well, surely you don't think one of my guests or one of our circle actually murdered Mrs Greenwood.'

'Don't distress yourself, Miss Marlow,' he replied, feeling terribly sorry for the poor woman. 'We've formed no opinion as to the identity of the murderer whatsoever. We'll speak with the other members of your circle tomorrow. What we really need now is someone to show us the way to the third-floor balcony.' Though she really shouldn't have taken it upon herself to let everyone leave, he couldn't be annoyed with her. The dear lady looked so terribly distraught.

'That's most kind of you, Inspector,' she said,

giving him a brilliant smile. 'I'll have the butler take you upstairs.'

The balcony opened off a large, wood-floored passageway that bisected the top floor of the house. But the killer hadn't made any mistakes and left any evidence lying about, at least not as far as the inspector could tell.

He sighed and stared at the French doors, their panes grim and coated with dust, that opened out onto the balcony. 'The butler said that Miss Marlow had this door opened to keep the air circulating. He said she always did it when the house was full of people.'

'That sounds right, sir.' Barnes scratched his chin. 'With all that crowd milling about downstairs, it probably would get pretty warm, especially on a night like tonight. Mind you, I don't expect the poor woman thought one of her guests would wander all the way up here and get herself murdered.'

The balcony was small, round, and made of stone and mortar. Witherspoon and Barnes stepped outside.

'Blimey, sir,' the constable said as he squeezed into the tiny space behind the inspector, 'there's hardly room for a body to move. I wonder why Mrs Greenwood took it into her head to come up here.'

'Perhaps she wanted some fresh air,' the inspector suggested. 'Though I must say, that's a jolly good walk up all those stairs, and if she only wanted air, she could just as easily have gone outside.'

'Maybe she just wanted to look at the view.'

From where he stood, Witherspoon could see the garden in great detail. The illumination, so thoughtfully provided by Miss Marlow for her guests, brightened even the darkest paths and deepest shadows.

'The rail is a good height,' Barnes said thoughtfully. He slipped past the inspector and peered over the edge. 'Even with a knife in her back, it must have took some doing to get her over the top here.'

The inspector looked up sharply. The constable was a tall man, close to six feet. The side of the balcony came up to his waist. 'You're right, Barnes. I think we can conclude our killer is probably a man. I don't think a woman would have the strength to have lifted Mrs Greenwood over the edge.'

'Course, she could've fallen forward,' Barnes suggested. 'And then whoever was standin' behind her could have just given her a good shove.'

'Possible,' the inspector said thoughtfully, 'but not likely. It's been my experience that stabbing victims usually fall backwards, not forwards.' Actually, he wasn't really sure of that fact. But it did sound quite clever.

Smythe knocked softly on Mrs Jeffries's door. He cocked his ear to the wood and heard a faint rustling sound. 'Mrs Jeffries,' he hissed, 'it's me. Smythe. Get up, I've got to talk to you.'

The door flew open and the housekeeper, wrapped in a heavy burgundy wool dressing gown, peered out at him. 'Gracious, Smythe, it's the middle of the night. What's wrong?'

'Nothing's wrong, Mrs J. But I think we might 'ave ourselves another murder. One of the guests at that fancy ball the inspector went to tonight took a tumble off the third-floor balcony. She's dead. And as she 'ad a knife stickin' out of her back, it weren't no accident.'

Mrs Jeffries brightened immediately. 'Get Wiggins and then get down to the kitchen. I'll wake Betsy and Mrs Goodge. But be very quiet; we don't want Mrs Livingston-Graves to hear us.'

He turned and tiptoed quickly toward the stairs leading to the fourth floor.

'Smythe,' she called out softly. 'When's the inspector returning?'

'He told me to come back for 'im in a couple of 'ours,' the coachman replied. 'So we've got a bit of time.'

Mrs Jeffries turned and crept down the hallway to rouse the maid and the cook.

Unlike most households, the female servants all had their own rooms. They were located on the third floor of the huge house. The housekeeper's rooms consisted of a small sitting room and a bedroom. Mrs Jeffries made certain the rest of the staff had full use of her sitting room if they wanted. Betsy's room was located nearest the stairwell, and Mrs Goodge, as befitting her station as the cook, had the larger, sunnier room next door. Up the staircase onto the fourth floor there was an attic on one side and a largish 'box' room on the other. Smythe, Wiggins, and Fred, when he wasn't sneaking down to the inspector's room, shared those quarters.

Within a few minutes they were gathered round the large table in the kitchen. Even Fred, looking sleepy and grumpy, had come down.

'What's all this, then?' Mrs Goodge mumbled. 'Should I put the kettle on?'

Betsy, her long blonde hair tumbling over her shoulders, yawned. 'Have we got us a murder?'

Wiggins, who didn't look like he was quite awake yet, mumbled something under his breath.

Smythe, who was staring at the maid, didn't say anything.

'Please, Mrs Goodge,' Mrs Jeffries said. 'I think a cup of tea would be wonderful. Now, Smythe.' She turned toward the coachman, but he didn't seem to hear her. 'Uh, Smythe,' she repeated, poking him lightly on the arm.

''Ave I got a wart on my nose?' Betsy asked grumpily.

Smythe flushed and drew his gaze away from the maid. 'Well, let's see now. As I told Mrs J, a woman took a tumble off the balcony at that fancy ball tonight. She had a knife in her back. Her name was Hannah Greenwood. She was one of the guests.'

'Doesn't sound like it was an accident, then,' Mrs Goodge muttered. She moved slowly toward the stove, teakettle in hand.

'As soon as I found out what were goin' on,' Smythe continued, 'I 'ad a word with this Mrs Greenwood's coachman. Nice bloke, works out of Piper's Livery . . . Well, this feller does a lot of drivin' for Mrs Greenwood. Said tonight she weren't upset or unhappy about anythin'. He claimed, if anythin', she were right pleased about somethin'. Besides, he says this Mrs Greenwood's a right old tartar. He didn't seem in the least surprised she'd got herself done in.'

Mrs Jeffries digested this piece of information. Mr Jeffries, the housekeeper's late husband, had been a policeman in Yorkshire for over twenty years. She'd learned a great deal about murder investigations from him. Unlike many of his colleagues, he hadn't assumed that because one was a servant, one was an idiot. On the contrary, when Constable Jeffries was working on a case, he took servants' observations very seriously. Mrs Jeffries made it a point to follow his lead. She'd found that servants were not all that different from their masters. True, some were stupid, lying and lazy. But many were intelligent, observant and perceptive. By respecting people and not status, she and the other members of the household at Upper Edmonton Gardens had solved several murders.

Not, of course, that they ever let on to the inspector. He thought he did it all himself. And they were all dedicated to keeping him thinking that way as well.

She glanced around the table, smiling slightly as she took in their sleepy but earnest expressions; Smythe and Wiggins had originally worked for the inspector's late aunt Euphemia. When she'd passed away, leaving her fortune and her home to Inspector Witherspoon, he'd kept both men on out of the goodness of his heart. He no more needed a coachman than he needed a hole in his head. And as for Wiggins – he was no more a trained footman than he was a dancing bear. But Gerald Witherspoon never considered tossing them out. He'd hired Mrs Goodge, a superb cook, but getting on in years, for the same reason – his kind heart. Betsy had shown up sick and penniless on his doorstep, and he'd given her employment as a maid, after hiring Mrs Jeffries to run his household and nurse the girl back to health. Was it any wonder they were all so loyal to the man?

But Mrs Jeffries didn't fool herself that their devotion to detection was totally altruistic. As Betsy once told her, dashing about following suspects and digging for clues was decidedly more interesting than scrubbing floors and ironing linens.

'So her own driver wasn't surprised she'd been murdered. That's a very interesting observation,' she said softly.

'And that's not all.'

The kettle whistled. Betsy got down the cups and Wiggins went to the cooling larder for a jug of milk. They waited until Mrs Goodge had poured the tea.

Again, Mrs Jeffries marvelled at how easily they all ignored the stringent codes most households followed. There was no hierarchy of false status here. No one needed to have their sense of worth bolstered by giving in to the foolish practices of most other households. They worked together as a team. Mrs Goodge didn't expect a maid or a footman to wait on her just because of her position as the cook, and Smythe didn't balk at doing anything asked of him.

The inspector's household was unique. Mrs Jeffries took some small pride in feeling that she'd helped make it that way. After all, she had been the first innovator. She remembered their shocked expressions the day she'd called them all to her sitting room shortly after the inspector had hired her. She'd told them precisely what their duties were, and then she'd told them she didn't give a fig when they did their chores as long as they got done properly. Once their work was finished, their time was their own. The only one who'd balked had been Mrs Goodge. But even she'd softened after Mrs Jeffries had announced she was getting rid of the odious practice of morning prayers. As far as the housekeeper was concerned, how one dealt with the Almighty was one's own business. And no one wanted to get up at the crack of dawn and gather in the drawing room for a Bible reading anyway. Least of all the inspector.

When they were all settled, they sipped their tea and waited for Smythe to tell them the rest.

'Well, go on,' Mrs Goodge urged. 'We've not got all night.'

'I found out a few other things about this Mrs Greenwood, too,' he said. 'But I'm not sure it 'as anythin' to do with her death.'

'Tell us anyway,' Mrs Jeffries suggested. 'As we've learned many times in the past, the most innocuous information can help us greatly.'

'This Mrs Greenwood, she weren't all that good a friend of the 'ostess, the lady who was havin' the ball.'

'And who is that?' Mrs Jeffries inquired. She wanted to get as many facts as possible.

'Lucinda Marlow.' Smythe's heavy brows drew

together in thought. 'I overheard the footman sayin' that Miss Marlow was havin' a go at a woman in a dark blue dress, and that's the colour that Mrs Greenwood were wearin'. So I'm wonderin' if this Miss Marlow and the victim 'ad been 'avin' words so to speak.'

Mrs Jeffries reached for her mug of tea. 'Did the footman actually identify the woman in the blue dress?'

He shook his head. ''E didn't know who Miss Marlow were talkin' to; 'e just 'eard the voices and saw a bit of blue stickin' out from behind the drawin' room door. They was standin' in a corner.'

From above, they heard the thump of heavy footsteps. 'Hello, hello.' Mrs Livingston-Graves voice could be heard from three flights up. 'Is anyone down there.'

'Oh, blast,' Betsy muttered. 'We finally gets us a decent murder, and we've got her hangin' about.'

Disgusted voices started babbling. Mrs Jeffries quickly shushed everyone. She got up and hurried to the foot of the stairs. 'It's all right, Mrs Livingston-Graves,' she called. 'Do go back to bed.'

'What are you doing up?' the woman screeched. They could hear her thumping down the second-floor stairs now.

'I couldn't sleep and I'm fixing myself a cup of hot milk. There's no need for you to trouble yourself.'

'You sure you're alone down there?'

Mrs Jeffries rolled her eyes. 'Quite sure. Please, do go back to bed. You'll catch a chill.'

'All right, then. But mind you, I'll have a word

46

with Gerald tomorrow. It's a bit of liberty, the house-keeper roaming about in the middle of the night and waking decent people.'

Smythe swore under his breath. Betsy's eyes narrowed in fury and Mrs Goodge snorted. Even Wiggins looked stunned by the woman's audacity.

'What are we going to do?' Mrs Goodge said. 'Tryin' to find out anything about this case is going to be bloomin' difficult with that old witch in the house.'

'You can say that again,' the coachman muttered darkly, 'Maybe it's time we figured out a way to send 'er nibs packin'.'

Everyone had a suggestion as to how to get rid of Mrs Livingston-Graves. When the ideas became too outrageous and involved shanghaiing and white slavery, Mrs Jeffries hid a smile behind her mug and raised her hand for silence. 'Don't worry about Mrs Livingston-Graves,' she said softly. 'She won't be interfering in our investigation. I'll see to that.'

CHAPTER THREE

IT WAS PAST two in the morning when the inspector arrived home. Rubbing his eyes, he crept to the coatrack and hung up his hat and coat. Every bone in his body was tired, his head ached, and he desperately wanted a nice hot drink.

As he turned for the stairs, he saw Mrs Jeffries coming down the hallway carrying a tray. 'Good gracious, Mrs Jeffries,' he whispered, 'it's very late. You didn't need to wait up for me.'

'It's quite all right, sir,' she replied. 'I've made a pot of tea. I thought you might need something to warm you up. Smythe said there had been a murder. How very dreadful for you. Shall we go into the drawing room?'

'This is most kind,' he said, following her. He watched her set the tray down on a table and pour two cups. 'It's been a very strange evening.' Settling down in his favourite chair, Witherspoon prepared to unburden himself. 'And I was having a jolly good time, as well. Did you know that Lady Cannonberry and I share a common interest? She's quite a railway enthusiast. Isn't that amazing?'

'Very,' Mrs Jeffries replied. She handed him his tea and picked up her own cup. As delighted as she was to hear that he'd enjoyed Lady Cannonberry's company, she didn't really want to talk about it now. She wanted to talk about murder.

'Now, sir, about your murder,' she prodded. 'Who was the victim?' Unfortunately, she didn't want the inspector to know she'd received any information from Smythe, so she was forced to waste time asking questions to which she already knew the answers. But it was a small price to pay to keep the dear man in the dark about the activities of his household.

'A lady named Hannah Greenwood.' He paused and took a quick sip. 'Older woman, possibly in her late fifties, and widowed. She's a member of the Hyde Park Literary Circle, so she was one of the guests this evening. The poor woman was stabbed in the back and shoved off an attic balcony. Horrible. I can't imagine why people do such diabolical things, can you?'

'No, sir.' But, of course, she could. Evil, greed, lust, revenge, and hatred had been part of the human condition since Adam. Mrs Jeffries thought it a true mark of the inspector's sterling character that after all his years with the police he was still genuinely shocked by the dark side of human nature. Most men in the inspector's position would have become extremely cynical.

'But, for once, we seem to have had a bit of luck. I mean, there were dozens and dozens of guests at the ball, but it appears that Mrs Greenwood wasn't acquainted with anyone other than the members of the literary circle.'

'How very clever of you to have found that out so quickly.'

He smiled modestly. 'Not so very clever, I'm afraid. One of the guests, Miss Mansfield, made a point of giving me that information.' He shook his head. 'Yet even with that bit of luck, I've a feeling this investigation is going to be very difficult. Very difficult indeed.'

'Of course it will be, sir,' Mrs Jeffries said briskly. 'They always are. But you must admit, you're at your very best when the case is complicated.' She gave him an encouraging smile.

'Thank you, Mrs Jeffries,' he murmured. 'Well, as I was saying, Lady Cannonberry and I were having this extremely interesting conversation out in the garden, when all of a sudden Mrs Greenwood comes hurtling off the balcony and lands on the terrace.'

'You actually saw it happen?'

He shook his head. 'Not really. I mean, we were outside, but my back was to the terrace. I didn't realize anything was wrong until I heard the screams.'

Mrs Jeffries clucked her tongue. There were dozens of questions she wanted to ask, but she'd learned from past experience that she was apt to get far more information out of the inspector by letting him talk at his own pace.

'Naturally, I took charge. Had to, really. I am the police.' He frowned. 'At first I assumed Mrs Greenwood's death was an accident. One doesn't expect to go to a fancy Jubilee Ball and find oneself dealing with murder, does one?'

'Of course not, sir,' she agreed, watching him

closely. He looked very anxious, very unsure of himself.

'I mean, I realized it was murder as soon as Mrs Putnam screamed out that there was a knife in the victim's back.'

'Who is Mrs Putnam?'

'One of the other members of the circle. Unfortunately, the, er . . . body landed only a few feet away from Mrs Putnam and two other ladies.'

'How very unpleasant.'

'Yes.' He sighed. 'I'm sure it was. Though I must say, the ladies took it surprisingly well. No one fainted. Odd, isn't it? We're so used to thinking of women as the weaker sex, yet it was Mrs Hiatt who got to Mrs Greenwood first. She didn't hesitate in the least. She leapt to her feet and dashed right over to see if she could be of assistance. You know, Mrs Jeffries, sometimes I have a very strong feeling that there is much we don't understand about the capabilities of females.'

Mrs Jeffries could spend the rest of the night lecturing him on exactly how capable women were, but she didn't really want to waste any more time. There was a murder to solve. 'I'm sure you're quite right,' she replied.

'Uhmmm . . . women. Sometimes they're not what they appear to be, are they? Then again, who of us is? Now, where was I?'

'You were describing the murder.'

'Oh, yes. Well, after I saw that Mrs Greenwood was dead, I asked Miss Marlow to send for the police and I told everyone to go into the drawing room.

But I'm afraid that I may have made a mistake at this point,' he said. 'Silly of me, I suppose. But, one assumes people will hang about after a murder.'

'Didn't the constables take statements from the guests and the servants?' Mrs Jeffries asked.

'Of course. But I really should have questioned the members of the literary circle tonight. I intended to, you see. Especially after I spoke with Miss Mansfield. Unfortunately, I must not have made my instructions clear. Miss Marlow, that's the lady who was our hostess, seemed to be under the impression that everyone could go home as long as they gave the constable their name and address. She told everyone to leave. So tomorrow I've got to start from the beginning. You know what that means – the trail will have started to go cold.'

'Now, now, sir. Don't be too hard on yourself. No one, not even the chief inspector, expects you to be omniscient. Furthermore, you were in a rather awkward position. You might be a policeman, but you were also a guest at the Marlow home.' She knew the inspector needed his self-confidence boosted a tad.

'Thank you, Mrs Jeffries. One doesn't like to think one is a complete incompetent.'

'Nonsense, sir. You're brilliant at solving murders and catching killers. I've no doubt whatsoever that you'll solve this one as well.' She smiled. 'You know how much I love hearing about your detection methods, so do tell me everything.'

Some of the anxiety vanished from his eyes. 'To begin with, it was dashedly hard keeping people straight tonight. Half the women there were in blue gowns. They all looked alike from the back. Most confusing. Every time I turned around I was losing track of Lady Cannonberry. But that's neither here nor there. As to the investigation, I did learn a few interesting facts. Mrs Putnam confirmed that Mrs Greenwood was only at the ball because she was a member of the circle. Which is most helpful. That fact will certainly narrow down the field of suspects, so to speak.'

'Really, sir?'

'Certainly. As the victim wasn't acquainted with the other guests, it's likely that she was murdered by someone from the circle. Why would a stranger lure her up to a dark balcony, stick a carving knife in her back, and then shove her over?'

Mrs Jeffries wasn't so sure the inspector's assumption was correct. So far, they knew very little about Hannah Greenwood. Despite what Cecilia Mansfield might have said about her not knowing anyone at the ball except for her own circle, she may well have had an enemy she didn't know about. Still, Mrs Jeffries did understand the inspector's reasoning. Unless the motive was robbery or the killer a madman, one was most likely to be murdered by someone one knew. 'Have you discovered if anyone in the circle had a motive?'

'Not yet. But Miss Mansfield, she was one of the ladies with Mrs Hiatt, did tell me that earlier in the evening she'd seen Mrs Greenwood having an argument with Dr Sloan. He's the president of the group and, I might add, the one in charge of the poetry contest. Miss Marlow also mentioned that Mrs

Greenwood wasn't very well liked. She was surprised Mrs Greenwood had shown up for the ball. I rather got the impression from both Miss Marlow and Miss Mansfield that Mrs Greenwood wasn't a very sociable person. As a matter of fact, Miss Marlow mentioned that the victim had gone out of her way on several occasions to be rude to one of the other members, a Mrs Stanwick.'

'I take it you weren't able to speak with either Dr Sloan or Mrs Stanwick.'

'They'd both already left. But I'll remedy that tomorrow.' He shrugged. 'We were able to account for several of the members' exact location when the murder occurred. Lady Cannonberry was with me, of course. Mrs Putnam was speaking with Miss Mansfield and Mrs Hiatt, so the three of them all have alibis, and Mr Putnam was standing over to one side of the terrace, sneaking a cigar. I remember seeing him myself.'

'So who hasn't been accounted for?'

Witherspoon frowned. 'Dr Sloan, of course, and Mrs Stanwick. Our hostess, Miss Lucinda Marlow . . .' He paused, trying to recall the other names in the circle. Drat, he should have written them down. But Barnes always took down those details in his notebook, and he didn't have the constable here to refresh his memory. He sighed and rubbed his eyes wearily. 'There's several other names but, honestly, I'm simply too tired to remember them right now. I'll start afresh tomorrow.'

'So the case is definitely yours?' Mrs Jeffries held her breath. On the inspector's last few cases, one of the other police inspectors, an odious man named Nigel Nivens, had made such a fuss that she'd feared her dear employer would get the next murder snatched right out from under his nose. Inspector Nivens was foaming at the mouth to investigate a homicide. But as Mrs Jeffries didn't think Nigel Nivens had the intelligence to find a potato in a greengrocer's, she sincerely hoped he would keep his paws off the inspector's case.

'I expect so,' he replied glumly. 'As I was "on the scene", so to speak, I'm sure the chief will insist I continue the investigation. That's not going to make Inspector Nivens very happy. He's always hinting that I'm hogging all the homicides.'

'Don't worry about Inspector Nivens,' Mrs Jeffries said firmly. 'You've far more experience in these matters than he does. Were you able to get any useful information out of the servants? Had anyone seen anything suspicious?'

'We haven't finished questioning them yet,' he admitted. 'They were all most upset. Two of the maids were weeping hysterically. Mrs Craycroft, the housekeeper, was attending to Miss Marlow, and the butler had been totally occupied with the ball. We'll try again tomorrow. Once everyone calms down we should be able to learn something useful.' He sighed again. 'I tell you, Mrs Jeffries, unless we can find an eyewitness or someone comes forward to confess, this might very well be the case I don't solve. We've practically no physical evidence.'

'What about the murder weapon?'

'That won't do us much good, I'm afraid. The

killer used a carving knife from the cold buffet table. Anyone in the house could have picked it up.'

Despite yawns and sleepy expressions, there was an air of suppressed excitement a few hours later. Mrs Jeffries told the other servants what she'd learned from the inspector in the wee hours. She gave them every single bit of information she'd wormed out of her employer, leaving out nothing, no matter how insignificant the detail.

'So you see,' she said, 'I think our first task is to learn everything we can about Mrs Greenwood and the Hyde Park Literary Circle.'

Smythe frowned thoughtfully. 'What are them names again?'

'Dr Sloan, Mrs Stanwick, Miss Lucinda Marlow . . .' She paused. 'There are others, but the inspector had already determined that Mr and Mrs Putnam couldn't have done it, as they were on the terrace. Nor could Miss Mansfield or Mrs Hiatt. As he was with Lady Cannonberry when the crime occurred, she's not involved, either.'

'What about Edgar Warburton and Shelby Locke?' the coachman asked.

'Who are they?' Betsy demanded, annoyed that Smythe always seemed to get the jump on her.

'Two members of the circle,' he replied smugly, giving her a cocky grin. 'I overheard Lady Cannonberry mention them when I brung her home last night.'

'Thank you, Smythe,' Mrs Jeffries said quickly. She wanted to nip any incipient rivalry in the bud.

Devoted as they all were to the inspector, they weren't above trying to outdo one another when it came to digging up clues. 'That's most helpful. But I think I'd better have a word with Lady Cannonberry today in order to get a complete list of names. There may be one or two more who were at the ball.'

'Cor,' muttered Wiggins, rubbing the sleep out of his eyes. 'That's a right lot of suspects we've got. What if this woman got herself stabbed by someone else? You know, one of them lunatics.'

'Now, how would a lunatic get himself invited to a fancy ball?' Mrs Goodge said impatiently.

'It don't have to be a 'im,' Wiggins argued. 'It could be a 'er. And 'ow do we know there ain't lunatics running about loose? Sometimes they look as right as you or me. My old gran told me about a woman who used to live in her village. She were a right respectable lady, too. No one thought there was anythin' wrong with 'er. But one day she locked 'erself in the church and started painting all the walls blue. She even painted over all the pretty stained-glass windows. Claimed that God had told her to do it 'cause he were gettin' right sick of seein' the same old buildin' Sunday after Sunday.'

'Don't be daft, boy,' the cook snorted. 'That's the silliest story I ever heard. If there's anyone who's not right in their head's around here, it's you.'

'I'm not so sure about that,' Betsy muttered. 'I'm beginnin' to think I'm losing my mind.'

Surprised, they all stared at her.

'Whatever do you mean?' Mrs Jeffries asked.

Betsy sighed. 'It's the silliest thing, really. I

shouldn't have mentioned it. I guess I'm just tired and it popped out.'

'Go on, girl, tell us the rest,' Smythe urged.

'It's my shoes,' Betsy said. She stared at the top of the table. 'There was a big hole in the bottom of one of my good black leather walking shoes. I kept meanin' to take it down to Mr Conner's and get it fixed. But I never got around to it. Well, a couple of days ago, I got the shoes out to make sure they was clean and the hole was gone. There was a brand-new sole on it.'

Smythe laughed. 'Is that what was worryin' you? Someone just did ya a favour, that's all.'

'But why would someone do that for me and not say anything about it?' Betsy shook her head. 'I think that's right strange.'

'I think Smythe's right,' Wiggins said. 'Someone's just doin' somethin' nice for ya, but don't want to say nuthin'. It's probably the same person who brought me that new packet of paper.'

'Someone's bought you paper?' Mrs Jeffries asked. She suspected she knew who'd fixed Betsy's shoes, but she didn't think that person would bother buying the footman more writing paper.

Wiggins nodded. 'Last week it was. I come in and found the paper in me drawer. Come in right handy as well.'

'Are you sure you didn't buy the paper yourself?' Smythe asked. 'Admit it, lad, sometimes you're a bit on the forgetful side.'

'Sometimes I might forget to clean the back steps or polish the doorknocker,' Wiggins protested. 'But

I've never once in me life forgot spendin' me money. And this 'ere was good quality paper. Whoever bought it paid a pretty penny for it.'

'Can we get on with the business at hand?' Mrs Goodge asked tartly. 'We've got a murder to solve. Time's gettin' on. If we don't get crackin', Mrs Nosy Parker will be down here screaming that we're takin' too many tea breaks.'

Mrs Jeffries stifled her own curiosity. They could learn the identity of this mysterious gift-giver later. 'Mrs Goodge is right. We must get busy.'

'So what do we do first?' Wiggins reached down and scratched Fred behind the ears.

'As we have several names already, I think it would be best if we learned what we could about the other members of the literary circle.' Mrs Jeffries drummed her fingers on the tabletop. 'Smythe, why don't you see what you can find out about this Shelby Locke and Edgar Warburton. Betsy, I think you ought to get over to the Marlow home and see if you can find out anything about what went on last night at the ball. Try talking to the maids. Wiggins, why don't you nip around to Mrs Greenwood's house and see what you can learn about the victim herself.' She turned to the cook.

Mrs Goodge grinned. 'Don't worry. I've got half of London troopin' through this kitchen today. I'll learn what I can about the members of that literary circle . . .' Her smile faded. 'But what am I going to do about her nibs? Mrs Livingston-Graves is always poking her nose down here. I can't get much out of anyone if she's hanging about all day, watching how much tea I serve and how many buns I let the delivery boy eat.'

'Nonsense, Mrs Goodge!' Mrs Jeffries exclaimed. 'You're being far too modest about your own abilities. If anyone can hold Mrs Livingston-Graves at bay, it's you.' The housekeeper wasn't exaggerating. She did think Mrs Goodge was remarkable. Without leaving her kitchen, the cook was able to learn the most intimate details about the suspects in their cases. She ruthlessly pumped information out of a veritable army of delivery boys, rag and bone merchants, chimney sweeps, and men from the gasworks. Additionally, because she'd cooked in so many grand households herself, she had sources of information from a huge network of other servants spread all over the city. There wasn't a morsel of gossip about anyone of importance in London that didn't pass through her kitchen.

'Mrs Goodge can probably 'andle the old girl, all right,' Smythe muttered. 'But what about the rest of us? Every time she lays eyes on me, she starts rantin' and ravin' about me cleanin' them attic windows.'

'What are we going to do?' Betsy moaned. 'We can hardly come and go as we please with her here! She's been after me for two days to air out them bloomin' linen cupboards upstairs. I don't want to air out cupboards; I want to get out and about and find out who killed Mrs Greenwood.'

'Don't worry.' Mrs Jeffries grinned mischievously. 'As I told you last night, I'll take care of Mrs Livingston-Graves. I do believe she'll be getting a special invitation today. An invitation she can't refuse.'

★ ★ ★

By ten o'clock Witherspoon and Constable Barnes were back at the Marlow home. His superiors, after learning that the inspector had been a guest at the ball, had instructed him to investigate the matter. Inspector Nivens hadn't been pleased. Witherspoon wasn't sure he was all that pleased about it, either. He'd rather hoped to sit this one out.

'I do hope Miss Marlow is feeling better this morning,' the inspector said to Constable Barnes as they waited in the drawing room for the lady of the house. He squinted at the portraits on the far wall. A stern-faced, elderly gentleman with deep-set eyes and white hair, and a grim-looking woman with a thin, flat line of a mouth seemed to glare back at him disapprovingly.

'Thank you, Inspector,' a soft voice said from the doorway. He whirled around to see Lucinda Marlow standing just inside, a faint smile on her lips.

'I'm feeling quite well today.' She continued as she advanced into the the room. 'I noticed you staring at my parents' portraits. Lovely, aren't they.'

That was hardly the adjective the inspector would have used, but he was far too much a gentleman to say so. 'Yes, Miss Marlow, they most certainly are.'

'They were done by Creighton, you know,' she said, smiling softly in the direction of the portraits.

As the inspector hadn't a clue who Creighton was, he wasn't sure what to say. Actually, he didn't really have to say anything. Miss Marlow whirled around, her dark green skirts swishing noisily, and said, 'But you're not here to look at paintings, are you? I presume you want to ask me more questions about last night's unfortunate incident.'

'I'm afraid I must.'

'I don't think there's all that much I can tell you, Inspector,' Lucinda replied with a shrug. 'I can't think of any reason why Mrs Greenwood would go up to the third floor, let alone why someone would want to kill her.'

'When was the last time you saw Mrs Greenwood?' Witherspoon asked. He saw Barnes whip out his notebook.

She frowned slightly. 'Let me think. It must have been close to ten-fifteen. Yes, that's right. I distinctly remember seeing Mrs Greenwood talking with Mrs Stanwick.'

'Did they see you?'

She shook her head. 'I don't think so. They were rather involved in their own conversation . . .' She paused. 'Both ladies had their backs to me, so I don't think they knew I was there.'

'Did you happen to hear what the ladies were discussing?' Witherspoon smiled slightly. 'One does occasionally overhear a conversation. Not, of course, that I'm implying you were deliberately trying to listen, but in a crowded room, sometimes one can't help but hear what's being said.'

Lucinda Marlow arched one eyebrow. 'How very diplomatic you are, Inspector. But as it happens, I was too far away to hear what they were discussing.'

'Did you happen to notice, Miss,' Barnes asked, 'if anyone else was standing close enough to hear the two women?'

'Not that I recall.' She cocked her chin to one side. 'Are you implying that Mrs Stanwick murdered Mrs Greenwood?'

'We're not implying anything of the kind,' Witherspoon said. 'We're trying to establish the facts. Any information about Mrs Greenwood's movements may be very helpful to us in catching her killer.'

'But you are assuming she was killed by one of the other guests, aren't you?'

'As I said, Miss Marlow,' the inspector replied patiently, 'at this point in the investigation, we're only interested in facts. We're not making any assumptions at all.'

'Good.' She smiled. 'I wouldn't like to think one of my guests had been murdered by one of my other guests or a member of the household. There were dozens of people coming and going during the ball. Extra serving staff, tradesmen making last-minute deliveries and, of course, dozens of coach drivers. I see no reason why some completely unknown person couldn't have slipped inside and done the foul deed.'

Witherspoon nodded politely. Miss Marlow could well be correct. However, he thought it most unlikely. People were generally murdered by those nearest and dearest to them, and from what he'd heard of the victim, he suspected she wasn't the sort of woman to be overly close to her coach driver or her maid. 'Did you see Mrs Greenwood after she'd finished conversing with Mrs Stanwick?'

'No, I was too busy with my other guests.'

'Can you give us a list of names of everyone who was in your house last night, please?'

'I gave a copy of my guest list to one of the constables last night. Surely you haven't lost it.'

'I'm sorry, Miss Marlow,' the inspector said. 'I didn't make myself clear. We haven't lost the guest list, but we would also like to know who else was in the house. As you just mentioned, there were dozens of outside servants and tradesmen coming and going. I'd like their names, please.'

'I'll need to consult with the butler and my housekeeper, Inspector,' she said. 'It may take me several hours to compose the list. Will that be satisfactory?'

'I'm sorry to put you to any extra trouble, Miss Marlow,' the inspector apologized. 'However, one never knows what one will find out unless one takes the trouble to look.'

'All right, you'll have your list by this afternoon. Is that all your questions? I don't really think there's anything more I can tell you.'

'I've only a few more. Where were you at ten-thirty last night?' he asked.

'Me?' Lucinda Marlow yelped. She was clearly outraged. 'What an impertinent question. I don't think I've got to answer that.'

'Please, Miss Marlow, we're only trying to find out what really happened.' Witherspoon had no idea why some people were so offended by the least little inquiry.

'I was in the ballroom,' she said coldly, 'seeing to the welfare of my guests. Where else would I be? After all, I was the hostess.'

★　★　★

Mrs Jeffries timed herself to arrive at the corner at precisely the right moment. She smiled in satisfaction as she spotted Lady Cannonberry coming out of her house, her cocker spaniel at her heels.

Shifting her basket to the other hand, the housekeeper crossed the street. 'Good afternoon, Lady Cannonberry,' she called cheerfully.

Lady Cannonberry, a woman of medium height with light brown hair, smiled broadly, her placid features and blue eyes expressing delight. She wore a mother-of-pearl grey gown trimmed with cherry-red silk stripes and a standing collar of matching crimson. The colour did wonders for her ivory skin. At forty-five, she was well past the first flush of youth, yet remained a very attractive woman. She was also a very nice woman, completely unaffected by her status as the wife of a late peer.

'Hello, Mrs Jeffries.' The cocker began to strain on its leash and bounce up and down. 'Boadicea, don't jump up on the lady.'

Boadicea, a caramel-coloured dog, immediately stopped leaping and flopped down onto her back. She wagged her tail in frantic delight at the sight of the housekeeper.

'Oh, do get up, you silly girl,' Lady Cannonberry continued. 'I'm so sorry. She doesn't act at all like her namesake, does she?'

Mrs Jeffries laughed and knelt down to rub the cocker's belly. 'No, but I expect she's a great deal more satisfying to have about than some horridly aggressive warrior queen.'

'She loves everybody.' Lady Cannonberry sighed.

'And she certainly gives me a great deal of company. So I mustn't complain.'

Mrs Jeffries stood up. 'I'm so dreadfully sorry your evening was spoiled last night.'

Lady Cannonberry shook her head in agreement. 'It was perfectly awful. The inspector and I were having such an interesting conversation, too. Do you know, he likes trains!' She made this announcement as though it were the most wonderful thing in the world. 'Then all of a sudden, poor Mrs Greenwood, came tumbling down off that balcony. I must say, it quite put a damper on the evening.'

'Yes, I rather expect it did.'

She nodded emphatically. 'But Gerald was wonderful. He took charge immediately. Kept everyone from going into a panic.'

Mrs Jeffries waited patiently while Lady Cannonberry extolled the inspector's many virtues. She nodded sympathetically, tut-tutted in the appropriate spots, and clucked her tongue in agreement when her companion expected it.

'The whole thing must have been dreadfully shocking,' Mrs Jeffries said, 'and not just for you. I'm sure your entire group was utterly appalled by what happened. And on the night of your poetry contest, too.' She wanted to get Lady Cannonberry gossiping about the other members of the Hyde Park Literary Circle.

'Oh, they were. Miss Marlow almost went into shock – she was as pale as a ghost. I don't blame her. It's not as if the poor woman has much social life at all. Her first party in ages and look what happens

'– one of her guests is murdered. And Mrs Stanwick. Goodness, she was so upset she had to lean on Mr Locke's arm when he escorted her to her carriage.'

'How awful,' Mrs Jeffries agreed.

'Oh, it was,' Lady Cannonberry said earnestly. 'The ball wasn't all that much of a success even before Mrs Greenwood's fall.'

'Really?'

'Personally, I was having a wonderful time,' She smiled and ten years seemed to melt off her age. 'Gerald is such an interesting companion. But I noticed that practically everyone else in our group was nervous. I expect it was the contest.'

'Competitions do sometimes bring out the worst in people, don't they?'

'They most certainly do,' Lady Cannonberry agreed. 'Mr Richard Venerable, you know, the poet, was to be our judge. Naturally, I hadn't a hope of winning, but I enjoyed writing the piece in any case. But several others seemed very anxious. Our president, Dr Sloan – he's had poems published before – I think he thought he stood the best chance. And, of course, Mr Locke was most annoyed . . . he claimed his best poems were lost. He didn't exactly come right out and accuse anyone, but supposedly he'd left his notebook at Miss Marlow's home at our last meeting. But no one had seen it. He virtually implied someone stole the notebook, and of course what he was really implying was that someone stole his poems. But, I can't believe anyone in our group would stoop to such a thing. Another thing for Miss Marlow to worry about.'

Mrs Jeffries nodded sympathetically. She quite liked Lady Cannonberry and she was delighted that the lady seemed so enamoured of the inspector. She was even more delighted to find her so very informative. 'Poor Miss Marlow. First a theft and then a murder,' she murmured.

'Honestly, Mrs Jeffries, it was a very peculiar evening. Mr Warburton – he's one of our newer members – was in a rage over something. He didn't even say hello when he arrived, and Mrs Greenwood—' She broke off. 'Oh, dear, one shouldn't speak ill of the dead.'

'Please, Lady Cannonberry, do get it off your chest,' Mrs Jeffries said soothingly. 'If you saw something amiss with the deceased, you really ought to talk about it. Perhaps what you noticed might have something to do with her murder.'

'Well, Mrs Greenwood had words with Mrs Stanwick.' Lady Cannonberry looked guiltily over her shoulder, as though she expected the ghost of the dead woman to come sneaking up on her. 'And I think it was over this silly contest. You know, the next time anyone suggests a literary contest, I shall put my foot down. It brings out the worst in everyone. Even Mrs Putnam, and she's a very good soul, was muttering about how unfair it was that those of us who were amateurs should be judged in the same category as Dr Sloan.'

'I believe this Mrs Putnam may have a point,' Mrs Jeffries said quickly. She wanted to get back to Mrs Greenwood's argument with Mrs Stanwick. 'Why do you think the two ladies were arguing over the contest?'

'I'm not certain they were. But I happened to come up behind them when I went to fetch my handkerchief, and I distinctly overheard Mrs Greenwood say to Mrs Stanwick that she'd never set foot in one of our meetings again.'

Fifteen minutes later Mrs Jeffries waved to Lady Cannonberry and turned to go home. Deep in thought, she walked slowly, putting all the small pieces of information that Lady Cannonberry had just given her into some semblance of order. She shook her head as she climbed the stairs. It was no good. The information that she had, while interesting, was far too sketchy to form any conclusion. The best that could be said was now she had a complete list of the members of the literary circle. And from what Lady Cannonberry had said, the inspector was correct earlier when he'd said no one else at the ball had any connection to Mrs Greenwood. She was a guest solely because she'd been a member of the literary circle. Mrs Jeffries wasn't discouraged, though. Once she heard what Betsy, Mrs Goodge, Smythe and Wiggins had found out today, the pieces would all start coming together.

Mrs Livingston-Graves met her at the door. 'It's about time you got back,' she snapped. 'There isn't a soul in this house except for that tight-lipped cook. The housemaid's disappeared, I haven't seen hide nor hair of that lazy footman, and even you had the audacity to desert me.'

'I had some household matters to see to,' Mrs Jeffries replied. She smiled slightly as she saw the white linen envelope in Mrs Livingston-Graves's hand. 'Is there something I can do for you?'

'Yes, I need someone to help me bring my trunk down.' Her narrow eyes gleamed with excitement. 'I've been invited to a house party. In Southampton. It seems a mutual friend happened to mention to someone of great importance that I was here in London. So I've been invited.'

'How very nice. Does the inspector know you're leaving us?'

She dismissed that with a wave of her hand. 'Not yet. But Gerald won't mind. It isn't every day one gets an invitation like this. He wouldn't want me to miss it.'

'I'm sure he wouldn't.' Considering that the inspector had taken to tiptoeing around the house to avoid his cousin, Mrs Jeffries was certain he wouldn't mind her going in the least. 'He'd want you to go.'

'If you can find that lazy good-for-nothing footman, have him bring my trunk down and then make sure the coachman brings the coach round. I want to catch the evening train.'

'You're taking your trunk?' Mrs Jeffries forced herself to keep her expression blank. 'Does that mean it will be a long visit?'

'Of course not.' Mrs Livingston-Graves stamped off toward the stairs. 'It means I'm taking all my clothes. One doesn't go visit an earl without proper attire.'

CHAPTER FOUR

'I QUESTIONED THE SERVANTS again, sir,' Barnes told the inspector as they left the Marlow house. 'The footman claimed the carving knife was still on the table at ten-fifteen. He specifically remembers because he overheard one of the guests askin' the time.'

'Ten-fifteen. Hmmm.' Witherspoon frowned slightly. 'The murder occurred at ten-thirty. Did the footman happen to notice when the knife went missing?'

Barnes shook his head. 'No, he were too busy servin' people. He didn't know it was gone until he saw it stickin' out of Mrs Greenwood's back.'

'Drat. Well, did he notice who in particular was hanging about the buffet table?'

'That end of the table was right beside the door. The lad says there were more traffic by that spot than hansoms at a railway station. What with guests trompin' up and down the stairs and goin' to and fro down that hallway, he didn't see a bloomin' thing.'

'What about the other servants? Did any of them see anything suspicious, anything out of the ordinary?'

Barnes pulled open the front door and stepped back to let the inspector pass. 'None of the house servants can remember seein' or hearin' anything unusual. The uniformed lads are interviewing the rest of them, the ones that were brought in to help with the ball.'

Witherspoon nodded and started down the steps. 'We'll just have to keep digging, Barnes.'

'This isn't goin' to be an easy one, is it?' Barnes said gloomily. 'What with half of London inside the Marlow house, we're goin' to have a devil of a time finding us a witness.'

The inspector cringed. He rather suspected the constable was right.

'Where to now, sir?' Barnes asked.

Witherspoon came to a full stop. Goodness, he thought, where should they go next? There was no point in going back to the station. They didn't really need to know the details of the autopsy report to investigate this murder. Witherspoon knew exactly how and when the victim had died. Besides, he really didn't want to risk running into Inspector Nivens.

'We'll go see the president of the Hyde Park Literary Circle,' he announced confidently as he stepped off the bottom step. 'Dr Oxton Sloan.'

He stopped again as he suddenly remembered something his housekeeper had once told him when they were sipping a companionable glass of sherry before dinner. 'Sometimes', she'd said, 'the best place to start an investigation isn't with the suspects; it's with the victim.'

'Shall we take a hansom to Dr Sloan's?' Barnes asked hopefully. He looked down at his feet. His shoes, new enough so that the shine hadn't rubbed off, pinched his toes.

'What? Oh, no, Constable,' Witherspoon replied airily. 'We've no need of a hansom. I've changed my mind. We'll see Sloan later. Right now we must get over to Bolton Gardens. That's not far from here. I daresay the walk will do us both good. I want to interview Mrs Greenwood's household.'

'How come you've been hanging about all mornin'?' The impudent boy stared suspiciously at Wiggins and Fred.

Wiggins stepped out from the tree trunk he and Fred had been lurking behind. The dog woofed softly at the intruder. 'Quiet, boy,' Wiggins hissed as he stared across the small clearing between the two rows of houses and studied his adversary.

The lad stared right back at him. With pale skin, blue eyes, and unkempt red hair sticking out of a grimy porkpie hat, the skinny child dressed in over-sized clothes couldn't be more than twelve.

'What's it to you?' Wiggins shot back. 'This is a public street. My dog and I can 'ang about 'ere as long as we like.'

'Yeah,' the boy sneered and wiped one dirty hand under his nose. 'But you ain't been stayin' on the street; you've been goin' in and out of them gardens there.' He broke off and gestured to his left in the direction of Bolton Gardens.

Fred growled low in his throat and the boy stepped back a pace. Wiggins laid a reassuring hand on the animal's head. 'That's none of yer business,' he replied, then decided to try to see what information he could get out of the youngster. He'd been hanging about the Greenwood house for hours now and hadn't seen hide nor hair of a servant or even a tradesman.

Wiggins was getting desperate. He couldn't go back to Upper Edmonton Gardens with nothing to report. 'But if you must know' – he jerked his thumb at the Greenwood residence – 'I'm tryin' to talk to someone from that 'ouse.'

'That's Mrs Greenwood's,' he said, looking warily at the dog, but by this time Fred had reverted to his natural good-natured self. He wagged his tail. The boy smiled and tentatively reached out a hand.

'Go ahead,' Wiggins urged. 'You can pet 'im. 'E's a good dog, Fred is. He were only growlin' 'cause you startled 'im. Did you know Mrs Greenwood?'

''Course I knew 'er. I worked for 'er, didn't I? 'Course, now that the silly old cow's gone and got 'erself done in, all of us is out of a job.' He knelt down and petted Fred, his small face creased with worry. 'I can't see that pie-faced sister of 'ers keepin' us on. She'll 'ave the 'ouse sold and all of us out in the streets before you can say Bob's Your Uncle.'

'What's your name?' Wiggins asked softly. He could see that beneath the boy's bravado was fear. A wave of sympathy washed over him; he knew exactly

74

what it felt like to be afraid you weren't going to have a roof over your head or food to fill your belly.

'Me name's Jon.'

'What did you do for Mrs Greenwood?'

Jon lifted his chin, suspicion clouding his eyes. 'What'cha want to know for and why you askin' all these questions? You ain't a copper.'

Wiggins knelt down beside him. Fred immediately licked his cheek. 'Get off, you silly dog,' he murmured. He smiled at Jon as he pushed Fred's snout out of his face. ''Ow do you know I'm not a copper?'

Jon grinned. 'Fer starters, you're too young to be anythin' but a peeler, and you couldn't be one of them, 'cause you ain't dressed like one.'

They were kneeling on a small strip of grass and sheltered from view by a low hedge. From the other side of the hedge Wiggins could hear the sounds of the busy street. He wondered how many other people might have spotted him hanging about the neighbourhood. 'Clever boy. You're right. I'm not a copper, but I do want to ask you some questions about Mrs Greenwood. I'm sorry you're goin' to be out of work, but ifn' you help me some, maybe I can help you.'

Jon stared at him, his expression a mixture of hope and suspicion. 'Why should you do anythin' to 'elp me?'

Wiggins shrugged. 'Let's just say I've been out of work a time or two myself,' he admitted casually, careful to keep his sympathy for the lad from showing.

'I'm not trained,' Jon warned. 'Mrs Greenwood

only kept me on because me dad used to work for her son. But there's lots I can do and I'm willin' to work like the devil. There's lots I can tell you about 'er, too. It weren't no surprise to me that she got 'erself murdered. She's been actin' peculiar for months now. Ever since . . .'

From the other side of the hedge, Wiggins heard a familiar voice. Fred did, too. The dog broke away from them and leapt in the direction of the road, barking at the top of his lungs.

Hoping to avoid disaster, Wiggins rushed after him, but he was too late. Fred dashed around the corner of the hedge straight into the inspector.

'Gracious,' yelped Witherspoon as Fred bounced happily up and down on the inspector. 'What on earth are you doing here, boy?' He glanced up as Wiggins came flying into view. 'Wiggins? Goodness, whatever are you and Fred doing round here? We're miles from Upper Edmonton Gardens.'

'Good afternoon, sir,' Wiggins stammered, his mind racing furiously. 'And you, too, Constable Barnes. Come on, Fred, get down. You'll get the inspector's trousers muddy.'

'Oh, that's all right,' Witherspoon said kindly. He reached down and scratched the animal behind the ears. 'Fred's just happy to see me and I'm quite pleased to see him, as well.' He broke off and cooed at the dog for a few moments. Wiggins used the time to try to come up with a reasonable excuse for being at Bolton Gardens.

'Now, young man . . .' With one last pat on Fred's head, the inspector straightened and stared curiously at his footman. 'What are you doing all the way over here?'

'Uh, uh, I was runnin' an errand for Mrs Goodge,' he sputtered frantically. 'She wanted me to pick up that fish you like so much, sir. You know, that special cod from that expensive fishmonger's over on the Brompton Road. Well, me and Fred spotted you a ways back, sir. We was tryin' to find a shortcut like. And, uh, well, you know how fond of you Fred is, so we darted up this way. You know, to surprise you like.'

Witherspoon beamed. He was quite touched. In the past Wiggins had always seemed a tad jealous of his close relationship with the animal. 'How very thoughtful of you, my boy. Isn't that nice, Constable?'

'It certainly is, sir,' Barnes replied, his eyes gleaming with amusement.

'And how very thoughtful of Mrs Goodge to remember how much I liked that cod,' the inspector finished, not wanting to leave anyone out.

'Well, ifn' that'll be all, sir, me and Fred best be on our way.' He whistled softly and Fred, after bumping the inspector's knees one last time, trotted over to him. 'See you at 'ome, sir,' he called.

'Righty ho, Wiggins. You and Fred be careful now.'

Wiggins nodded and then scurried off as fast as he reasonably could in the opposite direction. 'You almost give us away there, Fred,' he chided the dog, who trotted unconcernedly along at his heels. 'Next time I might not be able to come up with somethin' so fast.'

Wiggins cocked his head slightly, listening for the inspector's footsteps going the other way. After a few moments he turned and spotted the inspector and Barnes rounding the corner. He swivelled around and dashed back to where he'd left the boy.

'Blast and damn!' he muttered as he skidded to a stop behind the hedge. The clearing was empty. Jon was gone.

Inspector Witherspoon and Constable Barnes waited in the gloomy drawing room for the maid to fetch Hannah Greenwood's sister, Amelia Hackshaw. Witherspoon frowned uneasily. 'I say, Constable,' he whispered. 'This place does look a bit . . .' He stopped, not wanting to be rude, 'morbid.'

'Well, sir,' Barnes replied as he turned to stare at the black-draped windows, 'there has been a death in the family.'

'Of course. I know that, but Mrs Greenwood was only murdered last night. How did they get all this up so fast?' Witherspoon exclaimed. He gaped at the mourning cloth draped on every available surface. 'And really, this is a bit much. Why, I've seen families lose half their numbers and not put this much black in the house.'

Black crocheted antimacassars were draped on the back of the elegant brown settee and the matching chairs. The tables were covered with black fringed cloth, and on the carved mantel, black ribbons were tied around the brass candlesticks. On the wall over the mantel stood a row of portraits, their frames edged in black mourning cloth.

'Did you notice the foyer, sir?' Barnes asked. 'The mirrors were covered as well. I think they take death right seriously in this house, sir.'

Shaking his head, the inspector said, 'Apparently so. You know, I, too, believe in respecting the dead, but really . . .'

'You wanted to see me.'

At the sound of the voice, Witherspoon whirled around. His jaw dropped open with shock. Standing in the doorway was a middle-aged, blond-haired woman with thin hawk-like features and cool blue eyes. Ye Gods. It was Hannah Greenwood.

She smiled mockingly when she saw his expression. 'Don't be alarmed, inspector,' she said calmly as she advanced into the room. 'I'm Mrs Greenwood's sister. We were twins.'

'Blimey, sir,' Barnes muttered in the inspector's ear. 'That give me a right turn.'

'Do sit down,' she invited, gesturing toward the settee.

Grateful for something to do so he could get his bearings, the inspector and Barnes plopped themselves down. 'Er, first of all, Mrs Hackshaw, please accept my condolences for your loss.'

Amelia Hackshaw gave them a tight smile. 'Thank you.' She smoothed out the skirt of her elegant emerald-green gown and then gazed directly at the inspector. 'I appreciate your condolences, but we've no need to waste any more time. Why don't we dispense with the preliminaries, Inspector? Presumably, this isn't a social call. You're here to question me concerning Hannah's murder. I'm not squeamish nor easily upset. So please, do let's get this over with.'

Again Witherspoon was taken aback. The house was edged in black, for goodness' sakes. Yet the victim's own sister, whom he presumed must have been up half the night digging mourning cloth out of the attic, was as cool as a dish of lime sorbet. 'Er, yes, of course.' He cleared his throat. 'Did your sister have any enemies?'

'Enemies?' She arched one pale eyebrow. 'That's a rather silly question, Inspector. Obviously she had an enemy. Someone murdered her, didn't they? Hardly the act of a friend.'

'Yes, yes, of course,' he replied. 'What I meant to say was, do you know of anyone specifically who wished your sister harm?'

'If you meant to say that, then why didn't you?' she said impatiently. 'My sister wasn't an easy woman to get along with. She was much like me – she didn't suffer fools gladly.' She gave the inspector a withering look. 'But I don't know of anyone who actually had a reason to murder her.'

'Er, did she have any particular animosity toward anyone in the Hyde Park Literary Circle?'

'Not that I know of.' Amelia Hackshaw smiled. 'She hated all of them. Thought they were a pack of idiots.'

'Then why did she join the group?'

'She had her reasons.' Mrs Hackshaw shrugged. 'She didn't share those reasons with me.'

The inspector realized this line of questioning was getting him nowhere. 'How was your sister's mood yesterday?'

'The same as it always was – bad.'

'So she wasn't excited about the Jubilee Ball or the poetry contest?'

'Excited? No, I don't think so.' She paused and frowned thoughtfully. 'But I could be wrong about that. I think perhaps Hannah had actually gotten interested in poetry. Last week I found her reading one of those dreadfully pompous little literary publications. Some sort of poetry collection from the United States. Nonsense it was, too. I can't imagine why Hannah was interested in it.'

'Miss Hackshaw,' the inspector began.

'Mrs Hackshaw,' she corrected. 'Like my late sister, I am a widow.'

Somehow, that didn't surprise him. 'Did your sister have many friends or other outside activities?' He decided he might as well get as much information about the victim as possible. One never knew what one might stumble across unless one asked.

She snorted in derision. 'Hannah didn't have any friends at all. Her only activity outside this house was the circle. She hasn't been interested in much of anything since Douglas died.'

'Douglas?' The inspector straightened. Someone else was dead? Drat. 'May I ask who this Douglas person is and how he died?' He sincerely hoped he was an old man who'd died from natural causes.

'Douglas Beecher, Hannah's son. He died in a train accident this past spring. Hannah was devastated.'

'I'm sorry to hear that,' the inspector mumbled. 'Er, Mrs Hackshaw, do you know of anyone who benefits from Mrs Greenwood's death?'

'I do,' she said bluntly. 'Since Douglas is dead, I'll get it all. It's a considerable amount, Inspector. My sister outlived two husbands. She did well by both of them.'

'Thank you for your candour, Mrs Hackshaw,' Witherspoon said. He hoped he didn't look as shocked as he felt. 'Can you tell me what Mrs Greenwood did yesterday? Knowing her movements might be helpful in finding her killer.'

'No, I can't.' She smiled smugly. 'I wasn't here. I was visiting a friend in Croydon and I didn't get home until after Hannah had left for the ball.'

By the time they left the Greenwood home, the inspector's head pounded and his stomach growled. He knew very little about the victim and even less about her activities on the fateful day of her death. Mrs Hackshaw was a peculiar woman, to say the least, and the rest of the household seemed too frightened of their new mistress to answer more than the most perfunctory of inquiries. None of them seemed to know much about Mrs Greenwood's activities, either.

'I'd like to talk to the boy, Jon,' Barnes muttered as they trudged down the stairs. 'According to the maid, he's the only one who does know what Mrs Greenwood did yesterday. He were with her.'

'Yes, well, we'll come back and speak to him later. If he was with Mrs Greenwood, perhaps he can enlighten us as to her movements. I daresay, so far we've no evidence she did anything except go to the dressmaker's or whatever it is that women do before going to a ball.'

'We do know she were gone most of the afternoon, sir. That's something.' Barnes winced. His shoes were killing him now. 'Where to now, sir?'

'Let's go have a bit of lunch, Barnes. After that, we'll pay a call on Dr Oxton Sloan.'

Dr Sloan occupied rooms on the second floor of a house on a small square off the Marylebone High Street.

A smiling and talkative landlady, Mrs Nellie Tepler, escorted them up the stairs to Sloan's quarters.

'We don't get the police around here very often,' she chirped. 'Actually, we've never had them here before. Truth is, we don't get too many visitors. Pity really. Some of my gentlemen lodgers are so lonely.' She stopped in front of the first door on the second floor. Raising her fist, she pounded against the wood. 'Dr Sloan, you've got some visitors!' she screeched. 'It's the police. They want to talk to you.'

Witherspoon's ears tingled. Barnes rolled his eyes.

There was no answer. Mrs Tepler pounded again. 'Yoo-hoo, are you in there, Doctor?' She kept right on screeching and pounding until the door flew open.

'I heard you the first time, Mrs Tepler,' Sloan said irritably.

'Oh, sorry.' She laughed. 'You've some gentlemen to see you.'

'Thank you, Mrs Tepler,' he replied. The landlady, with one last curious glance, turned and strolled slowly down the stairs.

Sloan looked at the two policemen standing in his

doorway. 'I suppose you've come about that awful business last night,' he said. He opened the door wider and motioned them inside,

'Yes, sir, we have,' the inspector replied. He introduced himself and Barnes.

They entered a nicely furnished sitting room. In one corner stood a rolltop desk and a glass-fronted bookcase. Next to that was a small fireplace with a mustard-coloured settee and two matching chairs grouped in a tidy semicircle.

'Well, have a seat, then,' Sloan offered, gesturing toward the settee. He went behind his desk and sat down. 'And let's get on with it. I've not much time today.'

'Are you a medical doctor, sir?' Witherspoon asked.

Sloan looked surprised. 'I'm licensed. But I don't practise.'

'I see.' The inspector wondered why, but he couldn't think of a pertinent reason to ask. It didn't take a physician to stab someone in the back and toss them over a balcony. 'Could you tell me, how long have you known Mrs Greenwood?'

'I didn't really know Mrs Greenwood,' he replied. 'Except in the sense that she's a member of our literary group.'

'How long has she been a member of the group, then?' the inspector asked patiently.

Sloan frowned. 'Let me see, I believe she joined us in February. Yes, that's right. She came about a month later than Mrs Stanwick, and she joined the group in January.'

'So you've known the victim since February,' Witherspoon stated. 'Do you know if she had any enemies?'

'How would I know that?' Sloan said irritably. He drummed his fingertips on the desktop. 'I've already told you, I didn't know the woman personally. She wasn't overly popular in the group, but I don't think anyone hated her enough to kill her.'

'Someone did,' the inspector reminded him.

'Yes, I suppose someone did at that.' Sloan shrugged, as though the matter was of no concern to him. 'But I don't see what it's got to do with me or our circle. There were dozens of people in the house. The killer could have just as easily been someone completely unconnected with our group. Probably some madman.'

Witherspoon ignored that statement. Really, this case was most difficult. No one seemed to be in the least forthcoming. He decided to charge full ahead. 'Where were you at ten-thirty last night?'

Sloan eyed him warily. 'I was in the drawing room.'

'Really, sir? Are you sure? Mrs Putnam has already told us she looked in the drawing room and didn't see you.'

'Of course, how stupid of me.' Sloan smiled briefly. 'I'd forgotten. I'd been in the drawing room . . . oh, it must have been about ten twenty-five, when I suddenly realized I had to speak to Mr Venerable. So I went looking for him. At ten-thirty I was probably out in the garden.'

'If you were out in the garden, sir,' Witherspoon

asked, 'then why did Mrs Putnam not find you? She searched there, too. She specifically said she was concerned because it was almost time to announce the winner of the poetry contest, and she was alarmed because you'd disappeared.'

'I most certainly did not disappear. It's not my fault that confounded woman didn't find me,' Sloan snapped, an angry flush spreading over his cheeks. 'Now see here, Inspector, are you implying I had anything to do with Mrs Greenwood's death?'

'Not at all, sir.' He sighed inwardly. 'We're merely trying to establish where everyone was at the time of the murder.'

'I've told you where I was. The garden.'

'Where specifically were you in the garden?' Barnes asked quietly.

Sloan closed his eyes for a brief moment. 'For God's sake, I was all over the place. I've told you, I was looking for Mr Venerable. That garden is huge. I searched every path and practically shook the bushes looking for the man.'

'Did you see anyone?' the inspector asked.

'I saw dozens of people.'

'Could you name them, please?' As Witherspoon himself had been on the terrace with Lady Cannonberry, he wanted to see if the man would remember seeing him.

'I recall seeing Mrs Hiatt and Miss Mansfield. They were on the terrace. Mrs Hiatt was sitting on a bench.'

Witherspoon nodded. He wasn't certain he accepted Sloan's words. Miss Mansfield and Mrs

Hiatt had been on the terrace for a good half hour. He and Lady Cannonberry had seen them out there talking since ten o'clock. The inspector straightened his spine, rather proud of himself for remembering this particular detail. 'Did anyone see you?'

'Lots of people saw me. I expect some of them will remember. I am, after all, the president of the literary circle.'

'Did you find Mr Venerable, sir?'

'No.'

'When was the last time you spoke to Mrs Greenwood?' Witherspoon asked.

'Let me see,' Sloan murmured, his forehead creased in thought. 'I suppose it was at our last meeting. Yes, that's it. I spoke to her then.'

'Dr Sloan, you were seen having an argument with Mrs Greenwood only minutes before she was killed.'

'That's a lie!' he cried. 'We weren't having an argument. We were having a discussion.'

'Then you admit you did speak to her last night. What was the discussion about?'

'The contest. Mrs Greenwood asked me to clarify one of the rules. It was such a minor incident, I'd forgotten all about it until you mentioned it.'

'You're absolutely certain you weren't arguing with her?' the inspector pressed.

'Of course I'm certain.' He suddenly smiled. 'But if I were you, Inspector, I'd have a word with Mrs Stanwick.'

'We intend to speak to all the members of the literary circle.'

'Yes, but you should be especially interested in talking to Mrs Stanwick. She was quarrelling with Mrs Greenwood. To be blunt, Inspector' – Sloan picked a piece of lint off his tweed coat – 'they looked like a couple of hissing cats.'

'She gone, then?' Mrs Goodge asked. She darted a quick glance toward the stairs.

'We can speak freely. Mrs Livingston-Graves is on her way to a tea party,' Mrs Jeffries announced. She took her usual seat at the head of the table. 'I don't expect she'll be back for quite a while.'

'But a tea party only lasts a few hours,' Betsy said.

'Not when it's in Southampton,' the housekeeper replied calmly.

Betsy laughed. 'Cor, that's rich. Getting rid of her that way.'

'I don't know how you managed it, Mrs Jeffries.' Mrs Goodge shook her head in admiration. 'I can't imagine anyone inviting that old biddy out, but my hat's off to you.'

'I didn't do it alone,' she admitted. 'I had some help from Hatchet.'

'I thought he was in America with Luty Belle!' Betsy exclaimed in surprise.

'He's back. Luty'll be back next week.' Mrs Jeffries reached for the teapot and began to pour.

'Poor Luty,' Betsy said as Mrs Jeffries passed her a steaming mug. 'She'll be ever so annoyed she missed this murder.'

'If we've got it solved by then,' the cook muttered darkly. 'And if my mornin' is anything to go by, we've got a long road ahead of us. I didn't get nothing out of anyone.'

Mrs Jeffries smiled sympathetically. 'Don't despair, Mrs Goodge. The investigation's just started. The murder only happened last night.'

Betsy leaned forward. 'If it's any comfort to you, I didn't find out all that much, either. Right miserable mornin', it's been.'

'Nor have I,' Mrs Jeffries said firmly. 'But I've no doubt we will. Now, Betsy, tell us about your inquiries. Were you able to make contact with anyone from the Marlow household?'

'I didn't have any luck findin' someone from the house, so I popped into a couple of shops out on the Richmond Road, that's the nearest place to Redcliffe Gardens where I thought anyone might have had some gossip about the Marlow family. One of the girls knew a bit about Miss Marlow, but it isn't very interestin'.'

Mrs Goodge clucked her tongue. 'Nonsense, Betsy, all gossip's interestin'.'

Betsy smiled. 'Well, it seems Miss Marlow's had more than her share of tragedy. Her only brother died of pneumonia the winter before last, and six months later her parents were killed in a carriage accident.' She shrugged. 'Not much, is it? Do you want me to keep trying?'

'Yes,' Mrs Jeffries replied, 'I think so. Mrs Greenwood's killer was at the ball. He or she had to have taken the carving knife and followed the victim up the stairs and out onto that balcony. Somebody must have seen something. So do keep at it.'

'Maybe Wiggins or Smythe will have learned something useful,' Mrs Goodge mused.

'Perhaps the inspector will have found out something as well,' Mrs Jeffries said brightly. 'In any case, we mustn't give up and we mustn't feel defeated. As I've said before, the most inconsequential piece of information can lead us in the right direction.'

They heard the back door opening, and a moment later Smythe appeared. ''Ello, 'ello me lovelies. Beautiful day, isn't it?'

'He's found out something.' Betsy sighed. She hated it when the coachman got the jump on her. 'You can tell by the big, cocky grin on his face.'

'That I 'ave.' He pulled out a chair and sat down. 'Not that my news is all that interestin', but considerin' I only started diggin', so to speak, I'm right proud of myself.'

'Excellent, Smythe.' Mrs Jeffries smiled. She was rather glad that someone had some information. 'We're all ears.'

'It's about Shelby Locke. Accordin' to the housemaid—'

'Housemaid!' Betsy yelped. 'Why was you talkin' to a housemaid? You usually talk to hansom drivers and footmen.'

Smythe grinned. 'Well, sometimes, my girl, one's got to be resourceful. But, as I was sayin', Rosie told me that two weeks ago Locke left his case at the literary circle meetin' at the Marlow 'ouse. In that case was all of 'is poems and papers. Rosie claims Locke's been goin' out of 'is mind, tryin' to get the case back. Now Miss Marlow claimed she never saw the thing, and no one else in the circle will own up to seein' it, either.'

'Maybe one of the Marlow servants picked it up,' Mrs Jeffries said thoughtfully.

'A case full of worthless poems?' Smythe gave her a pitying look. 'The only reason a servant would take it would be to try and sell the case itself, but it weren't valuable. At least not enough to risk losin' a position.'

'But why would anyone want a bunch of papers?' Betsy asked.

'That's the point, isn't it?' Smythe poured himself a mug of tea. 'Rosie reckons someone pinched the notebook to keep Locke from winnin' the poetry contest.'

'That's daft.' Mrs Goodge sniffed. 'Even if someone stole his ruddy old poems, if it happened two weeks ago, there's no reason Mr Locke couldn't have done another one.'

'Rosie claims Locke were so rattled by the theft, 'e couldn't concentrate.' He shook his head. 'And not only that, but 'e's got woman trouble, too.'

'Now, that's a piece of important news!' the cook exclaimed, 'What kind of woman trouble?'

'The worst kind a man can 'ave; 'e's in love with one, but courtin' another.' Smythe grinned. 'Seems 'e and Miss Marlow 'ad some kind of understandin', and all of a sudden Mrs Stanwick appears out of nowhere and steals 'is 'eart. Rosie thinks 'e was goin' to propose to Mrs Stanwick last night.'

'What a cad!' Betsy cried. 'Poor Miss Marlow. She puts her trust in the bloomin' feller, and what does he do? He betrays her. Men!'

'Easy, lass.' Smythe's grin evaporated. 'Don't tar us all with the same brush. Not all blokes is like that.'

'Humph,' she sniffed.

'I wonder if Mr Locke told Miss Marlow of his intentions,' Mrs Jeffries murmured.

'I don't see that it matters all that much,' Mrs Goodge replied. 'It weren't Miss Marlow that was murdered.'

'True.' The housekeeper shook her head slightly. 'And it probably doesn't have anything to do with Mrs Greenwood.' She looked at Smythe. 'Did Mr Locke know Mrs Greenwood well?'

'I don't think so,' the coachman answered. 'When I asked Rosie about 'er, she weren't familiar with the name. But I'm going back to that neighbourhood tonight. I thought I might ask about at the pubs, see if anyone knew anything else about Shelby Locke. I figured I'd start askin' about Mr Warburton tomorrow mornin', if that's all right with you.'

'That's fine, Smythe,' Mrs Jeffries replied. She turned to Betsy. 'Would you mind having another go at the Marlow house?'

'I don't mind,' she said, her expression uncertain. 'But it seems quite a strange place. There's not much comin' or goin' for such a large house. It may take me some time to find someone.'

'I realize that, Betsy. But it's imperative that we find someone who can verify people's exact whereabouts at the time of the murder.' She drummed her fingers on the tabletop. 'Someone had to have seen the killer leaving the room, even if he doesn't realize what he saw.'

CHAPTER FIVE

B ARNES MOANED SOFTLY and tried not to limp. Hoping his superior hadn't heard him, he glanced at Witherspoon's back as they followed a maid into Rowena Stanwick's drawing room. His ruddy feet were killing him. As soon as he got home tonight he'd take a hammer to these wretched shoes.

'Inspector Witherspoon.' A lovely blonde came forward to greet them. 'I'm Rowena Stanwick. My maid says you wish to speak to me about poor Mrs Greenwood's unfortunate . . .' She paused, her blue eyes mirroring her confusion.

'Death,' the inspector supplied helpfully. 'Yes, indeed, we do have a few questions for you.' He gazed around the room, momentarily captivated by its utter charm.

Late afternoon sunlight streamed in through gauzy white curtains. Tables covered in rich, cream-coloured fringed shawls were dotted between overstuffed blue velvet chairs and settees. Fresh flowers adorned the top of the mantelpiece. Delicate figurines and crystal trinkets were elegantly displayed in china closets and on tabletops. The inspector had never been in such a completely feminine room in his life. Charmed as he was, he was also just a tad uneasy. He was afraid to move.

A tall auburn-haired man came through the archway. 'I expect you'll have a few questions for me as well,' he said without preamble. 'I'm Shelby Locke.'

Witherspoon was momentarily flustered. 'Er, yes, Mr Locke, we will have some questions. However' – he cleared his throat – 'we'd planned on calling round to see you later this afternoon.'

Locke smiled. 'Then I've saved you a trip.' He gestured toward the chairs near the settee, 'Do please sit down. Rowena, dear, will you ring for tea?'

Barnes scrambled into the nearest chair. Witherspoon gave his constable a puzzled glance and then sat down himself. He was at a loss – he didn't really wish to interview Mr Locke and Mrs Stanwick at the same time. It wasn't good police procedure. Yet, he didn't want to appear rude. Drat. Why was he always finding himself in these awkward situations?

He waited until Mrs Stanwick had instructed the maid to bring them tea before he started speaking.

'Mrs Stanwick,' Witherspoon began, 'perhaps it would be best if we spoke to you alone.'

'Alone?' Her eyes widened in alarm. 'But why?'

'It's rather standard procedure,' he said softly, not wishing to distress the lady unduly.

'What nonsense,' Locke interrupted. 'This whole episode has been most upsetting for Mrs Stanwick. I don't care what your silly procedures are; I'm staying here. I'll not have the police browbeating her.'

'Mr Locke,' Witherspoon said patiently, 'we're not in the habit of browbeating anyone. We'd merely like to ask Mrs Stanwick a few questions.'

'Oh, please,' she pleaded. 'Can't Mr Locke stay? This has been so terribly distressing.' Her eyes filled with tears.

'Yes, of course he can stay,' Witherspoon said quickly, terrified she was going to cry. 'We're not here to upset you any further, Mrs Stanwick.' He paused. 'How long have you been acquainted with Mrs Greenwood?'

She sighed and fidgeted with the lace edging on the sleeve of her lavender day dress. 'Not very long at all. I first met her at the literary circle. I believe that was in February or March.'

'And how long have you been a member of the circle?' Witherspoon asked. He wanted to see if her answer jibed with what Dr Sloan had told them. Then he realized that was a rather silly idea. What difference did it make how long the women had been involved in a poetry circle?

'Since January. I joined right after I came to London.' She glanced down at her hands.

'And where did you come from?' Barnes asked softly. He wanted to make this interview last as long as possible. Sitting in a nice overstuffed chair was much better than battering his poor feet any more than he had to.

'I'm sorry,' she replied, her expression puzzled. 'But what's that got to do with Mrs Greenwood?'

Witherspoon wondered the same thing. But he wasn't going to let his constable down. He frequently encouraged Barnes to ask questions during interviews. The fact that this question didn't appear to have any bearing on this case was irrelevant. Or perhaps it wasn't. 'Actually, Mrs Stanwick, the constable's question is quite routine.'

She shrugged. 'I'm from Littlehampton; that's near Worthing.'

'Thank you, Mrs Stanwick.' Witherspoon cleared his throat. 'Now, can you tell me if you saw anything out of the ordinary at the ball last night?'

'Nothing, Inspector. Up until Mrs Greenwood's death, it was like any other ball I've attended. The guests seemed to be enjoying themselves. Everyone was dancing and having a good time.'

'Had you seen Mrs Greenwood earlier in the evening?'

'Oh, yes,' she replied. 'Several times.'

Witherspoon smiled. 'Did you speak with her?'

'Only to say hello when she first arrived.' She glanced at Shelby Locke and blushed prettily. 'I was with Mr Locke for most of the time. Shelby's a wonderful dancer.'

'Thank you, my dear,' Locke replied, patting her hand. He turned to the inspector. 'I escorted Rowena to the ball. Once we arrived, I didn't leave her side.'

Witherspoon gazed at them curiously. It sounded awfully like these two were trying to give themselves an alibi. 'That's most odd, Mrs Stanwick,' he said, 'for Dr Sloan has told us he saw you and Mrs Greenwood having an argument only a few minutes before Mrs Greenwood was killed.'

'That's a lie.' Locke jumped to his feet. 'Sloan couldn't have seen any such thing. Rowena was with me.'

'Shelby, please,' Rowena implored. 'Do sit down.'

With an effort, Locke brought himself under control. He sat back down next to Mrs Stanwick. 'I'm sorry. It's most ungentlemanly of me to call Dr Sloan a liar. What I meant to say is that he must have been mistaken.'

'He seemed most certain of his facts,' the inspector persisted. 'Furthermore, he isn't the only person to report seeing Mrs Stanwick speaking with Mrs Greenwood. Miss Marlow also saw the two ladies together. Her impression was also that they were having a rather heated exchange.'

'I don't care who claims to have seen Rowena with that woman,' Locke began. 'She had nothing to do with . . .'

Witherspoon held up his hand. 'Mr Locke,' he said, 'I do understand you're wanting to protect Mrs Stanwick. But this is a murder investigation. We must have the truth. Two separate witnesses saw Mrs Stanwick arguing with the victim.'

'Forgive me, Inspector,' Rowena interrupted smoothly. 'You're quite right, I did speak to Mrs Greenwood.'

All three of them stared at her.

She sighed audibly and bit her lip. 'It's so silly of me, really. I didn't mean to mislead you, Inspector. But considering the later events of the evening, the incident quite slipped my mind.'

'Rowena,' Locke said sharply.

'It's all right, Shelby,' she said. 'The inspector is correct. I did speak to her.'

'Were you and Mrs Stanwick arguing?' Witherspoon asked.

Rowena gave a shaky laugh. 'Gracious, no. Admittedly, to someone observing us, it may have looked as if we were having a difference of opinion. But the truth is, Mrs Greenwood and I were discussing the poetry contest. She was so excited when she was telling me about her poem, she got carried away. Her voice got a bit too loud, she was waving her hands about, and her face became very expressive, but, honestly, that's all it was.'

Witherspoon pursed his lips. He supposed Mrs Stanwick could be telling the truth. Drat. If there were only some way of knowing for sure. 'So Mrs Greenwood wasn't angry at you.'

'Heavens, no. Why should she be angry at me? We barely knew each other.' Rowena gave Witherspoon a dazzling smile.

His next question went right out of his head.

Barnes coughed lightly. 'Excuse me, Mrs Stanwick,' he said, 'but would you mind tellin' us exactly what time it was that you was speakin' with Mrs Stanwick.'

'I'm not really sure, but I think it was . . .' She turned and gazed at Locke. 'It must have been when you went to speak to Miss Marlow, Shelby. Do you recall what time that was?'

Locke thought for a moment. 'I think it was around ten o'clock. Yes, I know it was. Lucinda and I went into the library. Just as we got inside, the clock finished chiming the hour, I remember that. We were only there a few minutes, though. Then I went back to Rowena.'

'How long did you and Miss Marlow stay in the library?' Witherspoon asked.

'I wasn't watching the time, Inspector,' Locke said impatiently. 'But as I just said, it was only a few minutes. I don't really think that a brief conversation with Miss Marlow a good half hour before the murder was committed has any bearing on it.'

'Exactly what were you and Miss Marlow discussing?' the inspector asked.

'That's not really any business of the police.'

'During a murder investigation', Witherspoon said calmly, 'everything is the business of the police. Please answer my question.'

Locke's eyes narrowed in anger. 'We discussed a private matter.'

Witherspoon decided to change tactics. He'd learned it sometimes startled people when you asked them questions they weren't expecting. 'Were you speaking with Miss Marlow about your missing notebook?'

Locke started in surprise. He and Rowena exchanged glances. 'How on earth did you hear about that?'

Witherspoon gave him what he hoped, was a mysterious smile. 'We have our ways, Mr Locke.'

'Apparently so,' he murmured. 'And, of course, you're correct. We were discussing my missing notebook. It's a trivial matter, I'm sure, and of absolutely no interest to the police.'

'And had Miss Marlow found it?' The inspector had no idea why he was asking these questions, but he couldn't quite think of anything else to ask just yet.

'No, she hadn't.'

The maid entered and served tea. The inspector used the time to gather his thoughts. As Mrs Stanwick handed him his cup, he looked at Locke and asked, 'How long have you known Mrs Greenwood?'

'I met her at the same time Rowena did, when she joined the literary circle.'

'And how long have you been a member of the circle?' Witherspoon asked. He knew it was another silly question, but this case really didn't make any sense at all.

Locke shifted uncomfortably. 'Actually, I joined the group last year. That's when it started.' He glanced uneasily at Rowena. 'I'd heard about it through Miss Marlow. We were . . . friends. We shared a mutual interest in literature. Once Miss Marlow knew of my interest, she invited me to join.'

'Where were you at ten-thirty last night?' the inspector asked bluntly.

Locke jerked in surprise. 'What do you mean? I was with Rowena. I've already told you that.'

'Yes, but where? In the gardens? The ballroom?'

'We were in the ballroom,' Locke said firmly. 'I was just getting ready to ask Mrs Stanwick to dance.'

Witherspoon stared at the two people on the settee. He reached for his tea. 'Do you know of anyone who hated Mrs Greenwood?'

It was Rowena Stanwick who answered. 'Hate is

a rather strong word,' she said slowly. 'But she wasn't very well liked. I don't think she and Dr Sloan got on all that well. I do know that she mentioned she'd had words with him earlier that day.'

Witherspoon's cup halted halfway to his mouth, 'Excuse me, Mrs Stanwick, but did Mrs Greenwood actually tell you that? Did she say she'd seen Dr Sloan before the ball?'

'Oh, yes,' Rowena smiled prettily. 'She said she'd gone to his rooms and talked to him. It had something to do with the contest.'

'You know, Constable,' Witherspoon said thoughtfully as they left the Stanwick home, 'I've the strongest feeling that everyone is lying to us.'

'Hmmm.' Barnes groaned as he stepped carefully down the stairs. His toes were on fire, and he could feel a blister bubbling on the side of his heel.

'So you agree with me,' the inspector continued. 'Yes, I thought you would. Well, I'm not having it. I know all of them couldn't have killed Mrs Greenwood, and I suppose they've their own reasons for not telling me the truth, but I'm determined to get to the bottom of this. In the ballroom, indeed. Mrs Putnam has already told us she searched the ballroom high and low. She certainly has no reason to lie to us. We know she didn't commit the murder. None of them could have been where they claimed to be. Mrs Putnam isn't blind. She didn't see hide nor hair of any of them, not Dr Sloan, Mr Locke, Mrs Stanwick, or Miss Marlow.' He snorted indelicately. 'We must find someone who can tell us where

101

everyone was at the time of the murder. Someone observant. Someone interested in the activities of the other guests.'

'A busybody?' Barnes suggested helpfully. To ease the pressure off his toe, he bowed his legs as he hobbled down the stairs.

'Precisely! What we need is a good busybody. Someone who sat there and did nothing but watch the other guests. Any suggestions?'

Barnes sighed. It was bloomin' hard to think with his feet throbbin' the way they was. But he didn't want his inspector to know that. He wasn't a complainer; he had his pride. 'Well, Mrs Putnam was dartin' about like a bluebottle fly; maybe she saw more than she realized. Maybe we should talk to her again. Miss Mansfield and Mrs Hiatt was outside. They struck me as the kind that'd keep a close eye on what everyone else was up to. Maybe they saw more than they think.'

'But we've already spoken to them,' Witherspoon said doubtfully.

'Maybe we ought to do it again, sir,' Barnes suggested. 'Remember, they'd just seen a body come flyin' through the air and practically land on top of 'em. Could be they'll recall things a bit better now that they've had some time to get over the shock.'

'You might be right about that, Constable,' the inspector replied. 'But it's getting late and we really must interview Mr Edgar Warburton today. He's the only one we haven't talked to yet.'

'He didn't give a statement last night, either,' Barnes groused. 'By the time we had the complete list of names for the literary circle, he'd gone.' Witherspoon came to a decision and immediately felt better. Any decision, even a bad one, was better than dithering. 'We'll interview Mr Warburton now. If we've time, we'll speak with the others again.'

'Uh, where does this Mr Warburton live?' Barnes fervently hoped he lived far enough away for them to have to take a hansom cab.

Witherspoon pulled the list of names and addresses out of his pocket. 'Oh, not far at all. It's a street just near Regent's Park. It's only a short walk.'

Barnes moaned.

Concerned, the inspector stopped and peered anxiously at his constable. 'I say, is something the matter?'

'It's nothing, sir.'

'Now, now, don't be so reticent, Constable.' Witherspoon studied him closely. Barnes didn't look right. 'It's not like you to make such odd noises. Are you ill?'

'It's my shoes, sir,' Barnes admitted. 'They're new and pinchin' me ruddy toes like the very devil.'

'Well, why didn't you say so? We can't have you in pain, man! Let's go find a hansom cab.'

Edgar Warburton wasn't in the least happy to see the police. 'I suppose I've no choice but to talk to you,' he muttered when his butler had escorted the men into Warburton's study. 'But do make it quick.' He gestured for them to take a seat.

'As you're in a hurry,' the inspector said, 'we'll do our best to get this over with. Mr Warburton, were you well acquainted with Mrs Greenwood?'

'No.'

'How long have you known her?'

'A little over two months. I met the woman when I joined the Hyde Park Literary Circle.'

'And that was two months ago?' Witherspoon asked.

'I've just said that.' Warburton frowned. 'Perhaps I should just make a statement and you gentlemen' – he sneered slightly as he said the last word – 'can be on your way.'

'As you wish, sir.'

'Fine. I didn't know Mrs Greenwood well at all except in my capacity as secretary for the group.'

'You only joined two months ago and already you're the secretary?' Barnes interrupted.

Warburton gave him an irritated glance. 'Correct. Frankly, it's not often a group such as that one attracts a member of my calibre.'

'You're well versed in literature, then?' the inspector interjected.

'Really, sir, are you going to let me make a statement or keep interrupting me with questions?' Warburton snapped. 'But you miss my point, Inspector. I'm not particularly well versed in literature, though I do, of course, have a degree from Oxford.'

'Then what did you mean?'

'Well, if you'd stop interrupting, I'd tell you. What I meant was that for a group like that to actually attract someone of my social standing to become a member was in itself unusual. They were very fortunate I joined.'

'So that's why they made you the secretary?' Barnes put in. 'Because of your social standing?'

Warburton sighed angrily. 'That and the fact their previous secretary had just left, so I volunteered to take on the task. Now, as I was saying—'

'Why'd the last one leave?' the inspector asked.

'How should I know? Perhaps he was a flighty fellow.'

Witherspoon made a mental note to ask the name of this person the next time they spoke to Dr Sloan.

Warburton folded his arms over his chest. 'As I was saying, Inspector, I joined the group and made the acquaintance of the members. That was the sum total of my relationship with Mrs Greenwood.'

'How did you find out about the circle?' Barnes asked.

Warburton paced over to stand in front of the window. For a moment he didn't say anything, merely stared out at the garden. Finally he said, 'From Mrs Stanwick.'

Witherspoon sensed that he was on to something here. Warburton was still standing with his back to them, so the inspector couldn't see his face. But there was something decidedly different about his tone of voice, and he was standing so rigidly one would think someone had shoved a poker up his spine. 'You were acquainted with Mrs Stanwick before you became a member of the circle?'

'Yes.' He turned and faced them. 'We've known each other for some time. I've property in Littlehampton. I knew her there. We happened to run into each other after she moved to London. She mentioned this group she belonged to, and though it isn't my usual sort of activity, I thought it sounded interesting.'

'Did you see anything unusual last night?' the inspector asked softly. Drat. The man looked completely normal now.

'Nothing at all,' Warburton stated.

'Did you see Mrs Greenwood go up the stairs to the balcony?' Witherspoon asked. He might as well take the bull by the horns. If Mr Warburton didn't know the woman, he probably hadn't murdered her.

'No, there were dozens of people milling about. It was a warm evening; people were coming and going up the stairs to the second floor all night.'

Witherspoon decided to hurry this interview along. 'Where were you at ten-thirty?'

'At ten-thirty?' He shrugged. 'I can't recall.'

Barnes and the inspector looked at each other curiously.

'I mean', Warburton corrected hastily, 'I don't know exactly where I was standing. I'd just gone into the ballroom from the drawing room when I heard the screams.'

'Did you see or speak to any members of the circle during the course of the evening? Did anyone say or do anything unusual?'

Warburton hesitated, 'I spoke to everyone. There was a good deal of excitement over the contest. The only unusual occurrence was Locke worrying about his wretched notebook. I overheard him asking Miss Marlow if it had turned up yet. Has anyone told you about that?'

Witherspoon nodded. 'We understand it had been missing for some time.'

'It drove Locke mad,' Warburton said with relish.

'I don't wonder, either. The man was always going on about how he refused to put anything on paper unless he felt it deeply. Quite pretentious about the whole thing, if you ask me. My personal feeling is that, as he was making such a fuss, he must have written something quite . . . well, let's just say personal.'

The inspector frowned slightly. He wasn't sure what the fellow was getting at and, furthermore, he didn't see that a bunch of silly poems written a considerable amount of time before Mrs Greenwood's murder could have any relevance to the case. 'Did you see anything else?'

'Not really.' Warburton shrugged. 'The only other thing of interest was my conversation with Mrs Stanwick. But I don't see what relevance it could have to Mrs Greenwood's murder.'

'Perhaps you should tell us anyway,' Witherspoon said politely.

'I spoke to Rowena, Mrs Stanwick, fairly early on in the evening.' Warburton smiled coldly. 'We had quite an interesting conversation. She told me she and Mr Locke were going to be married.'

Witherspoon was stunned. Neither Mrs Stanwick nor Mr Locke had mentioned this to him. 'Did you speak to Mrs Stanwick alone, or was Mr Locke present?'

'Alone.'

'And where did this conversation take place?'

'In the library.'

'What time?' From the corner of his eye, Witherspoon saw that Barnes was scribbling furiously in his notebook.

'I'm not sure. I think it might have been close to ten o'clock, or perhaps a little after. I really couldn't say. Mrs Stanwick also mentioned that Mr Locke would be telling Miss Marlow the news as well. I expect they were going to announce it to everyone after the poetry prize had been given.'

'Do you know if Mr Locke did mention his impending marriage to Miss Marlow?' The inspector couldn't see that Mr Locke's nuptial plans had anything to do with Mrs Greenwood's death, but one never knew. But he did know that if Warburton was telling the truth, then both Mrs Stanwick and Locke had lied. This was twice that the couple had been separated during the course of the evening. But why tell such a stupid lie? What purpose did it serve? Witherspoon stifled a sigh.

'Undoubtedly. I saw Mr Locke and Miss Marlow going upstairs toward the second-floor reception room when Mrs Stanwick and I were coming out of the library.' He suddenly began pacing back and forth in front of his desk. 'I don't think Miss Marlow was going to like hearing Mr Locke's news. He'd been courting her, you see.'

'Mr Locke was courting Miss Marlow while he got engaged to Mrs Stanwick?' The inspector was deeply shocked. Even with his limited experience of the opposite sex, he'd realized Shelby Locke was more than casually interested in Rowena Stanwick. But this was the first he'd heard that Locke had been involved with Miss Marlow as well.

'Oh, yes,' Warburton sneered. 'But I don't suppose he let that worry him. Men of his class have very little character. Locke took one look at Rowena, and poor Lucinda was left at the post. Women. Such stupid, fickle creatures! A silly, romantic fop like Shelby Locke comes along, and any ounce of good sense they have completely disappears.' He laughed harshly. 'Rowena's like all the rest. A handsome face and a few silly poems, and she thinks she's in love. I suppose it isn't surprising that she'd be taken in by the man. Her late husband was a great deal older than she. Since his death, well, one doesn't like to be ungallant. But there have been a succession of men. Some of them quite young.'

'Really?' Witherspoon muttered.

'That's one of the reasons she left Littlehampton,' Warburton continued bluntly. 'Her reputation was becoming scandalous.'

'How very unfortunate for the lady.' The inspector began to think that Edgar Warburton, despite his pretentions and obvious wealth, was no gentleman.

'I say, Inspector, I don't think this really has anything to do with Mrs Greenwood's death,' Warburton said, his expression indicating just the opposite. 'But I did see the two of them in a rather intense conversation last night. Perhaps you ought to ask Mrs Stanwick what she and Mrs Greenwood were talking about. You might find her answer very interesting.'

Witherspoon stared at the man. 'We already have.'

'Where to now, sir?' Barnes asked as they left Warburton's house.

The inspector sighed. 'Oh, dash it all. Let's call it

a day, Constable. I've much to think about and your feet are hurting.'

'They're feelin' a mite better, sir,' Barnes replied. But he winced as he walked.

'My good man, it's obvious you're in pain. Go on home and soak your feet. We'll start again early tomorrow morning.'

'But it's Sunday, sir. I thought you told me you were going to escort your cousin to see some of the Jubilee preparations.'

Witherspoon cringed at the mention of Mrs Livingston-Graves. 'That was before we had a murder to solve, Constable. But if you've promised to take Mrs Barnes out and about, I think I can manage on my own.'

'Wouldn't hear of it, sir, I'll be round your house at eight sharp, if that's convenient for you.'

The inspector's mood brightened when he arrived home to find his cousin gone. 'You say she's gone to Southampton for tea?' he asked incredulously, a wide smile creeping across his face. He handed Mrs Jeffries his hat.

'Indeed, sir. She received an invitation early on today and immediately packed up and dashed off for the train. I expect she'll spend the night there.'

'I've never heard of anyone going to Southampton for tea,' he murmured. 'It's a bit of a long way.'

Mrs Jeffries pushed the shaft of guilt that pierced her to one side. 'I do believe the invitation was from an earl.'

'An earl?' Witherspoon gaped at his housekeeper. 'Why would an earl invite my cousin to tea?'

'I've no idea, sir. I believe she mentioned something about a mutual friend. But you look absolutely exhausted. Do come in and have a rest before dinner. Mrs Goodge has made a lovely steak and kidney pudding.'

'Steak and kidney?' He stared at her in surprise. 'But I thought we'd be having cod.'

'Cod?' she repeated.

'Why, yes. I was quite looking forward to it, too. I ran into Wiggins today, and he said Mrs Goodge had sent him to the fishmongers over on the Brompton Road.'

'Oh, she did, sir,' Mrs Jeffries said quickly. 'But they were out of cod.'

He nodded. 'I see. Oh well, it can't be helped, I suppose. And Mrs Goodge does make a superb steak and kidney pie. I'm sure I'll enjoy it very much.'

They went into the drawing room, and Mrs Jeffries poured them both a glass of sherry. 'Now, sir, do tell me all about your day.'

The inspector was glad to. He sighed in pleasure, sipped his drink, and told her every detail.

By the time he was finished talking, Mrs Jeffries was shaking her head. 'It does sound like Mr Warburton was hinting about something, doesn't it?'

'Yes, I thought so, too,' Witherspoon replied, delighted that Mrs Jeffries was so very perceptive. But then, that was one of the reasons he did so like talking to her. She was perceptive and intelligent.

Why, there were times in his previous cases when

it was almost uncanny how she could say one little thing and the whole solution to a murder would fall right into place. 'But I can't see that Mrs Stanwick and Mr Locke's engagement had anything to do with Mrs Greenwood's death. The only thing the three of them had in common was that they were all widowed.'

'All of them?' Mrs Jeffries thought that an odd coincidence. Witherspoon shook his head. 'Shelby Locke's wife died of consumption two years ago, Mrs Greenwood's husband passed away from a heart attack a long time back, and Mrs Stanwick's husband died of a stroke.' Perhaps it wasn't so odd, Mrs Jeffries amended silently. Many people were left alone at a fairly young age. Furthermore, it was generally lonely men and women who joined organizations like the Hyde Park Literary Circle.

'But what I found peculiar about Mr Warburton's statement was his hinting that Mrs Stanwick had something to hide. He virtually claimed that the woman had to leave Littlehampton because she'd acquired a less than admirable reputation.'

'Why did you find that strange?'

'Not so much strange as . . .' He stopped speaking, trying to find the right word to describe the feeling he'd had when he was interviewing Warburton. 'It was as if the fellow was trying to make us think a certain way.'

'You mean you thought he was trying to manipulate you?'

'Yes, that's it exactly. It seems to me, if the man had something to say, he should have come right out with it. Instead, he dropped sly little hints and damned the poor woman through innuendo. Most unfair.' He sniffed the air. 'I say, do you think dinner is ready yet?'

Betsy cleared the dessert dishes and Mrs Jeffries reached for the teapot. Suddenly there was a pounding on the front door. 'Do you want me to get that?' the maid asked.

'No,' Mrs Jeffries said as she headed toward the hall. 'You take those dishes downstairs. I'll see to the door.'

She pulled the door open and saw Lady Cannonberry standing there, a hesitant and slightly embarrassed smile on her face. 'Good evening,' Mrs Jeffries said politely.

'Good evening. I do hope I'm not disturbing your dinner. But I'd like to speak to the inspector.'

'Please come in.' Mrs Jeffries opened the door wider. 'If you'll go through to the drawing room, I'll get him.'

She hurried back to the dining room. Witherspoon looked up from his teacup. 'Who was at the door?'

'Lady Cannonberry.'

Witherspoon's cup rattled against the saucer. 'What does she want?'

'She wants to talk to you,' Mrs Jeffries said calmly. She pulled a silver tray out of the top shelf of the sideboard and placed the teapot on it. 'I expect it's important. She's been our neighbour for a long time, and this is the first time she's called around unexpectedly.'

Witherspoon swallowed nervously and rose to his feet. 'Yes, of course. I mustn't keep the lady waiting.'

He dashed toward the drawing room. Mrs Jeffries was hot on his heels.

'Lady Cannonberry.' His voice squeaked slightly as he said her name. 'How very nice to see you.'

'Thank you, Inspector,' she murmured. 'I'm so sorry to disturb you, but it's really quite important.'

'Please have a seat,' he invited, gesturing toward the two wing chairs by the fireplace. 'Let's do be comfortable.'

As soon as they were seated, he said, 'Now, what's all this about?'

'It's about Mrs Greenwood's murder.' Lady Cannonberry demurely folded her hands in her lap.

'The murder.'

'Oh, yes, well, I heard today that you're interviewing all the members of the circle.' She smiled. 'I understand we're all suspects.'

'Suspects?' Witherspoon gaped at her. 'Oh, no, Lady Cannonberry. Nothing could be further from the truth. Of course you're not a suspect. I know you couldn't have had anything to do with Mrs Greenwood's death. You were with me when it happened.'

'Does that mean you don't intend to question me?'

'Well, I might have a few questions for you,' he said doubtfully. 'But you've already told me what you know of Mrs Greenwood, so I don't really see much point in it.'

'I still think you ought to interview me.'

'Yes, well . . .'

'I don't think it's fair to leave me out,' she persisted.

'Leave you out?' Witherspoon exclaimed. 'Lady Cannonberry, I really don't understand.'

'I could have hired someone to do it,' she insisted. Witherspoon's jaw dropped.

'I beg your pardon?'

She gave him a bright smile. 'I said, I could have hired someone to kill Mrs Greenwood.'

CHAPTER SIX

Wiggins took a deep breath and knocked at the back door of the Greenwood house. He'd just ask to speak to Jon. No harm in that. He glanced up the small passageway in which he stood. Fred was still sitting obediently at the end, his attention riveted to a dripping drainpipe.

The door opened a crack and a dark-haired kitchen maid, her cap slipping to one side and her eyes suspicious, stuck her nose out. 'What do you want, boy?' she asked sharply.

'Good evenin', miss,' he replied, giving her his best smile. 'If you don't mind, I'd like to see Jon.'

'I do mind. What you wantin' with Jon?' The door wedged open another inch.

'Uh, I need to tell him something,' Wiggins said, taking care not drop his h's. 'I've got a message for him.'

'From who?' the maid asked sarcastically. 'Who'd want to give that boy a message? Well, you can't see 'im. 'E ain't here.' She started to close the door, but he stuck the toe of his boot out.

'Do you know where 'e is?' he asked, not bothering to mind his speech. 'It's right important I talk to 'im.'

'Get yer bleedin' foot out of me door,' she yelped. 'I've told you, Jon's not here. He took himself off early this afternoon, and we ain't seen him since. The mistress is furious.'

Wiggins hastily complied and the door slammed in his face.

'Blimey,' he muttered as he walked back towards the street, 'she weren't very nice.' Fred trotted along at his heels as they rounded the house and came out onto the street.

He glanced up at the sky; the day was fading fast. But he didn't want to give up, not yet. Not until he'd found the lad. Jon had tried to tell him something. Something important about Mrs Greenwood's movements yesterday. Wiggins was determined to find out what it was.

Fred woofed softly and wagged his tail. Wiggins turned and saw a group of boys playing at the corner. They ran to and fro, screaming and tagging one another. He hesitated a moment; maybe these boys knew where Jon had gone. No harm in asking, he thought. 'Come on, boy,' he said to the dog, 'let's see what these nippers can tell us.'

The four boys stopped and stared as he and Fred approached. 'Any of you know where Jon is?' he asked casually.

A blond-haired child of about ten wiped a grubby hand under his running nose. 'Jon's gone.'

'Gone where?'

'Don't know.' He reached down and scooped up the ball, his pale face sober. 'He's just gone. Not that we got to play with him all that much. The lady he works for kept him plenty busy, that's for sure. Wouldn't hardly let him out.'

Wiggins tried another line of questioning. 'How do you know 'e's gone? Did you see 'im leave?'

'What'cha want to know fer?' a second boy asked warily.

Wiggins saw the child's eyes weren't straight. He felt a momentary rush of pity. He knew all about these boys. They weren't the sons of the families from some of the fine houses around here. They were the children of housemaids and clerks, washerwomen and hansom drivers. He tilted his chin so that he could see that just beyond the corner was a narrow cobblestone alley fronted with small, grimy brick houses.

He smiled kindly at the cross-eyed boy. 'I'm a friend of 'is,' he explained. 'It's real important that I find 'im.'

The boy appeared not to have heard him. He was too busy watching Fred. All the boys were watching Fred, and Fred, who loved being the centre of attention, was eating it up. He wagged his tail, bounced at their feet, and generally slobbered all over their shoes.

'It's all right to pet 'im,' Wiggins said, thinking that if he could get them petting the animal, he might keep them talking longer. He had a bad feeling about Jon's disappearance. If, of course, it was a disappearance.

'Does 'e bite?' the blond boy asked, but he was

already stepping closer and reaching out his dirty hand. Fred sniffed the boy's fingers and wagged his tail harder. The urchin laughed in delight, dropped to his knees, and stroked the dog's smooth fur.

'Course 'e don't bite,' Wiggins replied.

They all crowded in a tight circle around Fred, who continued lapping up the attention as if he were the Prince of Wales.

'So where's Jon gone now?' Wiggins tried again.

'Don't know,' the blond boy said, shrugging his shoulders. He didn't take his eyes off the dog. 'But 'e might 'ave gone over to 'is cousin's place in Clapham. 'E were carryin' a bundle of clothes with 'im when 'e left, so I don't reckon 'e's comin' back. Not with Mrs Greenwood dead.'

Curiously, Wiggins stared at the boy. 'What does Mrs Greenwood's death have to do with 'im comin' 'ome? 'E works in the 'ouse, don't 'e?'

The boy lifted his chin, his eyes hard and cynical. 'That don't mean nuthin' when one mistress dies and another takes her place. Mark my words, now that old Mrs Greenwood's gone, that sister of hers will sell off everything, toss the servants out into the street, and be off before you can snap yer fingers. I know, 'cause me mum's the washerwoman there. I heard her tellin' me dad that they're all scairt of losin' their positions. Me mum weren't too happy, either.'

Wiggins frowned. 'What makes your mum so sure everyone's going to be sacked?'

'She overheard Mrs Hackshaw talkin' to some bloke who come to the 'ouse with some papers for her to sign.'

'A solicitor?'

The boy shrugged. 'I dunno, I guess that could be it.'

Wiggins was shocked. Hannah Greenwood had been killed only last night and already her sister was making plans. Cor blimey, the woman weren't even decently buried yet. He pushed the thought out of his mind and concentrated on his present problem. 'So you think Jon may have gone to 'is cousin's?'

'He might. Couldn't much blame him if he did, what with Mrs Greenwood gettin' murdered right under his nose.'

Aghast, the inspector's jaw dropped even farther. He couldn't believe this. 'Lady Cannonberry, have you any idea what you're saying?'

'I know precisely what I'm saying,' she retorted brightly. 'I'm pointing out possibilities you appear to have overlooked.'

'I beg your pardon?'

'What I'm trying to tell you, Inspector,' Lady Cannonberry said patiently, 'is that you haven't questioned me. I might have seen or heard something about poor Mrs Greenwood's murder.'

'But how could you have?' Witherspoon was truly mystified. 'We were together the entire evening.'

'That's not true,' she corrected. 'You left me alone twice. Once while you got us some punch and once while you went back for another slice of cake.'

'But I was only gone for a few minutes . . .'

'Nevertheless,' she persisted, 'you still must

question me. It's not fair that you've spoken to everyone else in the literary circle.'

'I assure you, Lady Cannonberry,' Witherspoon sputtered, 'fairness has nothing to do with how and when I speak to witnesses. We are talking about a murder here.'

'I take it you won't be confessing to Mrs Greenwood's murder?' Mrs Jeffries queried from the doorway where she'd been standing. She was certain Lady Cannonberry was perfectly innocent and she was equally curious to hear what she had to say.

'Of course not,' she admitted. 'I only made that outrageous statement to get the inspector's attention. I felt so very ignored.'

Witherspoon blushed, coughed, and cleared his throat. 'I'm truly sorry,' he stammered. 'I . . . er . . . I would have got round to you sooner or later, you see. But there were other, more important inquiries . . .' He stopped speaking and turned an even brighter red. 'Goodness, I didn't mean that the way it sounded. Of course your evidence is important . . . it's just that as you were with me when the crime occurred, I didn't see how you could possibly know anything . . . Oh dear, this isn't coming out right at all.'

'That's quite all right, Gerald.' Lady Cannonberry smiled kindly and patted his arm. 'I understand what you meant to say.'

Mrs Jeffries rolled her eyes. Really, she had the urge to box her employer's ears. Poor Lady Cannonberry was so keen to see him she'd come running over here on the silliest of pretexts. She sighed silently. Young love was painful enough to observe, poor Wiggins was proof of that. But middle-aged infatuation was positively excruciating. Whatever hopes she had of hearing anything useful about the murder began to diminish as she watched the rapt expression on Lady Cannonberry's face as she gazed at the inspector. Mrs Jeffries coughed delicately.

Lady Cannonberry blinked. 'I expect you want to know what I saw.'

'Er, yes,' the inspector replied. He sounded very relieved.

'Do you remember when you went to get me a glass of punch?' she asked. At Witherspoon's nod, she continued. 'While I was waiting for you, you remember, I was sitting on the settee in the drawing room? The settee that faces the door into the library? Well, as I was sitting there, I saw Dr Sloan coming out of the library. He was carrying a satchel.'

Witherspoon's brows drew together. 'What's odd about that?'

'It wasn't his satchel,' she stated.

'How do you know it wasn't his?' Mrs Jeffries asked curiously.

'Because when the inspector and I arrived at the Marlow house, Dr Sloan and Mr Venerable were getting out of the hansom in front of us. I noticed them because Mr Venerable seemed to be leaning to one side. He was holding the satchel, and I remember thinking it must be jolly heavy to cause him to lean so far to his left.'

'Perhaps Mr Venerable was carrying Dr Sloan's satchel for him.' Witherspoon suggested.

Lady Cannonberry shook her head. 'No. As they were going up the stairs, I saw Mr Venerable stumble. Dr Sloan helped him and then tried to take the satchel from Mr Venerable. He wouldn't let it go. He snatched it right back.'

'Perhaps Dr Sloan was getting the satchel from the library to take to Mr Venerable,' Mrs Jeffries said thoughtfully.

'Why would he do that? I saw Dr Sloan coming out of the library close to ten o'clock. By then, Mr Venerable was so drunk, he was asleep.'

'Then you've solved your mystery,' Mrs Jeffries said cheerfully. Both of them stared at her.

'Don't you see,' she explained, 'it's precisely because Mr Venerable was drunk that Dr Sloan had the satchel. He is the president of the circle; therefore, if Mr Venerable was incapacitated and unable to give out the prize to the winner of the poetry contest, Sloan would naturally have to take his place.'

Lady Cannonberry shook her head, her expression stubborn. 'He was up to something, I know it. Otherwise, why would he have tried to hide the satchel under his jacket when he went up the stairs?'

'As you instructed, Mr Smythe,' the banker said timidly as he handed over the small pouch, 'it's all in shillings and half-crowns.'

'Thank you, Mr Babbit,' the coachman replied. He was the only customer left in the bank, and that was precisely the way he wanted it. The fewer people there were, the less chance that anyone would see him.

'Er, a . . .' Mr Babbit cleared his throat. 'Do you mind if I make a suggestion, sir?'

'I'm in a bit of a 'urry,' Smythe replied, picking up the pouch and dropping it into his pocket. Blimey, if he didn't get a move on, he was goin' to be late.

'This won't take long, Mr Smythe,' the banker said quickly. 'It's about your investments in those American cattle ranches. I really don't think this is a good time to sell.'

'Good time or not, sell 'em anyway.'

'And what shall we do with the money from the sale? At the current market value, there will be a goodly profit.'

'Put it in my account. I'll be back in a couple of weeks . . .'

'Weeks!' Mr Babbit exclaimed. 'Really, Mr Smythe, I would like to see you again as soon as possible. There are decisions you must make. Money doesn't look after itself, you know. And you've quite a lot of it.'

Smythe sighed. Money. Bloomin' pain in the neck it was, too. Just look at the grief it was causin' him now. Mr Babbit complainin' that he 'ad to make decisions, havin' to sneak around just to walk in the bank, and worse, the worst of all, havin' to hide the fact that he had more money than he'd ever spend from the people he cared about most in the world.

'All right, all right.' Smythe's brows drew together as he tried to think of when he could get back here. 'I'll try and get in next Tuesday even—'

'We'll be closed then,' Babbit interrupted. 'It's the Queen's Jubilee Day. The parade.'

'Oh, yeah. All right, I'll be 'ere Thursday evenin' just before closin'.' He hoped they'd have the case solved by then. He wasn't going to give up huntin' a murderer just to keep this ruddy old bank manager happy.

'Fine.' Mr Babbit beamed his approval and stood up from behind his desk. 'I'll look forward to seeing you, then, Mr Smythe. There will be a number of papers for you to sign.'

'There always are,' Smythe muttered. He quickly left the bank, pausing only long enough before he stepped out into the street to make sure there was no one who might recognize him. He hurried off, wanting to make it back to Upper Edmonton Gardens in time for supper.

He leapt over a pile of rubbish as he crossed the road, the coins jingling in his pocket. The sound made him wince. Guilt pierced his conscience. He hated keeping this part of his life secret. Living a lie didn't sit well with him. But there was nothing he could do about it now. Smythe shook his head. Damnation. How the ruddy hell did he end up in this fix? He should have told them right from the start, but the time were never right. Once Euphemia knew she were dyin', she'd made him promise to stay on and keep an eye on the inspector and Wiggins. After she were gone, the only way he could hang about was to go on bein' a coachman.

Then Mrs Jeffries and Mrs Goodge and Betsy had come and settled in. Before you could slap a fly off a horse's bum, they was investigatin' murders and growin' to like each other. By then it was too late.

Everyone at Upper Edmonton Gardens had come to mean too much to him. He didn't want to go back to livin' on his own again; it were too bloody lonely.

And, of course, the thought of never seein' Betsy again was too awful to think about.

Smythe scowled and a street Arab quickly dodged out of his way. He reached into his pocket and pulled out a shilling. ''Ere, lad,' he called, tossing it in the boy's direction. 'I didn't mean to scare you.' He knew his frown was frightenin' enough to scare the fleas off a dog. But there weren't much he could do about that.

The urchin easily caught the coin. 'Thanks, guv!' he yelled, his eyes gleaming in delight at the unexpected bounty.

Smythe sighed. He wished he could remedy the situation at Upper Edmonton Gardens as easily as he'd soothed the child. But he couldn't and that was a fact. Telling them the truth would change everything. They'd feel differently towards him. Treat him differently. And he didn't want that. For the first time in his adult life, he felt like he had a home, a family. And he wouldn't risk losin' that for all the world.

Smythe stopped at the corner and stared at a line of hansoms waiting for fares. He fingered the heavy pouch in his pocket. At least his money was goin' to be put to good use, he told himself as he headed for the beginning of the line. This case wasn't goin' to be an easy one, he could feel it in his bones. It might take a good bit of lolly and a lot of greasin' palms before he could get anyone to give him any useful information at all.

Decision made, Smythe waved at the driver of the first cab and then glanced at the sky. If he hurried, he might be able to have a word or two with someone from the Warburton household before he had to get back to Upper Edmonton Gardens.

Supper was late that night. Mrs Goodge muttered darkly under her breath as she and Betsy finished dishing up the food.

'What are you on about?' Betsy asked as she took a platter of beef and placed it in the centre of the table.

'It's nothing really,' the cook mumbled. She averted her gaze and reached for the pot of potatoes, but not before Betsy saw the genuine worry in her eyes.

'Something's botherin' you, Mrs Goodge. It's written all over your face,' she persisted. 'What is it? Are you ill?'

'It's not that.' Mrs Goodge sighed. She and the maid were alone in the kitchen. 'It's that.' She jerked her head toward the kitchen sink.

'Something's wrong with the sink? Well, have Smythe in to have a look at it—'

'It's not the ruddy sink,' the cook cried. 'It's my medicine.'

Suddenly Betsy understood. 'Is that what's worryin' you? For goodness' sakes, Mrs Goodge. I know how expensive it is. If you're a bit short, I can loan you a few shillings—'

'That's just it. The bottle's full and it shouldn't be.' She plopped down in a chair.

Betsy frowned in confusion. 'What?'

'This is the third time it's happened,' Mrs Goodge said wearily. 'And I'm beginnin' to think I'm losin' my mind. I use that liniment every day, so I know how much I've got. Well, for the past few months or so, every time it gets low, I remind myself I need to get more. I write myself a little note and leave it on the counter with me provisions list. But before I can even get to the chemist's, another bottle appears. A full bottle.'

'I should think that'd make you happy,' Betsy said slowly. She wondered if perhaps the cook wasn't getting forgetful. Mrs Goodge was no spring chicken.

'The first time, it did,' she said. 'I thought maybe Mrs Jeffries or the inspector had got it for me. But I asked them, and neither of them knew a thing about it. Then it kept happening. I'm beginning to wonder if maybe I bought the bottles and . . .'

'And forgot about it?' Betsy finished bluntly.

Mrs Goodge nodded slowly, her shoulders slumped, dejected. 'That'd mean I'm gettin' like me old granny,' she said softly. 'She went right off her head before she died. Kept thinkin' she were ten instead of ninety. Couldn't remember where she'd put things or what she'd eaten for breakfast.'

'Don't be silly,' Betsy said firmly. 'You're not goin' off your head. It's just like my shoes or Wiggins's writin' paper, that's all. Someone in the 'ouse is doin' us favours. But they don't want to own up to it.'

'But writin' paper and gettin' soles mended is a bloomin' sight cheaper than buyin' that medicine,' Mrs Goodge replied, 'And who around here has that kind of money?'

'There's an explanation for what's happened,' Betsy persisted, determined to make the cook feel better. 'Maybe the inspector's been gettin' it for you but don't want to say anything about it. You know what a kind man he is.'

'You won't say anything to anyone, will you?' Mrs Goodge asked, 'It wouldn't do for any of 'em to think . . .' She stopped speaking as she heard Mrs Jeffries's footsteps coming down the stairs.

'I won't say a word,' Betsy promised quickly.

Mrs Jeffries hurried into the room. 'Where's Smythe and Wiggins?' she asked as she took her seat. 'We've much to talk about this evening.'

'They'll be here shortly,' Mrs Goodge replied. She placed a bowl of steaming vegetables next to the roast beef. 'They may be late sometimes, but they hardly ever miss a meal.'

Mrs Goodge was half right. Smythe arrived a few moments after they started eating, but Wiggins didn't show up at all. By the time they'd cleared the table and sat back down to discuss the case, all of them were throwing anxious glances at the passage leading to the back door.

When a loud knock sounded, they all jumped.

'I'll get it.' Betsy leapt to her feet. She hurried down the hallway and threw open the door. 'Why, goodness!' she exclaimed. 'It's you.'

Hatchet smiled politely and took off his shiny top hat, revealing a full head of white hair. 'Good evening, Miss Betsy. May I come in?'

'Course you can.' She led him back to the others.

Everyone greeted him effusively. Hatchet worked

for their friend, Luty Belle Crookshank. He was allegedly her butler, but in reality, his relationship with his eccentric and elderly employer was far more complex than that of butler and mistress. Tall, ramrod straight, and excruciatingly proper, he was still a popular and much beloved friend to the staff of Upper Edmonton Gardens.

'Do sit down, Hatchet,' Mrs Jeffries invited. 'Would you care for a cup of tea?'

'Thank you, but no.' He smiled slightly, amusement apparent in his clear blue eyes. 'I've come to help you.'

'Help us?' Betsy gave him a puzzled frown. 'With what?'

'With this murder,' Hatchet replied evenly. 'You certainly didn't think that just because madam is out of town I had no interest in furthering the cause of justice?'

'Bored are you, Hatchet?' Smythe challenged with a cocky grin.

'Extremely. Now,' he said, his expression serious, 'I am here to place myself completely at your disposal.'

'You've already done a great deal for us,' Mrs Jeffries said. 'Thank you again for arranging that invitation for Mrs Livingston-Graves.'

'No thanks are necessary,' Hatchet replied. 'Using my contacts to rid your good selves of that odious personage was almost as amusing as it's going to be when the madam gets back and finds out she's missed a murder.' He grinned slowly. 'I can't wait. She'll be fit to be tied, as she would say. It serves her right as well. I told her not to go gallivanting off to America.

130

But would she listen to me? Oh, no, claimed she couldn't stomach the Jubilee.'

'She left because of the Jubilee?' Betsy yelped. 'But why? All London'll be celebratin'.'

'Madam considers herself a Jeffersonian democrat,' Hatchet explained. 'She's morally opposed to the idea of a monarchy. And, of course, she did it to annoy me.'

'Women'll do that,' Smythe muttered.

Betsy threw him a glare and then turned her attention to the butler. 'How would her goin' off to America annoy you?'

'I do not approve of the madam travelling without me.'

'Then why didn't you go with her?' Mrs Goodge asked.

Hatchet's eyes narrowed. 'I couldn't. She cleverly arranged her trip to coincide with my annual trip to Scotland. I go there once a year to visit my brother. By the time I arrived home, she'd left.'

'You've got a brother?' Betsy said, looking interested.

Mrs Jeffries quickly interrupted. 'He's just told us he has, dear,' she said gently. 'But we really must get on with our discussion. It's getting late and we've much to talk about. Hatchet is more than welcome to stay and help. No doubt his services will come in very handy.'

'If you would be so good as to enlighten me as to the progress you've made thus far?' Hatchet said. 'I'll endeavour to offer what assistance I can.'

Mrs Jeffries quickly told Hatchet everything they

knew about the murder and their circle of suspects. She then went on to share what she'd learned from the inspector and Lady Cannonberry.

'So Dr Sloan were hidin' the satchel under his coat,' Smythe mused. 'I wonder why?'

Mrs Jeffries sighed. 'I shouldn't put too much credence in that evidence. Lady Cannonberry . . .' She hesitated, searching for the right words. 'Well, she wanted the inspector's attention, and she could easily have misconstrued what she saw.'

'You mean she might have just seen him pickin' up the satchel and walkin' off?' Mrs Goodge asked. 'Only she didn't want to be left out, so she made more of it than it really was?'

'That's it precisely.'

'Silly woman,' the cook murmured. 'Anyways, can I go next? I've found out some interestin' bits. Or should we wait for Wiggins?'

'Go right ahead,' Mrs Jeffries replied. 'We'll just have to fill Wiggins in later.'

'Daft boy,' Mrs Goodge muttered. 'Bloomin' inconsiderate of him to be late and worry a body so. But as I was sayin', I've learned quite a bit today. Mrs Jeffries has already told us that Mr Warburton was acquainted with Rowena Stanwick before she come to London. But I've found out he weren't just acquainted with the woman; he were in love with her.' She paused dramatically. 'And he's been in love with Mrs Stanwick since afore her husband died. He didn't just happen to run into her after she moved here; he followed her to London.'

'That's why he joined the literary group,' Smythe

added. 'He's no more interested in poetry and books than Bow and Arrow,' he mused, referring to the inspector's horses. 'But once he found out Mrs Stanwick were in the group, he couldn't join fast enough.'

'Am I tellin' this or are you?' Mrs Goodge yelped. She glared at the coachman.

'Sorry.' He grinned, not looking in the least bit contrite. 'Didn't mean to step on yer toes.'

'Humph. Anyways, that's not all I learned. Warburton's got plenty of money. He were fixin' to ask Mrs Stanwick to marry him, and he'd almost wore her down to the point where she was goin' to say yes. But then she met Mr Locke and dropped Warburton like a hot potato,' Mrs Goodge finished with relish.

'Did Mr Warburton take his rejection like a gentleman?' Mrs Jeffries asked. She'd frequently observed that when it came to matters of the heart, one's social class had no bearing at all on how one acted.

'He didn't take it well at all,' Mrs Goodge answered. 'He went over to her house and had a right old set-to with her about it. He accused Mrs Stanwick of leadin' him on and triflin' with his feelings. The whole neighbourhood heard him shoutin' at her.'

'When was this?' Hatchet asked.

'Less than a fortnight ago. I couldn't find out the exact date. Do you think it's important?' Mrs Goodge asked, looking anxiously at the housekeeper.

'I'm not sure,' Mrs Jeffries said slowly. 'I don't see how it could have anything to do with Mrs Greenwood's murder.'

'Exceptin' that Mrs Greenwood had a row with

Mrs Stanwick right before she was killed,' Betsy chimed in. 'Could be they was arguin' about Mr Warburton. Maybe Mrs Greenwood liked Mr Warburton herself.'

'Warburton barely knew Mrs Greenwood,' Smythe said. 'Besides, he liked 'em young – ' He broke off as he realized what he'd said. 'Uh, I mean, uh . . .'

'Are you, perhaps, referring to the fact that Edgar Warburton has a penchant for young females?' Hatchet asked helpfully.

'Mrs Stanwick isn't all that young,' Betsy protested. 'She's at least thirty.'

'She's twenty-eight,' Smythe countered, recovering quickly. 'But she looks much younger.'

'Smythe,' Mrs Jeffries interrupted before the discussion got out of hand, 'you've obviously learned something about Mr Warburton. Would you like to share it with us?'

Smythe glanced at Betsy and shook his head. 'It don't have anythin' to do with the murder.'

'How do you know?' the maid demanded. She turned to Mrs Jeffries. 'Aren't you always tellin' us that we don't know what's important and what's not? Shouldn't Smythe 'ave to tell us everythin' 'e's learned?'

In her anger she was dropping her h's again. Mrs Jeffries drummed her fingers on the table-top. Betsy was right. 'I think you ought to tell us, Smythe,' she said gently. She never ordered them about. Their participation in these investigations was totally voluntary.

Smythe shifted uncomfortably. 'It's not very nice and it don't have a ruddy thing to do with Mrs Greenwood gettin' murdered.'

'Nevertheless,' she said softly, 'Betsy is right. We don't know at this point what is or isn't important. If you've learned anything about Mr Warburton you really must tell us all.'

He took a long, deep breath. 'Warburton likes women. Young ones, some of 'em barely old enough to be considered women, ifn' you get my meanin'. He pays 'em to go with 'im.'

'You mean he pays prostitutes,' Mrs Jeffries clarified. From the corner of her eye she saw Betsy blush.

Smythe nodded. 'There's some pretty nasty places in this city. Houses where a man can flash a bit of money about and get whatever he likes. Warburton's a regular customer.'

'Sounds as though the man frequents some of the most notorious brothels in the city,' Hatchet said calmly. 'How very disgusting.'

Smythe nodded but didn't volunteer anything else. He'd learned about a few of Mr Warburton's other habits, too, but nothing short of torture would get that information out of him.

'Had he gone to a brothel the night of the murder?' Mrs Jeffries persisted. 'The inspector told us he admitted he'd just learned Mrs Stanwick was going to marry Shelby Locke. Perhaps he left the ball and, well, sought solace in the arms of another woman.'

'But that would mean he couldn't 'ave done the murder,' Mrs Goodge said.

'Unless there's something about him and his

relationship with Mrs Greenwood that we don't know,' Mrs Jeffries replied. 'She might very well have found out about his, well, extracurricular activities and threatened to expose him. That's not the sort of gossip one wants spread about, you know. Furthermore, Warburton has no alibi for the time of the murder. As you'll recall, he claimed he was in the ballroom when Mrs Greenwood was killed. But no one can remember seeing him there.'

'I don't know if he went to a brothel or not,' Smythe replied. 'But I can find out.'

'I think you ought to,' Mrs Jeffries said.

'What difference does it make where he went after the murder was committed?' Betsy asked curiously. 'Shouldn't we try and find out where he was durin' it?'

'The victim was stabbed, Betsy,' Mrs Jeffries explained. 'Whoever committed the murder may have gotten some blood on his clothes. And no one recalls seeing Warburton after the killing. I know, because I specifically asked the inspector. Mr Warburton was gone by the time the inspector began questioning the guests.'

'But why would Warburton want to kill Mrs Greenwood?' she persisted. 'The worst she could do was spread some nasty gossip 'bout him. That don't seem like much of a motive for murder.'

'It's not much of a motive,' Mrs Jeffries admitted, 'but it should be looked into.'

'Seems to me, if 'is feelin's was hurtin' over Mrs Stanwick givin' him the boot,' Betsy continued, 'he'd murder her or Mr Locke.'

'We don't know that he'd want to murder any-body,' Mrs Jeffries explained. 'We're merely trying to establish where he was both during and after the murder, and, more important, why he lied to the police. Mrs Putnam claimed she searched the ball-room and Warburton wasn't there.'

They heard the back door open, and a second later Fred bounced in followed by a breathless Wiggins.

'It's about time you got here,' Mrs Goodge said, giving him a good frown.

'I'm ever so sorry to be late,' Wiggins explained breathlessly. 'But I couldn't come back until I found out what's 'appened to the boy.'

'What boy?' Mrs Goodge snapped. Her concern about Wiggins's absence had transformed to anger now that she knew he was all right. 'And where have you been? Your food's gone stone cold, and I'm not gettin' up and reheatin' it for you.'

'The boy's name is Jon!' he cried. 'We've got to find 'im. 'E's in danger, I know 'e is. 'E were with Mrs Greenwood at the ball. She's dead and now 'e's gone.'

CHAPTER SEVEN

'Do sit down, Wiggins,' Mrs Jeffries suggested. 'Surely, whatever it is you have to report can wait until you've caught your breath.' The lad was prone to exaggerating, so she was quite certain no one was in imminent danger.

'But that's just it, Mrs Jeffries,' he protested, 'I'm not sure it can. I think maybe that Jon knows who the murderer is and that's why he's disappeared.'

'Who's this Jon, then?' Smythe asked.

'And why do you think he's disappeared?' Betsy added.

'Do you suspect foul play?' Hatchet said doubtfully.

'I best get Fred his supper.' Mrs Goodge reached down and patted the animal on the head. The dog licked his lips and bounced up and down.

'Fred?' Wiggins yelped, outraged. 'What about me? I've not 'ad a bite to eat all day.'

'Really, Wiggins,' Mrs Jeffries said. 'I thought you were concerned about this Jon person.'

'I am. But that don't mean I'm not hungry.' He blushed. 'I mean, I don't think Jon's really in any danger. But I do think he might 'ave gone to ground, so to speak.'

Mrs Goodge chuckled as she got to her feet. 'Thought hearing me offer to feed the dog first would snap you back into shape, boy. Now just hang on a minute and I'll have you both tucking into a right tasty meal, not that you deserve it, mind you. I've half a mind to carry through on my threat and serve you your dinner cold.'

Smythe glanced at Wiggins and snorted in disgust. 'You had us worried there a minute, lad.'

'The way you come runnin' in here, you'd have thought this Jon person was bein' tortured,' Betsy chided.

'Ah, youth,' Hatchet said. 'So impetuous. So noble. So concerned with the satisfaction of their stomachs.'

As soon as Mrs Goodge had fed Fred and put a plate of hot food in front of the footman, Betsy cleared her throat. 'Well, I found out what happened to Shelby Locke's notebook.' She smiled triumphantly. 'Lucinda Marlow stole it.'

'So she did want to use one of Mr Locke's poems in the contest,' Mrs Goodge said.

'Oh, no,' Betsy said quickly. 'She didn't give a fig for the contest. Rupert told me she didn't even bother writin' a poem. She stole Mr Locke's poems so she could find out what he was up to.'

'Rupert?' Smythe asked softly. 'Who's 'e?'

'He's the Marlow butler,' Betsy admitted proudly. 'And he does like to talk. He hasn't worked at the house very long, but he's a right nosy parker, knows what's goin' on. Anyway, he thought it strange that Miss Marlow kept tellin' Mr Locke she hadn't seen his notebook, when she'd had it ever since their last meeting. Rupert saw her carryin' it out of the drawing room after the others had left. He didn't think much of it until the next day, when Mr Locke came round looking for it and Miss Marlow stood right there and lied to the man, bold as brass.'

'So 'ow does this Rupert reckon Miss Marlow was usin' the notebook to find out what Mr Locke was up to? It were a bunch of ruddy poems she had, not his diary,' Smythe challenged.

Betsy was ready for that question. 'One of Rupert's duties is to stand outside the door when the meetings are breaking up. You know, to see people out and hand them their coats and such. Well, he once heard Mr Locke telling Miss Marlow that his whole life is a poem. He writes about everything that's important to him and puts the poems in the notebook. That's why he was so upset at it bein' gone.'

'Do you think this Rupert knows what he's talkin' about?' Smythe asked.

'Of course he does,' Betsy replied irritably. 'He'd have no reason to lie to me.'

'If you was askin' questions, he might 'ave been tryin' to impress you. Act like 'e knew what was goin' on, tryin' to make 'imself look important.' Smythe crossed his arms over his chest. 'It wouldn't be the first time a man made up a few tales to impress a pretty girl.'

Betsy tried to look annoyed but couldn't. She was too flattered by his words. She'd never thought the coachman even noticed she was a female, let alone a pretty one.

'I think we must assume he was telling the truth,' Mrs Jeffries interjected. 'Do please go on, Betsy.'

'Rupert told me that after Lucinda Marlow found the notebook, she startin' acting right peculiar.'

'That's hardly surprisin', now, is it? The poor woman thought she had an understandin' with Mr Locke, and then she reads some ruddy poem and finds out she's been jilted.' Mrs Goodge made a face. 'Nasty, that is. Right nasty.'

'Did Rupert explain what he meant by "peculiar"?' Mrs Jeffries asked. She really didn't see where all this was leading, but that didn't bother her. It was one more piece of the puzzle.

'She got all quiet like, moody. Wouldn't smile, wouldn't eat much, and she took to going for long walks.' Betsy shrugged. 'She even took to wearin' her spectacles in public; that's how miserable she was.'

'Humph!' Mrs Goodge exclaimed. 'Doesn't seem to me that Lucinda Marlow acted any differently than any other young woman would behave if they'd just read a love poem about someone else.'

'But we don't know for certain that Lucinda Marlow did read such a poem,' Mrs Jeffries said.

'What else could it be?' Betsy argued. 'Rupert claims she were as right as rain until she found that notebook. She was makin' plans for her ball, sendin' out invitations and doin' up the menu, dashin' out to the dressmaker's, and orderin' a new gown. Then she finds that notebook and starts actin' like her best friend's up and died. She got so melancholy, she even sent her new gown back.'

Smythe said, 'Isn't Lucinda Marlow the one who's supposedly had such a tragic life? Blimey, there's so many people mixed up in this case it's hard to keep it all straight.'

'Her brother is dead and then she lost her parents, so she has had a tragic life,' Betsy said defensively. 'She's a nice woman, too. Her servants like her. It's right sad, her thinkin' she had an understandin' with Mr Locke and then findin' out he was just triflin' with her. No wonder she got all weepy and maudlin and had to work out her grief by goin' for long walks.'

'I bet I know where she were goin', too,' the coachman interrupted. 'I'd lay even money that she were snoopin' about Mr Locke's. Typical female trick.'

'What an evil thing to say,' Betsy snapped, incensed.

'For goodness' sakes!' Mrs Jeffries exclaimed. 'We don't know that she did anything except read Mr Locke's poems. We don't even know for sure that those poems had anything to do with Mr Locke's romantic interests.'

'That reminds me!' the cook cried suddenly. 'All this talk of bein' maudlin. I've forgotten to tell you what else I found out.' She shook her head in disgust. 'I must be getting old. Can't keep a thing straight these days.'

'It's all right, Mrs Goodge,' Betsy said quickly, then reached over and patted her hand. 'Everyone forgets things every now and again. You're not gettin' old.'

'How true,' Mrs Jeffries murmured and smiled kindly at the cook. 'Do go on.'

'I found out that Mrs Greenwood's been in mourning – that's why the house were done up in black. Remember,' she continued eagerly, 'you told us the inspector said they had mourning cloth draped everywhere. Well, it weren't put there by Amelia Hackshaw for her murdered sister. It were put there months ago by Mrs Greenwood herself for her son, Douglas. He died over a year ago, supposedly got hit by a train. But the gossip is, he got drunk and killed himself over a woman.'

Mrs Jeffries tried to keep it all straight in her head, but it was impossible. Dr Sloan hiding a satchel, a missing boy, Lucinda Marlow stealing notebooks, Mrs Greenwood visiting Dr Sloan, and now a suspected suicide. She took a short, sharp breath and promised herself that as soon as she gained the quiet of her room, she'd try to make sense of everything. 'That explains the mourning cloth being up so quickly. Mrs Greenwood did it for her dead son.'

'Supposedly, but if she were still in mournin', why'd she join the literary circle in the first place?' Mrs Goodge frowned. 'Don't make a lot of sense, does it? Especially as her sister told the inspector she didn't think Mrs Greenwood cared a toss for poetry and books and the like.'

'None of this makes sense,' Mrs Jeffries muttered. However, she felt a tiny tug at the back of her mind. Something that she couldn't quite put her finger on was falling into place.

'You can say that again,' Betsy said. 'And the inspector also said that Mrs Greenwood went to see Dr Sloan the day of the ball. Why? What reason could she have to go to his rooms?'

'Ah, but that's the mystery, isn't it? Why did she visit Dr Sloan, and, more important, why did she join a group she had absolutely no interest in?'

'Perhaps she was lonely.' Hatchet ventured.

'Lonely?' Betsy repeated. 'That doesn't sound like Mrs Greenwood.'

'I don't know,' Smythe put in, his expression thoughtful. 'Loneliness can drive a body to do lots of strange things.'

Mrs Jeffries detected an odd undertone in the coachman's words. But she didn't have time to think about it now. She had an idea. 'Mrs Goodge, can you find out where this train accident took place?' she asked. 'And see if you can learn the name of the woman involved as well.'

'I've already got my sources workin' on it,' she replied smugly. 'But it may take a day or two to get an answer.'

'Can I tell you about Jon now?' Wiggins asked.

'Of course.'

Wiggins told them about his meeting with Jon and his unfortunate run-in with the inspector. 'You'd best buy some cod, Mrs Jeffries,' he said, turning to the housekeeper. 'I had to tell the inspector somethin' when he caught me.'

'You're lucky he didn't ask where it was tonight,' the cook said sternly.

'He did ask,' Mrs Jeffries said. 'I told him the fish

mongers had run out. But we mustn't digress. Do get on with your account.'

'After the inspector left,' Wiggins continued, 'I tried to find Jon, but 'e were gone. So I asked about and found out that 'e'd been seen leavin' the Greenwood 'ouse carryin' a bundle of clothes. One of Jon's friends said 'e'd probably gone to 'is cousin's in Clapham, but this same lad also said 'e weren't in the least surprised that the boy had gone, seein' as 'ow Mrs Greenwood got murdered right under 'is nose.'

Smythe leaned forward. 'Jon had spoken to this lad you were talkin' to?'

'Right. The lad's name is Timmy Reston. His mum's the washerwoman for the Greenwood 'ouse. This morning Jon were jumpier than one of Fred's fleas – remember how bad 'is fleas were this summer?' He glanced fondly at the dog, who wagged his tail.

'Yes, yes, get on with it,' Mrs Goodge snapped irritably. 'We haven't got all night.'

'Anyways,' Wiggins continued, 'as 'e were leavin', Jon told Timmy 'e wouldn't spend a minute more in that 'ouse, not with Mrs Greenwood gettin' herself done in. He said he were scared the killer 'ad seen him in the Marlow 'ouse and 'e weren't 'anging about waitin' for the murderer to come after 'im.'

'Let me see if I understand you,' Mrs Jeffries clarified. 'Are you saying that Jon was with Mrs Greenwood in the Marlow house during the ball?'

Wiggins frowned impatiently. 'Didn't I tell you that at the beginnin'?' There was a collective moan.

'No, you most certainly didn't. Or if you did, you

didn't make it clear this young man was actually in the house with the victim.'

'Oh.' Wiggins looked embarrassed. 'I must o' left that bit out.'

'How the blue blazes did this lad get 'imself in the 'ouse?' Smythe asked. 'Or are you tryin' to tell us 'e were Mrs Greenwood's escort for the evenin'?'

'Jon got in like 'e always did. 'E nipped round the back and slipped in through the kitchen. Timmy told me that Jon boasted about 'ow he got the kitchenmaids and serving girls to feed 'im every time 'e went somewheres with Mrs Greenwood. Jon even did it a time or two when Mrs Greenwood went to 'er literary circle meetin's. Accordin' to what Jon told Timmy, the Greenwood 'ousehold was a bit on the stingy side with food. The boy 'ad learned a few tricks to get 'im a bit on the sly, so to speak.'

'Are you sure this Timmy was telling the truth?' Mrs Goodge asked, her expression suspicious. 'It's not unknown for young boys to stretch the truth a bit, either.'

Mrs Jeffries wasn't sure it was a good idea for everyone to start questioning one another's sources. 'I think', she stated firmly, 'that it would be in all our interests if we assumed that people were telling us the truth. Otherwise, we'll never make any headway on any of the inspector's cases.'

'You're right, Mrs J,' Smythe said, glancing apologetically at Betsy. 'Sorry, lass, I didn't mean anything earlier. You're a smart one — you'd be able to tell if this Rupert person were 'avin' you on.'

'Me, too,' Mrs Goodge admitted. 'I'm sure that Wiggins would know if this lad were tellin' tales.'

Wiggins nodded. 'Timmy was tellin' the truth. Mrs Greenwood took Jon with her everywhere. I know 'e were with 'er at the ball. Timmy saw 'im gettin' in the carriage.'

'She took a carriage to the Jubilee Ball, not a hansom?' Smythe asked.

'It were a hired one,' Wiggins replied. 'But it was a carriage.'

Smythe's expression grew thoughtful. 'Did this Timmy 'appen to know which livery Mrs Greenwood used?'

Wiggins shook his head. 'Timmy didn't say and I didn't think to ask, but Berry's Livery is just round the corner from the 'ouse.'

'I'll pop round there tomorrow,' the coachman muttered.

'Isn't that a bit odd, a young servant boy goin' with her to a fancy Jubilee Ball?' Betsy murmured.

'I suppose it is,' Mrs Jeffries said. 'But there are many odd people involved in this case and in that particular literary circle.'

'For one thing, none of them seems overly much interested in literature,' Hatchet said. 'Except, perhaps, for Shelby Locke and Dr Sloan.'

'I expect for most of the members the circle was merely a good excuse for a social occasion,' Mrs Jeffries said. 'However, that reminds me. We really must find out more from the other members of the circle.'

'But what about Jon?' Wiggins cried.

'I thought you said 'e'd gone to 'is cousin's 'ouse,' Smythe said impatiently.

'No, I didn't. I said Timmy thought Jon went there, but 'e didn't. That's why I'm so late. Fred and me went all the way to Clapham and we couldn't find 'ide nor 'air of the boy.'

'Did you actually go to the cousin's house?' Hatchet asked calmly.

'Course I did,' he protested. 'But no one answered the door.'

'Then I think we really ought to go back, don't you?' The butler smiled and turned to the housekeeper. 'You don't mind if I accompany young Wiggins on his search for the missing boy, do you? I may have some resources that can help should the relatives of the young man not be forthcoming concerning his whereabouts.'

Mrs Jeffries heaved a sigh of relief. In truth, she didn't like the idea of Wiggins searching for what could well be an eyewitness to murder on his own. Hatchet, she had found, was a good man to have about if trouble started.

'I don't mind in the least,' she replied warmly. 'We'll be very grateful for any assistance you can give us.'

'It will be my pleasure, Mrs Jeffries,' he assured her. He reached into his coat pocket and withdrew a cream-coloured envelope. 'Before I forget,' he said, handing it to her, 'I must give you this. Should Mrs Livingston-Graves return earlier than expected, this will no doubt keep her busy for a while.'

Mrs Jeffries grinned. 'What is it this time?'

'An invitation to Lord Willoughby's Jubilee Picnic. There will be several hundred guests, and, even better, it's in Richmond.'

'Thank you, Hatchet.' Mrs Jeffries glanced at the others around the table. She supposed she really ought to give them an explanation. But before she could speak, there was a bloodcurdling howl from outside.

Fred cringed and slithered under the table.

'What in blazes is that?' Mrs Goodge exclaimed, heaving herself to her feet.

'Sounds like a bunch of tomcats sniffin' after a—' Smythe broke off as another howl sliced through the air.

'Oh, no,' Betsy said, 'it's that wretched Alphonse. He sounds like he's being clawed to death.'

'What's Alphonse doing out?' Mrs Jeffries asked. She noticed that no one made a move to go and rescue the unfortunate feline.

'He pushed himself out through the kitchen window,' Mrs Goodge said calmly as she sat back down. 'Wouldn't have thought the blighter could do it. The window was only open a crack and his backside is bigger than a side of beef.'

'Well, isn't someone going to rescue the poor thing?' Mrs Jeffries demanded. 'I know none of us are fond of Mrs Livingston-Graves or her cat but, honestly, Alphonse is hardly able to defend himself.'

Meowww . . . another howl shook the air.

No one moved for a moment, then Smythe sighed and climbed to his feet. 'I'll do it. Mind you, if the bloomin' creature digs his claws in me, I'll let 'im spend the night outside. Do that foppy cat a world of good.'

The house was very quiet the next morning, but that was to be expected. Sundays were always quiet. Since Mrs Jeffries had taken over the management of the household, she'd made it clear that the day of rest wasn't just to apply to the master of the house, but to the servants as well. The inspector, naturally, hadn't seen anything wrong with this arrangement and had even offered to boil his own eggs for breakfast.

Mrs Jeffries wouldn't hear of that; she was quite adept at boiling eggs herself.

Everyone was out sleuthing; Hatchet had shown up several hours ago to pick up Wiggins and Fred, Betsy had decided to see what she could learn by concentrating on the other members of the literary circle, and Smythe had gone off on some mysterious errand he refused to tell anyone about. Mrs Goodge had taken to her room, claiming she needed to think but leaving the back door open in case any of her 'sources' showed up with information.

For all intents and purposes, Mrs Jeffries and the inspector were alone. As she brought his breakfast tray up from the kitchen, she went over the various pieces of information they'd gathered thus far.

She sighed as she nudged open the dining room door with her foot. So far, she had absolutely nothing. The beginning of the pattern she was starting to discern yesterday evening had completely unravelled. This crime simply had no motive.

Hannah Greenwood was not well liked, but they

could find nothing that would make anyone want to actually kill the woman.

Lucinda Marlow was a lovesick girl, but gracious, Mrs Jeffries thought as she put the inspector's eggs on the table, half of London was filled with lovesick girls. Nor was she the first young woman to rifle through a young man's belongings in hopes of learning his true intentions.

Shelby Locke was in love with Rowena Stanwick, but that gave him no reason to murder Hannah Greenwood. The victim hadn't been standing in the way of Locke's desire for Mrs Stanwick.

Dr Sloan's actions were suspicious and his story about being out in the gardens during the murder was probably a lie. But then again, he could be telling the truth. Mrs Putnam might have missed seeing him.

Mrs Jeffries paused, her hand hovering over the rack of toast. But Mrs Greenwood had visited Sloan on the day she died, and Sloan had not seen fit to mention this to the police. Perhaps Mrs Greenwood did know something about Sloan. Something he'd kill to keep secret.

And then there was Rowena Stanwick. Mrs Jeffries frowned. Both Warburton and Locke were in love with her. Warburton followed her to London from the country. When she spurned his affections, he was bitter enough to cast aspersions on her reputation. Was he bitter enough to kill? She shook her head. Perhaps he was, except that Mrs Stanwick wasn't the victim.

And what about Edgar Warburton? Where did

he fit in? He certainly hadn't cared about the Hyde Park Literary Circle. So why didn't he leave once Mrs Stanwick had made it clear her affections were engaged elsewhere? According to what she'd learned, Mrs Stanwick and Mr Locke's association had been going on for several months.

The inspector bounced into the room. 'Good morning, Mrs Jeffries.' He spotted the delicate china coddlers. 'I say, coddled eggs this morning; that is most good of you.'

'Not at all, sir. You need a hot breakfast.' She poured herself a cup of tea and sat down beside him. Despite spending half the night thinking about this case, the best course of action she'd come up with was to get the inspector to double-check where everyone was at ten-thirty. Furthermore, it was becoming increasingly apparent that everyone's story must be verified in some fashion. And, of course, she had to find a discreet method of letting the inspector know about Lucinda Marlow's theft of Locke's notebook. 'Will you be continuing your investigation today?'

'It may be the day of rest for the rest of the world, but the pursuit of justice never stops.' He reached for his teacup. 'Barnes should be here soon and we'll be off.'

Mrs Jeffries clucked her tongue sympathetically. 'Are you going back to the Marlow house, sir?'

As the inspector had no idea where he was going this morning, he shrugged. 'Er, well, I'm not sure.'

'The only reason I mention it is because of what you told me on your last case, sir.' She calmly sipped her tea and waited for him to take the bait.

'My last case?'

'Why, yes, sir. Don't you remember? You told me that whenever you got stuck in the middle of an investigation, you always went right back to the source, the scene of the crime, the circle of suspects.' She smiled.

'I said that?' Witherspoon gave her a puzzled frown.

'So, naturally, I assumed that you'd be going back to the Marlow house and questioning the servants again.' She sighed. 'It's so very easy for one to forget the most important things when one is rattled. Being present in a house where a murder is committed would naturally upset the staff. But once one gets over the shock of the event, then one can quite clearly remember details that had completely slipped one's mind.'

As understanding dawned, his confused expression cleared. 'I say, that's a jolly good idea. I was considering going back to Dr Sloan's this morning. I mean to ask him about Mrs Greenwood's visit to him the day of the ball. I want a look at those contest poems, as well. Lady Cannonberry's statement got me to thinking. If Dr Sloan was hiding that satchel, then I'd better find out why. But that can wait until after I've questioned the Marlow servants again.'

'You know, sir,' Mrs Jeffries said cautiously, 'I've been thinking about that missing notebook.'

'What notebook?'

'Mr Locke's.'

'Oh.' Witherspoon dug into his eggs. 'That one. What about it? I'm not certain it's all that important.

It probably doesn't have anything to do with Mrs Greenwood's murder.'

'I'm sure you're right, sir,' she continued. 'But I've been thinking about it anyway.' She laughed airily. 'It seems to me that there's really only one place it could be. The Marlow house.'

Before she could explain, they were interrupted by a loud pounding on the front door. Mrs Jeffries started. 'Gracious, Constable Barnes is making a racket.' She got to her feet and hurried toward the hall. Throwing open the door, her eyes widened in surprise.

'Well, don't just stand there gaping,' Mrs Livingston-Graves snarled. 'Help me in.'

Her elegant pink dress was muddy and torn at the sleeve and her plumed hat leaned to one side, its once white feather broken and hanging askew. Tendrils of lank brown hair straggled around her neck, and as Mrs Jeffries helped her into the house, the woman hobbled precariously.

'Goodness, Mrs Livingston-Graves, what happened?'

'I say, Mrs Jeffries, is that Constable Barnes?' Witherspoon asked as he came out of the dining room. He stopped dead in his tracks at the sight of his cousin. 'Goodness, Edwina, what on earth happened to you? Are you all right?'

'Of course I'm not all right!' she yelled. 'I've spent half the night in the most wretched inn, and then I had to get up at the crack of dawn to get a seat on the train. But that horrid little toad of an innkeeper kept me haggling over the bill so long, I missed the train. Then I had to hire a carriage.'

'Oh, dear,' he murmured. 'You had to hire a carriage? But why didn't you just wait and take the next train?'

'Because I wasn't going to stay in that awful place another minute!' she cried. 'It was bad enough being stuck there as long as I was, but that's not the worst of it. As we were coming back to London, the carriage lost a wheel . . . I suspect the driver was drinking. Then I slipped and fell in the mud. To top it off, once that imbecile of a driver had repaired the wheel and we were on our way again, the blasted door flew open every time we rounded a curve. It was awful, positively awful. And I mean to do something about it!'

'Oh, dear.' The inspector started forward.

'Hello, hello,' the cheerful voice of Constable Barnes called from the doorway.

Witherspoon took one frantic look at his dishevelled and enraged relation and then leapt for his hat and coat.

'I'll leave you in Mrs Jeffries's capable hands,' he sputtered and hurried toward the door. 'We'll talk this evening when I return. I'm sure we can get everything sorted out then.'

'But you can't leave now, Gerald,' she protested. 'That carriage driver was drunk! Surely that's against the law. And that conveyance was certainly unsafe. There must be a law against that. You can't go now. You're the police. I want to press charges.'

Smythe pulled out a shiny new florin and waved it under the housemaid's nose. 'Does this 'elp your memory any?'

The girl smiled, revealing a half-broken front tooth. She snatched at the coin and dropped it into the pocket of her apron. 'By rights, I shouldn't be talkin' to ye,' she said, 'but seein' as how yer a feller that pays 'is way, I expect I can remember a bit more than I told them coppers.'

Smythe nodded. He wasn't surprised that the maid hadn't shared everything she knew with the police. Why should she risk her living for the sake of a murdered woman she didn't even know? 'So what can you tell us now, luv?'

'It weren't much.' The girl shrugged. 'I usually works down in the kitchen. I'm the second scullery maid. But because of all the people comin' for the ball, the 'ousekeeper sent me upstairs to work. I was supposed to keep the punch bowls filled.' She laughed softly. 'And it were a hard task, too, the way them toffs was drinkin'. Anyways, I 'ad to run back and forth between the second pantry and the dinin' room. Well, just as I was comin' out of the dinin' room, I saw that Mrs Stanwick havin' a right old row with Mrs Greenwood. The woman what was murdered.'

'Were you able to hear what they was arguin' about?'

'You'd a 'ad to be deaf as a post not to 'ear 'em,' she replied. 'Me name's Lena, by the way.' She gave him a coy smile.

Smythe, who was male enough to be flattered by her sudden interest, was also smart enough to realize that it was probably the coins from his pocket and not his person that piqued her attention. 'Lena's a nice name,' he replied, giving her a slow smile. 'Real pretty, like you. But you were tellin' me about the argument.'

'Oh, yeah. Like I was sayin', they was goin' at it somethin' fierce. Not screamin' or nuthin' but kinda hissin' at each other. I didn't reckon they'd appreciate me trottin' back and forth under their noses, so to speak. So I ducked behind the curtain and waited for 'em to finish.'

Right, he thought, and I'm the King of Spain. The girl'd been deliberately eavesdropping.

'And what was they on about?' he prodded. He schooled himself to be patient.

'Mrs Greenwood was tellin' the other woman, Mrs Stanwick 'er name is, that she'd see to it that she wouldn't be able to show her face at one of their meetin's ever agin.'

'Mrs Greenwood was threatenin' Mrs Stanwick then?'

Lena frowned impatiently. 'That's what I said, in't it? Then Mrs Stanwick claimed she didn't give a tinker's damn about their group. That didn't sit well with the old lady. She got all red in the face and said she'd see to it that some feller, I didn't quite catch 'is name, wouldn't be wantin' to come sniffin' after Mrs Stanwick no more. Not when 'e heard about 'er Douglas.'

'You're sure the name was Douglas?'

She nodded. 'There's nuthin' wrong with me hearin'. The name was Douglas, all right. Anyway, as soon as this Mrs Greenwood said it, Mrs Stanwick got all quiet. Didn't say nuthin'. Then Mrs

Greenwood started laughing, a right 'orrible laugh it was, too. She told 'er she was goin' to pay for what she'd done. She'd see to it that no one ever spoke to Mrs Stanwick again, and as soon as this feller 'eard about Douglas, 'e'd be finished with 'er, too.'

'And then what 'appened?' Smythe asked.

'Then Mrs Stanwick turned and run off.' Lena shrugged. 'I think she were cryin'. She were in such a state she ran smack into the buffet table.'

'Then what did she do?'

'She righted herself, took off down the 'all, and went up the stairs.'

'What time was this?'

'It must of been close to ten-thirty.'

'What did Mrs Greenwood do?' Smythe asked slowly.

'She went after 'er.'

'Are you sure this is the correct house?' Hatchet asked.

'I'm sure,' Wiggins replied.

They were standing in front of a small grey brick row house off Victoria Road in Clapham. The paint was peeling around the windows, the door stoop was dusty, and the street was littered with trash. They'd knocked several times to no avail.

Hatchet knocked again, this time pounding hard enough to make the windows vibrate.

'They's no one home,' a disgruntled female voice rang out from above.

They both looked up to see a frizzy blond-haired woman glaring at them from the top window of the house next door.

Hatchet took off his top hat. 'Excuse me, madam. I'm so sorry my knocking disturbed you. But do you have any idea when the family will return?'

'It's Sunday,' she replied irritably. 'They've gone to visit their gran. They'll not be back till tonight. Now quit that poundin' and let a body get some sleep.'

'We can't hang about till tonight,' Wiggins moaned.

The woman started to close the window. Hatchet yelled. 'Excuse me, madam, I'm so terribly sorry to be a nuisance. But did they have a young boy with them?'

'A young boy?' She stared at them suspiciously. 'Who are you and why you askin' all these questions about the Hickmans?'

Hatchet gave her his most engaging smile. 'The young man we're inquiring about is called Jon. He's cousin to the Hickman family. I'd like to offer him employment with my mistress, Mrs Crookshank. But she needs him to start working for her right away. She's leaving for Scotland early tomorrow morning and wants someone with her to look after her trunks. Jon was recommended to us as an honest lad in need of a position.'

The woman hesitated. She spent several seconds staring at Hatchet and then raked Wiggins with a hard glance. Finally she sighed. 'You'd best be tellin' the truth, because I'll remember what you looked like. If you're up to no good, I'll know about it. But I don't want to take the chance on Jon missin' out on gettin' work. Lord knows they' – she jerked her thumb at the Hickman house – 'can't afford another mouth to feed.'

'Thank you, madam,' Hatchet said solemnly. 'I assure you, we've only the boy's best interests at heart. If you would be so good as to tell us where the Hickmans went, we'll trouble you no further.'

'You'll be wantin' to find the Purty house, then. Their granny's name is Hazel Purty.' She started to shut the window.

'Could you be more precise, madam?' Hatchet called.

'She lives at Haggar's Lane in Clacton-on-Sea!' she yelled. With that, she slammed the window shut.

'Clacton-on-Sea,' Wiggins whispered. 'Blimey, that's miles from 'ere.'

Hatchet popped his elegant top hat on and leapt spryly off the door stoop. 'It's hardly the end of the earth.'

'We'd better just nip back and try to have a word with Jon tonight.'

'Don't be ridiculous,' Hatchet said as he hurried up the stone path toward the street. 'We're not going to waste a whole day.'

'Where are we goin', then?' Wiggins asked. He practically had to run to keep up with the stiff-backed butler.

'To Clacton-on-Sea.'

CHAPTER EIGHT

Inspector Witherspoon wished the young man would sit still. He gave the footman a kindly smile, hoping the poor soul would relax. Gracious, he was only asking a few questions. He tried again. 'Now, Ronald, you say you were too busy to notice anyone picking up the knife from the serving table, is that correct?'

Ronald's left shoulder twitched. 'That's right, sir. There was so many people milling around the cold buffet, I could barely keep up.'

'And how did the knife come to be lying beside the plate?' Witherspoon asked. 'I mean, if you were serving such a great number of people, shouldn't the knife have been in your hand so that you could carve?' That sounded like a good question.

'Oh, no, sir, we couldn't do it that way; we'd have people lined up all the way to Hyde Park.' He entwined his fingers and began to rotate his thumbs around each other, 'We'd carved off part of the beef down in the kitchen. I was heaping it on plates as fast as I could, you know, as the guests come up.

Every time I had me a bit of a lull, I'd hack off a bit more. I'd just run out of the last of the meat and I was reachin' over to pick up the knife. But just then I heard all the commotion outside.' Ronald stopped twirling his thumbs and began to pump his knee up and down. 'Naturally, I run out to see what was goin' on. And there was me carvin' knife, stickin' straight out of that poor lady's back. Blow me for a game of tin soldiers, I thought. I'll never use that ruddy knife again.'

Witherspoon sighed silently. Questioning the servants was turning out to be only minimally better than staying home and facing his cousin.

Ronald drummed his fingers against the table. The inspector concentrated fiercely, trying to think of some questions that would get the footman past his nervousness. Prime the pump, so to speak. But he'd been talking to the servants now for several hours, and he'd learned nothing new, nothing that seemed to have any bearing whatsoever on Mrs Greenwood's murder. No one, including Miss Marlow, had seen or heard anything amiss until the victim had come tumbling off the balcony with a knife in her back.

Miss Marlow had not been pleased to see them again, but he could hardly blame her for that. Having a murder take place at one's ball did tend to make one less hospitable than usual.

'Do you know which guests are members of the Hyde Park Literary Circle?' the inspector asked.

Ronald nodded. 'They meet here all the time, so I know most of them by sight.'

'Did you see any of them anywhere near your

serving table from the time you put the knife down until the time you heard the commotion outside?' The inspector tried another smile. 'Take your time before you answer. Take a deep breath and try to remember.'

'Let me see,' he murmured, a look of intense concentration spreading across his thin, pale face. 'Miss Marlow come up to check that we had plenty of food. But she'd done that all evening.'

'Isn't that the butler or the housekeeper's responsibility?' Barnes asked softly.

'Usually, yes,' Ronald explained. 'Miss Marlow ain't one for interferin' most of the time. But she was very anxious about this ball. Wanted it to go right and all. She watched over the preparations herself, even down to checkin' the linens and lookin' for spots on the crystal. But as for seein' any other members of the circle, well, I don't think . . .' He stopped. 'Wait a minute, I did see Dr Sloan scarperin' up the stairs.'

They'd already established that Ronald had a full view of the stairs from his position behind the buffet table. Unfortunately, Ronald was not the most observant of witnesses.

Witherspoon and Barnes glanced at each other. Finally the inspector asked, 'Was he carrying anything?'

'Yes, he had some sort of satchel or case in his hand.'

'Now, Ronald,' the inspector said gently, 'think carefully before you answer this question. Prior to your seeing Dr Sloan go up the stairs, had he come anywhere near the buffet table?'

'Now that you mention it' – Ronald chewed his lower lip – 'he did.' A proud smile spread across his face. 'Of course, that's why I remember seein' him go up the stairs. He'd been standing by my table only a minute before. He knocked into the leg with his foot when he scarpered off. That's right. I were a bit nervous, seein' as how Miss Marlow had just come by to make sure everything was runnin' smoothly.'

Witherspoon nodded encouragingly. 'So both Miss Marlow and Dr Sloan had been by the table. Do you know what time this was?'

'Near as I could tell, it were probably about ten-fifteen, maybe ten-twenty.' He shrugged. 'But I wouldn't want to swear to it.'

They continued questioning Ronald for a few more minutes, but were unable to get any additional information out of the young man.

For the next hour the inspector spoke to servant after servant. But it was the same as on the night of the murder. No one had seen or heard anything.

'How many more do we have to talk with?' Witherspoon asked Barnes.

The constable squinted at his notebook. 'Only two, a scullery maid named Lena Crammer and Rupert Malloy – that's the butler.'

A young woman appeared at the doorway. 'Mrs Craycroft says you want to ask me some questions.'

'Yes, please come in and sit down.' Witherspoon hoped this young woman could be of help. 'You're Miss Lena Crammer?'

She nodded, her dark head bobbing as she took the seat that Ronald had just vacated. Her face was narrow and sharp with a beaked nose, hazel eyes, and a slightly protruding mouth. 'Right. I'm a scullery maid. I've worked here for the best part of a year now.'

'And you were on duty the night of the Jubilee Ball, is that correct?'

'That's right.' Lena slipped her hands in her pockets and fingered the coins the big man had given her. She smiled, remembering how he'd told her to tell this copper everything she'd told him. Claimed this one was a good copper, not that there really was such a thing, but blimey, he'd paid good money for her to tell the truth, so she supposed she might as well, Lena thought. Strange feller, he was. Tall and raw lookin' with shoulders as broad as a bridge and muscles stretchin' from here to Sunday. She hoped she'd see him again. It weren't often a girl run into a feller that didn't mind splashin' his money about. 'Me job was to nip back and forth between the pantries and the buffet table. I was keepin' the punch bowl filled and makin' sure we had plenty of china and the like.'

'On the night of the ball,' the inspector began, 'did you see anything unusual?'

Lena smiled smugly. 'I reckon I did.'

'Really?'

'Course I didn't remember it when you was talkin' to us before,' Lena said quickly, thinking good copper or not, peelers didn't much like it when you lied to 'em. 'I was so rattled by the murder, I barely remembered me own name. We was all in an awful state.'

Witherspoon felt his pulse leap. Finally they were

getting somewhere. Perhaps he would be able to solve this murder after all. 'I quite understand, Miss. Now, what was it you saw?'

'It were a few minutes afore that Mrs Greenwood come tumblin' off the balcony – her having a row with Mrs Stanwick,' Lena explained.

'You saw Mrs Greenwood and Mrs Stanwick arguing?' Witherspoon clarified.

'They was hissin' at each other like a couple of she-cats,' she replied, her eyes glittering with excitement. 'Course, as they was standing in the hallway, blockin' me way to the pantry, I had to nip behind a curtain till they was finished.' She went on and told them everything she'd told Smythe earlier.

When she'd finished, Witherspoon pursed his lips. 'Are you absolutely sure about the time?'

'Course I am,' Lena replied promptly. 'I remember because I was supposed to have the rest of the champagne glasses upstairs to the ballroom by half past. That's why I was on me way to the pantry in the first place. As soon as they was gone, I nipped on down to the pantry. If them glasses was late and the guests had to wait to drink their ruddy toast, Miss Marlow would have me guts for garters. That's when I noticed the other funny thing.'

'Other funny thing?' Witherspoon prodded.

'Why, Mr Locke actin' so peculiar. Mind you, at the time I didn't think nuthin' of it, but later I got to thinkin' and it seemed to me he were actin' a mite funny.'

'You'd seen Mr Locke do what?' Barnes asked patiently.

'I'd seen him come down the hall and slip out the side door.'

The inspector frowned. 'What time was this?'

'About ten-twenty,' Lena replied. 'Now, there weren't much odd about that – guests slip in and out all the time. But we keep that side door bolted. Mr Locke threw the bolt and stepped outside. I thought he were after a breath of fresh air. So you see, what was odd was the door was unlocked. But a few minutes later, when I went to get them glasses, I noticed someone had bolted it again. Then I got to thinkin', if Mr Locke were after a bit of air, why didn't he go out to the terrace?'

'I see,' Witherspoon murmured. Actually, he didn't see a thing. 'I suppose one of the other servants could have bolted the door.'

She shook her head. 'Not likely. I was the only one going back and forth down that hall – the only place it goes is to the china pantry. The other servants was usin' the back stairs.'

The inspector wasn't sure what to make of the girl's story. If she was telling the truth, and he couldn't really think of a reason for her to lie, then it appeared as though they'd better have another talk with Mrs Stanwick. And with Mr Locke.

Lena cocked her head to one side. 'I reckon that's about it.' Witherspoon suddenly thought of something. 'You appear to be a most observant young woman,' he said. 'Do you remember seeing Mr Warburton during the evening?'

A sly look crossed her face. 'I saw him earlier in the evenin',' she said slowly. 'But after that, I'd say

167

you'd best speak to Dulcie if you want to know what he was up to.'

'Dulcie who?'

'Dulcie Willard. She's the upstairs maid.' Lena shrugged. 'She's out today. She won't be back until this evenin'. But if I wanted to know about Mr War-burton, I'd talk to her.'

'Did you get her nibs settled, then?' Mrs Goodge asked.

Mrs Jeffries nodded. 'Yes, finally. Gracious, I feel rather awful. I sent the woman off to get her out of our way, but I didn't expect she'd have such a wretchedly miserable experience.'

'Don't fret yourself over it,' the cook muttered. 'Probably do her good. Give her a bit of excitement in her life.'

'True, but I wasn't trying to get her killed.'

'She's exaggerating. Don't worry. Give her a few hours' sleep and she'll be right as rain. Did she take the bait?'

'That's why she's taking a nap,' Mrs Jeffries answered. 'She wants to be fresh for the Jubilee Picnic.'

'Cor, she isn't very bright, now, is she?' Mrs Goodge shook her head in disbelief. 'You'd think after what happened she'd be suspicious of any more invitations.'

'People believe what they want to believe, Mrs Goodge,' Mrs Jeffries replied thoughtfully. 'And Mrs Livingston-Graves desperately needs to believe that she's important enough to procure invitations merely on the strength of her connections.'

'What connections? Just because her late husband was related to some minor viscount! Nonsense.' Mrs Goodge put the teapot on the table. 'If you ask me, the woman's a half-wit.' She poured them both a cup of tea. 'Anyways, enough about her nibs. I've got a bit of news. A couple of my sources come through for me this morning while you and the inspector was havin' breakfast.'

'Excellent, Mrs Goodge. What have you found out?'

'To begin with, Miss Marlow's had a few problems in her life. Seems she's been sent off a time or two to one of them fancy places out in the country. She suffers from a nervous condition.'

'Are you talking about an asylum?'

'Nothing that horrible,' Mrs Goodge replied. 'More like a nursing home, I reckon. Mind you, there's good medical treatment there; it's one of them establishments the rich sends their relations when they're not quite right. I don't mean she were actin' crazy or anythin' like that. But she used to get real melancholy sometimes. She'd quit speakin' and wouldn't eat much. It used to be so bad her parents would pack her off to this place out in the country, make sure she got plenty of fresh air and rest. But she hasn't had one of her spells in a long time.'

'How awful for the poor woman,' Mrs Jeffries replied sympathetically.

'As for this Mrs Stanwick, she isn't quite the lady she makes out,' Mrs Goodge said with relish. 'It looks like Mr Warburton's nasty little comments might have more than a grain of truth to them. It seems Mrs Stanwick didn't leave her country house just to get away from her husband's memory. Seems there was a scandal hangin' over her head. Accordin' to what I heard, she were involved with some young man. Flirtin' with him and God knows what else. And this weren't the first time she'd done it, neither.'

'What's so scandalous about that?' Mrs Jeffries queried. 'Mrs Stanwick wouldn't be the first widow to have a few flirtations.'

'It were more than a few, but that's not what got tongues waggin'. With this last young man, Mrs Stanwick weren't in the least serious about him, but he was dead set to have her. He proposed and she refused. The next day he were dead. It were supposedly an accident. But there was some that whispered it was suicide.'

'Hmmm, I can see why people talked and why Mrs Stanwick felt it necessary to leave her home. Being the cause of a suspected suicide would harm any woman's reputation.'

'And that's not all. You'll never guess who the man was. . . .' Mrs Goodge paused dramatically.

Mrs Jeffries knew better than to rush her; she enjoyed her small triumphs far too much to be hurried along. Of course, she'd already guessed who the unfortunate young man was, but she wouldn't let on for the world. It would spoil the cook's whole day. 'Who?'

'Douglas Beecher. Hannah Greenwood's son.'

'Have you finished with your questions, Inspector?' Lucinda Marlow inquired politely. Sitting on the settee in the drawing room, she made a lovely picture of feminine beauty. On her lap was an embroidery hoop, and at her feet a fluffy white cat slept curled on the rug.

'Yes, Miss Marlow. We've finished for the present.'

'For the present?' She arched one eyebrow delicately. 'Do I take that to mean you'll be returning?'

Witherspoon didn't know. But he wasn't going to give up until he had this case solved. 'We may. Naturally, we'll try not to disrupt your household routine any more than necessary.'

'My household has already been interrupted,' she said with a faint smile. 'A murder taking place at one's ball virtually assures one's routine is disrupted.'

'I'm very sorry, Miss Marlow.' He wasn't sure why he was apologizing, but nevertheless, it seemed the thing to do. 'Now, I do have one question I'd like to ask you.'

She sighed delicately and picked up the embroidery hoop. 'Of course I'll answer any question you like, but I don't see what good it will do.'

'Your footman says you went to the cold buffet table a few minutes prior to the murder, is that correct?'

'I don't quite recall the time,' she replied. 'But I did check the table several times that evening. Why? Is it important?'

'Do you recall seeing the carving knife?'

She glanced up from her embroidery, her expression thoughtful. 'Now that you mention it, I don't recall seeing the knife. I think it must have been gone.'

Witherspoon stifled a spurt of irritation. Really, she should have mentioned this the first time she was questioned. Then he realized the poor lady was probably so distressed by having murder committed in her own home, it was a wonder she could recall anything. Women were such delicate creatures. 'Do you have any idea what time it was that you checked the buffet the last time?'

'I can't say for certain,' she said. She stuck her needle into the cloth and gave him her full attention. 'The nearest I could estimate is that it was quite close to ten-thirty. Perhaps ten twenty-five or so. Oh, yes, that's right. It must have been close to half past because I was getting concerned about Mrs Stanwick. I was afraid she'd miss the presentation.'

Witherspoon's pulse leapt. 'Why were you afraid she'd miss the presentation?'

'Well, you see, I'd forgotten until you mentioned me going to the table.' She laughed self-consciously. 'But that's why I went to the buffet. I'd seen Mrs Stanwick there only moments before and I was trying to catch up with her. Of course, once I was there, I did check the food supply. Then, when I turned around to try and find her again, she'd disappeared.'

'Cor,' Barnes muttered, 'if this case isn't right muddled, then I'm not a grey-haired copper with sore feet.'

'Are your feet still bothering you?' Witherspoon asked.

'I was speakin' figuratively, sir. Actually, I'm wearin' me old boots today. Mrs Barnes has got the new ones stuffed with coal.' Barnes led the way up the stairs to Dr Sloan's rooms.

'Coal?'

'Yes, sir. If your shoes are too tight, you slip some goodly sized lumps in an old sock, stuff the sock in the boot or shoe, and give the leather a good stretch.' He raised his hand and knocked on the door. 'Works every time.'

They waited for a few moments, but the door didn't open. 'That's odd.' Witherspoon muttered. 'His landlady said Dr Sloan hadn't gone out today. Try again, Constable.'

Barnes pounded harder.

From behind the door they heard a faint moan.

They looked at each other, and before Witherspoon could even get the words out, Barnes was racing down the stairs shouting for the landlady to come and bring her keys.

'Dr Sloan!' the inspector shouted through the keyhole. 'Are you all right?'

No answer.

'Do hang on, sir,' Witherspoon tried again. 'We're getting your landlady.'

A moment later a breathless Barnes and a red-faced Mrs Tepler, a ring of keys in her hand, pounded up the stairs.

'I do hope the gentleman's not gone off his head,' she said, putting the key in the lock and giving it a turn. 'They do that sometimes, you know.' Barnes pulled her back and pushed the door open. He and the inspector hurried inside.

Dr Oxton Sloan lay on the settee. His hair stood

on end, his shirt was pulled out of his trousers, and an empty whisky bottle lay on the carpet. He blinked several times, his red-rimmed eyes focusing on the trio standing by the doorway.

'Gracious me,' Mrs Tepler said irritably. 'He's as drunk as a lord.'

'Ah, I've been expecting you,' Sloan said, his voice slurred. He struggled to a sitting position. 'Forces of law and order and all that. Wondered when you'd get back round to me. Wasn't my fault, though. Never touched the old bitch. Someone else got her first.'

'Well, I never!' the landlady sputtered. 'What's got into the man? He never used to drink.'

'Thank you for your assistance, Mrs Tepler,' the inspector said. 'Perhaps you'd be so good as to bring us up a pot of coffee.' He ushered her out of the room.

'Blimey, looks like he's as tight as a newt.' Barnes shook his head. 'Do you want me to try and sober him up, sir?'

Sloan laughed. 'Sober me up? I'm not that drunk. I can hear you perfectly well. Who was it, then? That silly little housemaid? Or was it her nibs herself. Stupid really, should never have trusted her. God, I thought my luck had changed. Once she was gone, I thought I was safe.'

The inspector was totally confused, but he certainly didn't want it to show. 'I take it you're referring to . . .' He hesitated, wondering who Dr Sloan was babbling about, and afraid if he guessed wrong, it would shut the man up completely. Not that he was making much sense in the first place.

'I'm referring to that silly cow, Cecilia Mansfield.'
Sloan hung his head. 'She saw me, didn't she?'

'Yes,' the inspector said slowly. 'I'm afraid she did.'

Sloan covered his face with his hands. 'I heard her
coming up the stairs behind me. I knew I was taking
a risk, but God, I had no choice.'

Witherspoon wondered if he ought to caution Dr
Sloan.

'She was going to ruin me, you know,' Sloan continued. 'Absolutely ruin me. Then she was dead and
I thought I was safe, but I'm not. There is no safety
when you've done what I've done.'

'Dr Sloan, I must warn you that anything you say
can be used against you in a court of law,' the inspector said quickly. 'Do you understand that?'

Sloan raised red eyes and stared at the two policeman. 'Caution me? What for?'

Confused, Witherspoon said, 'Well, you are confessing to murder, aren't you?'

'Murder?' Sloan laughed 'Ye Gods, Inspector. I'm
not a murderer, I'm a plagiarist.'

''Ow much farther do you reckon?' Wiggins asked
Hatchet. He took a deep breath, enjoying the crisp
sea air of Clacton. Gulls screeched overhead, the sun
shone brightly between huge, puffy white clouds,
and the wind blew in off the water just enough to
keep them from being too hot. They walked down
a row of neat houses, each of them with their own
front gardens filled with bright red, yellow, and pink
summer roses.

'Haggar's Lane should be just at the end of the

175

road,' Hatchet replied. He walked faster. 'Once we get there, Wiggins, I do believe it might be best if you allowed me to conduct the conversation. Is that agreeable to you?'

'You want me to keep me mouth shut, then?'

'Of course not, my good fellow. Your insights and questions are, I'm sure, most invaluable. It's just that I have noticed people do tend to speak rather more freely to me. Perhaps it's because I'm older.'

They stopped at the first house, a small terraced building of brown brick, and asked where Hazel Purty lived. They were directed to the second-to-last house at the end of the road.

Hatchet boldly knocked at the door. It was opened by a pale, middle-aged woman. 'Excuse me, Madam,' he began, 'but I'm wondering if you could be of assistance to me. We're looking for a young man named Jon. I believe he is your cousin.'

'What do you want Jon for?' she asked, wiping her hands on the front of her apron. 'Has he done somethin? Well, if he has, that's hard luck for you, 'cause he isn't here.'

Hatchet smiled. 'Of course he hasn't done anything. I'm trying to locate him so that I can offer him employment.'

'Doin' what? Jon's not trained. He can't read nor write, neither.'

'Nevertheless, we do wish to offer him a position.'

'Are you daft?'

'Madam,' Hatchet said earnestly, 'I assure you, we're quite serious. Young Jon has been highly recommended to us, and I'd like to offer him a position.'

She stared at him. 'Like I said, he ain't here.'

Wiggins glanced down the row of houses. He saw a movement in the bushes in the front garden of the last house. He turned and stared, his eyes narrowing as he saw the top of the shrubs moving in a steady rhythmical motion that couldn't be the wind.

'We'd be most grateful if you could tell us where the young man has gone,' Hatchet continued. 'The offer of a position is most genuine, I assure you.'

The gate at the end of the garden creaked. From where Wiggins stood, his view was blocked by the bushes, but by standing on tiptoes and craning his neck, he did catch a glimpse of porkpie hat and tuft of red hair. 'There 'e is!' Wiggins cried.

Jon must have heard him, because a second later they heard the sound of footsteps pounding off down the road. Wiggins took off after him.

'Here now!' the woman shouted. 'You leave the lad alone or I'll have the police on you.'

Hatchet doffed his top hat as he joined the pursuit. 'Thank you for your assistance, madam,' he called as he charged after Wiggins. 'I think we can find the young man on our own.'

They raced after the boy. Jon's hat flew off, but he paid no attention, just continued hurtling toward the end of the road.

'Just a minute, now!' Wiggins shouted at the rapidly retreating figure. 'We ain't gonna hurt you. We just want to talk.'

Jon ignored them and kept running.

★　★　★

'Thank you, Mrs Tepler. I'm sure Dr Sloan will be fine in just a little while. The coffee smells delicious. It was so very good of you to bring it up,' Witherspoon said.

'Well, all I can say is this better not become a habit.' She sniffed and glared at her hapless tenant. 'Otherwise Dr Sloan can find himself another set of rooms. This is a decent house.'

As soon as she'd left, Witherspoon poured a cup of black coffee and handed it to Sloan. The doctor's fingers trembled as he took the cup.

'I suppose I should have told you everything before,' he muttered.

'Why don't you tell us now?' the inspector suggested. He wasn't terribly interested in recriminations, he just wanted to get some facts about this case.

'Oh, where to begin.' Sloan laughed harshly. 'You see, it's important that you understand.'

'We can't understand anything if you don't explain yourself,' Witherspoon said kindly. 'But we're not here to accuse anyone of anything. We're here to learn the truth.'

'Truth? What is truth?'

Witherspoon sighed silently. He did so hope Dr Sloan wasn't going to embark on a rambling philosophical discourse. That sort of thing gave him such a frightful headache. Really, even if he was supposedly brilliant at solving murders, it was moments like this when he longed for his old position back in the records room at the Yard.

A wave of nostalgia washed over him as he thought

of his neat rows of ledgers and file after file of tidy police reports. But he mustn't waste any more time wool-gathering, he thought, staring at Sloan's haggard face. No matter how distasteful, he really must get this over with. Truth was truth and it was his duty to find it.

'Dr Sloan,' he said patiently, 'the only truth we're interested in is what you saw or heard on the night of the murder. Please, this is no time to digress.'

Sloan nodded. 'Yes, you're right. And I'm not digressing, I'm delaying. Admitting one's weaknesses isn't very pleasant.' He closed his eyes briefly. 'It all began the day of the ball. I was up here in my rooms, working, when Mrs Greenwood arrived. She was in a state. Very excitable, almost giddy. I asked her what she wanted and she . . . she told me that if I didn't do as she asked, she'd make sure that everyone at the circle knew I was a plagiarist.'

'Does that mean you copied some other person's work and claimed it as your own?' Barnes asked curiously.

'Precisely.' Sloan laughed again, a terrible barking sound that didn't have a smidgen of humour in it. 'That's exactly what I'd done, and Hannah Greenwood had found out about it. She had a copy of an American publication with her. A small, rather obscure one, at that. God knows where she got hold of it. Unfortunately, it contained a poem I'd read as my own work less than a month ago at one of our meetings. I was amazed. I'd gotten the poem by corresponding with the author. He's a young fellow, very talented. Lives in Colorado. Naturally, I had no idea he'd submitted the poem for publication. If I had, I'd never have claimed his poem as my own.'

'What did Mrs Greenwood want you to do?' the inspector asked. He wanted to get on with it. Gracious, being a plagiarist wasn't very nice, but it was hardly in the same league as murder. He didn't really see why Dr Sloan was making such a terrible fuss.

'She threatened to expose me,' Sloan murmured. 'I couldn't let that happen. I just couldn't. I'd have nothing then. Absolutely nothing. I've little money and no position. They haven't let me practise medicine for years. All I have in my life is the circle. Being a published poet. And I didn't steal all of my poems. The first ones that were published were mine. All mine.'

'Yes, I'm sure you're a wonderful poet,' Witherspoon began.

'Don't you see? I know it was wrong. I know I shouldn't have done it, but I had no choice. No choice at all . . . but she wouldn't listen.'

'Dr Sloan, you're getting off the point . . .' the inspector interrupted.

'But you don't understand. She was going to tell them. She was going to announce it that night at the ball.'

'Dr Sloan!' Barnes yelled. 'You haven't answered our question.'

'Question?' He blinked groggily. 'But I'm answering it now. For God's sake, I'm baring my soul to you.'

'What did Mrs Greenwood want you to do?' Witherspoon persisted. 'You haven't told us that yet.'

180

'What did she want me to do? But I just told you.'

'No, you haven't. You've told us what she planned to do to you if you didn't cooperate with her.' The inspector took a deep breath and strove for patience. Really, back in the records room he never had to talk to maudlin men who'd had too much to drink.

'Oh, I'm sorry, I thought I had.' He took another sip from his cup.

'Well?' Barnes prodded.

Sloan put his cup down on the table. 'Hannah Greenwood wanted me to help her ruin Rowena Stanwick.'

CHAPTER NINE

Wiggins raced after the boy. Holding on to his top hat, Hatchet threw dignity to the winds and doubled his efforts to keep up the pace.

As they turned the corner onto a busy road, Wiggins saw Jon dodge behind a fruit vendor's cart and disappear between two buildings. 'There 'e is!'

They ran, oblivious to the stares of startled pedestrians as they rushed by. Wiggins reached the spot where the boy had disappeared and plunged after him with Hatchet hot on his heels. They ran down a narrow passageway lined with dustbins and mounds of refuse. Their feet pounded against the dry dirt, raising clouds of dust.

At the end of the passage Jon turned sharply to the right. Wiggins, breathing hard, blinked as he shot out into the bright sunlight and found himself in a paved courtyard surrounded by buildings. 'Blast,' he muttered, unable to see any spot where the boy could have escaped.

'There he goes!' Hatchet yelled. He pointed to a narrow wooden gate that was just now slamming shut and dashed toward it, Wiggins right behind him.

They emerged from the courtyard into the centre of the business district. Luckily, as it was Sunday, the streets were relatively empty. A few pedestrians wandered about, city folk up from London to take advantage of the sea air. A carriage rolled leisurely up the street and a group of men taking the sun in front of the hotel stared at them curiously as they burst out into view. But Jon paid them no heed. He simply ran as if the devil himself were on his heels.

Twice, Wiggins was almost in grabbing distance, but both times Jon managed to elude his grasp. The third time he was close to the fleeing boy, he shouted, 'I only want to talk to you!' He lunged for Jon's coat.

'Leave me be, you ruddy bastards!' Jon yelled. He jumped over a low wall. Wiggins hurdled the wall. His foot snagged on the top and he landed flat on his belly, gasping as the air was knocked out of him.

Hatchet ignored him and hurried after the retreating figure. 'Get up!' he shouted to the footman. 'He's headed for the train station.'

Wiggins grimaced, pulled himself to his feet and loped off after the butler.

They rushed up one street and down another, past shuttered shops and pubs and hotels. But no matter how fast they ran, the boy stayed well ahead of them.

As he rounded a corner, Wiggins saw Jon slip through the iron gate surrounding the station. Hatchet, red-faced and holding his side, pointed to the spot where he'd gone inside. 'Hurry, there's a train leaving. If that boy gets on it, we'll never get our hands on him.'

Wiggins charged toward the station, but he wasn't fast enough. Just as he reached the platform, he saw the boy nimbly leap onto the still-open baggage car.

'Well, hell's bells,' Wiggins said in disgust. His legs were on fire, he could barely breathe, there was a god-awful stitch in his side, and the ruddy train was on its way to bleedin' London.

And Jon was on it. Bloomin' Ada, as Smythe would say. They'd let the lad slip right through their fingers.

Shoulders slumped in defeat, he went back to where Hatchet stood by the gate. 'I didn't make it,' he admitted morosely. 'The little nipper got to the baggage car just as the train pulled out. He's gone. What'll we do now?'

Hatchet wiped his face with a pristine white handkerchief as he considered the matter. 'I think', he said slowly, 'we'd better get back to London on the next train.'

'What good will that do us?' Wiggins protested. 'We've already lost 'im. Who knows where 'e'll go next.'

'Well, he certainly won't be coming back here,' Hatchet said. He took off his top hat and smoothed a lock of white hair off his forehead. 'I had the distinct impression he was not a welcome addition to his cousin's household.'

Mrs Jeffries set the inspector's dinner in front of him. 'I'm afraid it's just cold beef and salad,' she said.

'This will be fine,' he replied. 'I say, I think I'm finally beginning to make progress on this case.'

'But of course you are, sir,' Mrs Jeffries poured herself a cup of tea and took the seat next to him. 'You always do.' It never hurt to bolster the inspector's confidence.

She wondered how she was going to slip him the information regarding Hannah Greenwood's son. She'd already decided to say nothing of the boy, Jon, accompanying Mrs Greenwood to the ball – they had acquired that information third-hand, so to speak, and before she involved a child in a murder investigation, she wanted to make doubly sure her facts were correct. But she really must tell the inspector about Douglas Beecher. At this point it was all she had. Wiggins and Hatchet still weren't back, Betsy was snooping around the Hiatt and Putnam households, and God knows where Smythe had got to.

'Thank you, Mrs Jeffries, I do my very best.' He sighed. 'I daresay, though, sometimes what one learns in the course of a murder investigation is enough to make one, well, a tad cynical.'

'Whatever do you mean, sir?'

'I mean, Mrs Jeffries, that appearances can be deceiving. People are rarely what they seem,' he said sombrely. 'Take this Hyde Park Literary Circle, for instance. One would naturally assume that all of the members came together for a common love of literature. You know, to discuss the great works of writers like Shakespeare or Mr Dickens or even that American fellow, Mr Edgar Allan Poe. But I don't believe that's at all true about this particular group. It seems to me that half of them joined just so they'd have somewhere to go and gossip, and the other half joined so they could avail themselves of romantic liaisons or to avenge themselves on one of the members.'

Mrs Jeffries regarded him curiously. 'Gracious, sir. That is a rather dark view.'

'Take our victim, Hannah Greenwood.' He waved his fork for emphasis. 'She wasn't in the least interested in books or poems.'

'I take it she was one of those more interested in the social aspects of the circle rather than the intellectual ones.'

'Worse than that!' Witherspoon exclaimed. 'She joined for the sole purpose of ruining Rowena Stanwick. According to what Dr Sloan told us today, Mrs Greenwood holds Mrs Stanwick responsible for her son's death. Seems the Stanwick woman was leading him on, and, when she refused him, he walked in front of a train. The chap's name was Douglas Beecher. He was Mrs Greenwood's son from her first marriage and her only child.'

'How dreadful.'

'And on top of that,' the inspector continued, 'Mrs Greenwood threatened to expose Dr Sloan as a plagiarist if he didn't help her ruin Mrs Stanwick socially.'

'I say, sir, you have been very busy today.' She gave him her most encouraging smile. 'You've learned an enormous amount of information. Why, now you've two members of the circle who had a motive to murder Mrs Greenwood. Now, sir, do tell me what else you found out.'

For the next half hour Mrs Jeffries listened closely. She was delighted she wouldn't have to bring up the subject of Douglas Beecher herself.

'So you see, at least now we've one suspect with a reasonable motive,' the inspector finished.

'Rowena Stanwick?' Mrs Jeffries guessed. She wondered why the inspector had discarded Dr Sloan.

'Correct.' Witherspoon sighed. 'We know from the maid's evidence that Mrs Stanwick knew that Hannah Greenwood was going to ruin her. And we know from Miss Marlow and the maid that Mrs Stanwick came close enough to the table to get the knife.'

'But didn't the maid say that she saw Mrs Greenwood follow Mrs Stanwick up the stairs?' Mrs Jeffries queried. Something about the sequence of events bothered her. 'If that's true, how could she have gotten the knife?'

Witherspoon frowned. 'I suppose she could have snatched it off the table when she bumped into it. The knife was sitting right on the end.' His expression brightened. 'Yes, I'm sure that's what happened. She pretended to stumble into the table so that she could get her hands on the murder weapon. That's probably when Miss Marlow saw her. Then she hurried up the stairs and waited for her victim.'

'Did she know that Mrs Greenwood was following her?'

'I'm sure she did,' Witherspoon replied. 'She'd just had a very ugly row with Mrs Greenwood – I expect she knew quite well that the woman would come after her. Mind you, I'm not sure she planned the murder, but I do think that she took advantage of the opportunity when it arose. Bumping into that table and seeing that knife lying so close to her hand was simply too much of a temptation to resist.'

'But according to the maid, Mrs Stanwick was crying by this point. Wouldn't that indicate she was more upset than enraged?' Mrs Jeffries had no idea where her train of thought was going, but she was determined to follow it through. Logic, rational thinking, and deduction were all very well, but sometimes, she'd learned, it paid to trust one's instincts.

Witherspoon drummed his fingers against the lace tablecloth. 'Mrs Jeffries,' he said, 'you may find this difficult to believe. I mean, you're such an honest person yourself I do think you find it hard to credit dishonourable behaviour in others. However, it has come to my notice there are some people who are very good at conveying one emotion while feeling another.'

Mrs Jeffries stared at him incredulously. Where the inspector had come by this amazing insight, she couldn't deign to guess. What startled her the most was that he'd had it at all. He was such a delightfully naive fellow. 'So you think that Mrs Stanwick was, shall we say, faking her response to Mrs Greenwood and hoping the woman would follow her upstairs so she could murder her?'

'I'm afraid I do,' Witherspoon replied. 'Several other people have told us that Mrs Stanwick's character is less than' – he paused and blushed – 'admirable.'

'Are you referring to Mr Warburton's statements?' she asked, mainly because it annoyed her that a female who had gentlemen admirers was always credited with the worst of character, while a man was considered masculine because of his conquests.

'Not just Warburton's,' Witherspoon protested. 'Several others have made comments regarding Mrs Stanwick's reputation. But that's not why I think she may be the murderer. We know she went upstairs and we know that Mrs Greenwood followed her. We also know she had access to the murder weapon. Besides, she's the only one with a genuine motive.'

'What about Dr Sloan?' she argued. 'It seems to me he might have just as compelling a motive. You told me yourself, sir, that Sloan was convinced that if the others learned of his plagiarism, he'd be ruined.'

'True.' The inspector smiled. 'But the man was quite drunk when he made those statements. I'm sure he was being overly dramatic.'

'But if he really believed she could ruin him, sir, perhaps he was driven to do something desperate. And what about Lady Cannonberry's evidence? She saw Dr Sloan hiding Mr Venerable's satchel under his coat. The footman stated that he saw Dr Sloan going upstairs, and he also said that he'd been near the table as well. He could just as easily picked up the carving knife as Mrs Stanwick.'

Witherspoon, his mouth full of salad, nodded. 'Sloan explained all that,' he finally said as soon as he'd swallowed his food. 'He admits to taking the satchel upstairs. That's why Mrs Putnam couldn't find him. He'd taken it to try and get his poem back before the contest. You see, he'd realized that Mrs Greenwood had only heard him recite the poem he'd stolen from the American chap at one of their earlier meetings. She didn't actually have any proof in hand, so to speak, except for the American magazine.'

'I'm afraid I don't understand.'

'She didn't have a copy of the poem he'd read aloud,' Witherspoon explained. 'But Dr Sloan had plagiarized another poem from this American fellow and it was in the publication Mrs Greenwood had. Sloan had changed a few words of the poem and submitted it as his Jubilee contest poem. He wanted to get the poem out of Venerable's briefcase before the winner was announced. You see, he had no intention of helping Mrs Greenwood. He'd already decided he wouldn't say a word about Mrs Stanwick's past.'

'Are you saying that Dr Sloan thought that if he got the poem back before anyone saw it, Mrs Greenwood couldn't harm him?'

'Of course.' Witherspoon smiled. 'Mrs Greenwood confronted Sloan based on her remembering a poem she'd heard him recite. The only written evidence of Sloan's plagiarism was his contest poem. Once he retrieved that and destroyed it, he could easily say that Mrs Greenwood was mistaken and that the poem she heard wasn't at all like the one in the magazine. So he pinched Venerable's satchel and nipped up to an empty bedroom on the second floor so that he could search it in private.'

'Did Dr Sloan find his poem?' she asked.

'Oh, yes. Of course by then he'd heard the screams and Mrs Greenwood was dead.'

'I see,' she said slowly. 'Do you believe Dr Sloan is telling you the truth?' To her way of thinking, confessing to a bit of plagiarism would be far less dangerous than being arrested for murder.

Witherspoon hesitated before answering. 'I think so. But naturally, I'm going to try and verify his story. He claims he left the satchel in the bedroom. He kicked it under the bed when he heard all the commotion outside.'

'So if the satchel's still there or one of the servants found it'll assume his story is true?'

'Yes.'

'Are you going to arrest Rowena Stanwick?'

'Perhaps,' the inspector hedged. 'But I'm not sure we've really enough evidence at this point.'

'Of course not, sir,' she said quickly. 'Forget I even asked that silly question. I know your methods; you would never arrest anyone on the minuscule amount of evidence you have now.'

'I don't believe it's all that minuscule,' he said quickly. 'Naturally, we'll keep digging to obtain more.'

'But what about Mr Warburton?' Mrs Jeffries continued relentlessly. 'We don't know where he was when the murder took place. He may have had a motive as well.' As soon as she said the words, she knew she was stumbling in the dark. So far they had absolutely no indication that Edgar Warburton had any reason to murder Mrs Greenwood. He barely knew the woman. Or did he? 'Have you established in fact that the two weren't better acquainted than appearances would indicate?' she asked. 'Perhaps Mr Warburton had something to do with Mrs Greenwood's son?'

She knew she was grasping at straws, but she desperately wanted the inspector to keep looking. He was a very good policeman, but unless some other suspect or evidence turned up, he'd eventually have to act on what he had now. Rowena Stanwick would be arrested for the murder of Hannah Greenwood. Perhaps she'd actually been the killer, but there was something tickling the back of Mrs Jeffries's mind, something that made her want to keep at it.

'I suppose we could follow up that course of inquiry,' he murmured softly. 'It certainly couldn't hurt. And, of course, one doesn't want to risk arresting the wrong person.

'I'm sure you'd never do that, sir.'

'I say,' the inspector mumbled as he reached for his water glass and took a sip, 'the house is awfully quiet. Isn't it a bit late for everyone to be out? I do worry about Betsy when it starts to get dark. She is a rather innocent young woman, and the streets aren't all that safe, you know, despite our best efforts.'

'Don't worry, sir. Betsy is doing some household errands, but she knows to take a hansom home once the sun goes down. And Wiggins is off with Luty Belle's butler, Hatchet. I do believe he's a tad lonely since Luty's been in America.'

'Good, good. I know I worry too much. But you must admit, Mrs Jeffries, policemen do see too much of the dark side of life.' He sighed dramatically.

They heard the front door open and then a moment later a highpitched giggle.

'I daresay that sounds like Betsy now,' Witherspoon said.

Mrs Jeffries didn't think so. For one thing, Betsy didn't use the front door, and for another, she certainly wouldn't come in laughing her head off. From the hallway they heard a feminine voice burst into the first stanza of 'God Save the Queen'.

'Gracious. That doesn't sound like Betsy, sir,' she declared, getting to her feet and heading for the door.

Before the housekeeper reached her goal, Mrs Livingston-Graves, a silly grin on her face and her bonnet askew, lurched into the room. She propped herself against the doorway. 'Good evening, Mrs Jeffries, Gerald.' Her voice was slurred. 'I've had the loveliest time.'

Mrs Jeffries stopped dead. From behind her she heard the inspector gasp. 'Mrs Livingston-Graves,' she said cautiously, 'are you all right?'

'Edwina?' the inspector said, rising from his chair.

Edwina burped. 'Oops!' She giggled and shoved away from the door. 'Guess that one slipped out.' Weaving slightly, she walked toward the dining table.

Mrs Jeffries looked at Witherspoon. His jaw gaped open as he stared at his dishevelled cousin.

'Edwina,' he said, 'perhaps you'd better sit down.'

She stumbled on the hem of her dress, and Mrs Jeffries, who was right behind her, grabbed her arm to steady her.

'Thank you,' Mrs Livingston-Graves said, giving

the housekeeper a big smile. 'I tripped.' She burped again. 'Oops, there goes another one. Mustn't do this on Tuesday,' she rambled. 'Mr Freeley's coming, you know.'

As Mrs Jeffries helped her into the chair, she caught the scent of liquor. The moment the woman's backside made contact with the chair, she sighed, placed her arms on the table, flopped forward, put her head down, and closed her eyes.

'Egads, Mrs Jeffries.' Witherspoon stared at his cousin with alarm. 'Do you think we ought to call the doctor? She seems quite ill.'

'She's not in the least ill,' Mrs Jeffries replied dryly. 'She's passed out. Drunk.'

'Are you sure it was Warburton?' Smythe asked. He gave the fat, greasy publican his most intimidating stare. He wanted to let him know he wasn't to be trifled with. It wasn't often he used his size to intimidate people, but he wasn't sure he trusted this bloke. Feller's eyes were shifty.

The barman pocketed the half crown Smythe had placed by his beer mug. 'It were Warburton all right,' he said. 'And that weren't the first time it'd 'appened, either. The man's got a bit of a reputation with some of the girls round 'ere now. Some of 'em won't go with 'im at all.'

Smythe hissed softly. This miserable, squalid pub was in one of the worst areas of the East End. Hard. Dangerous. And the girls who plied their trade round here were just as hard and frequently just as dangerous. If they'd put the word out about

Edgar Warburton, a rich mark if there ever was one, then the bastard had to be worse than he'd thought. 'What was the girl's name?'

'Don't know her proper name.' The barman shrugged and slapped a dirty teatowel at a fly that had landed on the counter. 'But she used to be known round these parts as Dolly Jane.'

'Used to be known?' Smythe didn't much like the sound of that.

'She's dead. Died right after it 'appened.'

'What'd she die of, Warburton's beatin'?'

'Nah, she were used to the beatin's,' he replied casually. 'Besides, he paid her well for her trouble. She died of the consumption.' He leaned forward, his small blue eyes glittering with greed. 'Look, if you're lookin' for somethin' like Dolly Jane, I can fix you right up. 'Alf the girls that come in 'ere'll—'

'No, thanks.' Smythe couldn't keep the contempt out of his voice. 'I ain't interested. I just want to be sure you're tellin' me the truth about Edgar Warburton.'

'Course I am, mate,' he replied. 'It's just like I said. He comes in here once a week or so. The girls start comin' in round six in the evenin'. Warburton flashes a bit of coin, they go off together, and the next time I see the girl, she's usually got a few bruises showin'.' He gave a short, ugly bark of a laugh. 'And Warburton's a real odd duck. Dolly Jane told me somethin' funny about 'im, right afore she took sick.'

'And what was that?' He wasn't sure he really wanted to know.

'She said the last time she were with 'im, he kept callin' her by another woman's name.'

'What name would that be?'

Wrinkles creased his fat, greasy face, as though he were concentrating and it really hurt. 'Don't know that I can remember,' he finally mumbled. 'It's been awhile, you know. A body can't recall every little thing.'

Smythe couldn't decide if he was angling for more money or if he was genuinely stupid. To be on the safe side, he reached into his pocket and pulled out another half crown. 'This help you remember?' he asked, slapping it on the counter next to the beer.

'Reckon it does, mate,' he said, snatching the coin. 'He kept callin' her Rowena. Nice name, ain't it?' He chuckled. 'One thing I'll say about Warburton, he's a right 'ard man to please. Only went with the pretty ones. Liked 'em young, too. Dolly Jane couldn'a been more than fifteen.'

By the time Mrs Jeffries got Mrs Livingston-Graves upstairs to bed, the inspector had retired and the servants were gathered in the kitchen.

'Was she really drunk, then?' Mrs Goodge asked.

'As a lord,' Mrs Jeffries replied. 'I must say, I was quite surprised. Mrs Livingston-Graves is the last person I would ever guess was a secret drinker. However, I do believe her overindulgence may work to our advantage. I don't think she'll be bothering us tomorrow. From the look of her, she'll probably stay in bed all day.'

'Cor,' Smythe said, 'if we'd known that was all it

took to keep the old girl out of our way, we could've been slippin' 'er gin all along.' He grinned to show he was jesting and Mrs Jeffries relaxed.

She'd been concerned about the coachman. He'd arrived back at Upper Edmonton Gardens looking like he was carrying the weight of the world on his shoulders. It was good to see him smile, even if it was at Mrs Livingston-Graves's expense.

As soon as they were all settled, Mrs Jeffries told them everything she'd learned from the inspector. 'So you see,' she concluded, 'unless one of you has come up with anything else, it appears as though Rowena Stanwick is our leading suspect.'

'Sounds to me like she probably did it,' Mrs Goodge said. 'Like the inspector said, she had a bloomin' good motive. For a woman like her to be ruined socially would be the end.'

'But she weren't the only one with a motive,' Smythe protested. 'What about this Locke fellow? Seems to me, if 'e was really in love with Mrs Stanwick, 'e'd want to protect 'er. And no one knows where 'e was during the murder.'

'Wasn't Mr Locke outside?' Hatchet ventured.

'That's what 'e says,' Smythe replied, 'but 'e could've come back in, seen the women 'aving a go at each other, and nipped up the back steps when 'e saw 'em going up the main staircase. Lena, the maid, admitted she were deliberately keepin' out of sight. Maybe Locke slipped in when she weren't lookin'.'

'But how would he have obtained the knife?' Mrs Jeffries asked. 'The footman didn't report seeing him anywhere near the buffet table.'

'But 'e couldn't say Mr Locke 'adn't been there, either,' Smythe argued. 'For all we know, Locke could've gotten the knife before 'e let 'imself out that side door.'

'But what about the maid?' Wiggins said. 'She claimed she saw Locke slip outside, and then a few minutes later the door were bolted, so how could 'e 'ave gotten back inside?'

Smythe shrugged. 'That's my point. Locke could've nipped back in and bolted the door 'imself.'

'Why did he go outside in the first place?' Mrs Goodge asked. 'That's what I want to know.'

'Could be', Smythe mused, 'that 'e saw Lena comin' and goin' from the pantry. Maybe he went out deliberately when he knew the maid would see him leave.'

'You think he was deliberately arranging an alibi?' Mrs Jeffries thought the coachman might be on to something. Shelby Locke did have an interest in Rowena Stanwick's reputation. He was planning on marrying the woman.

'It's possible, ain't it?' He leaned forward, crossing his elbows on the table. 'If Lena overheard Mrs Greenwood and Rowena Stanwick goin' at each other, isn't it possible that Locke 'eard 'em, too?'

'I suppose,' she replied doubtfully. 'But I'm not sure the timing is right. According to the maid, she was quite certain of the time. If she's correct, then Shelby Locke would have already been outside when the argument occurred. However, the inspector is going to be talking to Mr Locke again tomorrow.' She turned to Smythe and said, 'And I think it might be wise for us to try to find out exactly who is telling the truth here. If Mr Locke was outside, someone might have seen him.'

'I'll ask some of the drivers,' Smythe said. 'See if they saw 'im skulkin' about and, more important, exactly what time it was.'

'Were you able to learn anything today?' Mrs Jeffries asked. She was wildly curious as to what he'd been up to.

He hesitated and a slow blush crept up his cheeks. 'Not much,' he mumbled, looking down and studying the tabletop. 'Just a bit about Warburton. But I didn't hear anythin' that 'as any bearin' on what went on the night of the murder.'

'Well, I found out plenty about Edgar Warburton,' Betsy added. 'And it's not very nice, either.'

Smythe shot her a quick, sharp look.

Betsy ignored him and went right on. 'I had a little chat with Dulcie Willard – you remember, the other maid at the Marlow house.'

'And what did she tell you about Warburton?' Smythe demanded.

'Like I said, it's not nice, but I think she were tellin' the truth.' Betsy sighed. 'It seems he does have an alibi for the time of the murder. He were with Dulcie.' Her voice faltered and a rosy blush crept over her cheeks. 'They was in a bedroom up on the third floor . . .'

'I think we all understand what you're saying, Betsy,' Mrs Jeffries said hastily. Hearing about Warburton and the maid's amorous activities didn't particularly embarrass her, but she wasn't so certain about the rest of them. Mrs Goodge was listening with wide-eyed amazement, Wiggins's mouth was hanging open, Hatchet was staring straight ahead at a nonexistent spot on the wall, and Betsy and Smythe were both blushing furiously. 'Was Dulcie sure she was with Warburton at the time the murder actually took place? Not before or after?'

'She were sure,' Betsy replied. She glanced at Smythe. 'Unless Smythe heard differently, she'd have no reason to lie to me.'

'No, lass,' he said softly, 'I heard nothin' about that night.'

'Just a minute, now,' Mrs Goodge said before anyone else could protest. 'I thought we were all agreed that we'd share everything we learned. Seems to me Smythe isn't tellin' us all he knows.'

'I would if I'd learned anythin' worth repeatin',' he snapped. 'But what I 'eard today don't have nuthin' to do with the murder. It were just the same nasty old gossip I told you earlier, and I ain't repeatin' it in front of decent folk.' He clamped his mouth shut and sat back, his expression utterly determined.

'In that case,' Mrs Jeffries said soothingly, 'why don't we hear what the others have to say? Hatchet' – she smiled at the butler – 'you and Wiggins seem bursting with news.'

'Actually, Mrs Jeffries,' Hatchet began, 'we do have news of sorts.' He told them how he and the footman had successfully followed Jon's trail to Clacton. 'I believe', he concluded, 'that Wiggins's earlier information is correct. Jon did see something the night Mrs Greenwood was murdered.'

'Did he tell you that?' Mrs Jeffries asked.

'No. Unfortunately, as soon as we arrived at the Hickman home, he ran off.'

'Wouldn't a thought the little blighter could run so fast,' Wiggins muttered. 'I've still got a bit of stitch in me side from chasin' 'im all over Clacton.'

Mrs Jeffries ignored Wiggins's grumbling and looked at the butler. 'Then what makes you think Jon knows something?'

Hatchet smiled. 'He ran, madam. That means he was scared. The moment we appeared, he took off like a bat out of hell, if you'll pardon the expression. I believe he was genuinely afraid of us. Unfortunately, he managed to leap onto the London train before we could allay his fears.'

'Bloomin' boy slipped right through our fingers,' Wiggins muttered.

'However,' the butler continued, 'though we have momentarily lost the lad and his whereabouts are still unknown, we do have a plan.'

Wiggins snorted. 'Fat lot of good that's gonna do us.'

'Now, Wiggins,' Hatchet chided. 'Don't be such a naysayer.'

'I'm not,' he protested. 'But I don't see what good it's goin' to do 'angin' about the Greenwood 'ouse.'

'I take it that's your plan.' Mrs Jeffries interrupted.

Hatchet nodded. 'Precisely. My theory is that the boy will go back to someplace with which he's familiar.'

'Why not back to his cousins?' Betsy asked. 'Wouldn't he be more likely to go to his kin?'

Hatchet shook his head. 'I don't think so. I think he'd be afraid that would be the first place we'd look. My guess is that he'll go back to the Greenwood house. I suspect he might make contact with Timmy Reston or one of the other children in the neighbourhood.' He paused. 'Actually, Wiggins and I went there before we came here. We spoke to Timmy.'

'Had he seen Jon?' Mrs Jeffries asked.

'No. But Timmy did tell us something else,' Hatchet said gravely, 'something which leads me to believe that Jon could well have seen the murderer that night.'

''E could've been lyin' 'is 'ead off, too,' Wiggins protested.

'I don't think so,' Hatchet replied, shaking his head. He looked at Mrs Jeffries. 'Timmy Reston is Jon's friend. He wouldn't deliberately give us information that might land the lad in big trouble.'

'What kind of trouble?' Mrs Goodge asked.

'Well,' Hatchet said thoughtfully, 'from the start, I've wondered why Jon was so frightened. Then I realized it might be because he'd seen the murderer. But from what we know, the only way Jon could have seen the killer was if he was on the second or third floor of the house. But how could he possibly be there? He'd admitted going to the kitchens and talking a few cooks and scullery maids out of a bite to eat, but the kitchen in the Marlow house is two floors below the place he'd have to have been to see anything useful. So I asked Timmy about it. After a good bit of hemming and hawing and trying to evade the question, Timmy admitted that Jon probably had been on the second or third floor that night. He occasionally did a bit of petty pilfering.'

'You mean the lad's a thief!' Smythe exclaimed.

'I'm afraid so,' Hatchet replied. 'According to Timmy, Mrs Greenwood was so stingy with food, the lad was often hungry. Jon pilfered a bit here and there, sold the goods, and used the money for food.'

'That's disgusting,' Mrs Goodge snorted.

Hatchet held up his hand. 'Don't judge the boy too harshly,' he said. 'Jon didn't just feed himself. He bought food for Timmy and some of the other children. Once, he even bought a bottle of cough medicine when one of younger Restons had the croup.'

'That's no excuse,' the cook protested. 'Thieving is thieving.'

'It bleedin' well isn't!' Betsy cried. 'Not when you're starvin' to death.'

Shocked, they all looked at her.

'Sorry,' she mumbled, 'I shouldn't have yelled. But I don't think it's right to condemn the boy because he lifted a few trinkets to buy a bit of food. If that nasty old Mrs Greenwood had paid 'im a decent wage and fed 'im proper, he wouldn'a done it.'

'How do you know he wouldn't a done it?' Mrs Goodge asked. 'Maybe he just likes stealing.'

'Have you ever been hungry?' Betsy demanded, staring at the cook. 'Have you ever had to walk the streets with your belly touching your backbone and wonderin' if you was ever goin' to have a hot meal and roof over your 'ead again? Have you ever been so hungry and so scared that you didn't give a fig for what anyone else thought was right? You'd do what-ever you had to to stay alive.'

Smythe reached over and laid his hand on Betsy's arm. 'Easy, lass,' he said softly. 'No one's condemnin' the boy. We'll not be 'andin' 'im over to the police when we find 'im.'

Betsy sank back in her seat and stared at her lap. She was deeply embarrassed. Her outburst was so obviously personal that you'd have to be deaf, dumb and blind not to realize she'd been talking about herself. About her own past.

Mrs Goodge patted the maid's shoulder. 'I didn't mean to upset you, Betsy,' she apologized softly. 'Sometimes my tongue runs away with me. I know what you're sayin', though. Before the inspector give me a position, I was scared, too.'

Betsy lifted her chin and gave the cook a shaky smile. 'I'm sorry, too, I shouldn't have said anything – not to you, anyway. You feed half of London in this kitchen.'

Mrs Jeffries cleared her throat. 'Well, now that we've cleared the air, so to speak, perhaps Hatchet can continue.'

'There isn't really much else to tell you,' he said. 'Except to say that Timmy claims Jon was quite familiar with the Marlow house. He'd accompanied Mrs Greenwood there many times.'

'Lifted a few trinkets, too,' Wiggins murmured.

'Tomorrow I'll go back to the Greenwood house and Wiggins will keep an eye on the Hickman house, just in case Jon does show up there. We'll take care to conceal ourselves. When the lad shows up, we'll do whatever we can to earn his trust.' Hatchet looked at Betsy. 'I promise you, we won't scare him or threaten him, and we certainly won't be handing him over to the police.'

CHAPTER TEN

'HAS MRS LIVINGSTON-GRAVES come down?' Witherspoon asked Mrs Jeffries. He pushed his empty breakfast plate to one side.

'Not yet, sir,' she replied, turning her head slightly to hide a smile. When she'd walked past their house-guest's bedroom on her way downstairs, she'd heard the woman snoring loud enough to shake the walls. 'I expect she'll sleep quite late this morning.'

'Yes, well, that doesn't surprise me. But I do hope she's well enough to attend the festivities tomorrow.'

'Festivities?'

Witherspoon dabbed at his lips with a white linen napkin. 'The Jubilee,' he reminded her. 'Tomorrow's the Royal Procession. Surely you haven't forgotten? Why, the West End is ablaze with colour. There are flags in Trafalgar Square, all the clubs along the Pall Mall have put up box seats, and the houses along the procession route are decorated with crimson banners and festoons. Gracious, they're even going to have a gigantic mound of fresh flowers in the middle of Piccadilly Circus. It will be a magnificent spectacle.

I want the entire staff to have the day off. Everyone must get out and enjoy themselves.'

'Why, thank you, sir,' Mrs Jeffries replied honestly. 'How very kind of you. I'm sure it will be delightful.' Actually, in light of the fact that they were investigating a murder, she'd quite forgotten about the Jubilee celebration. 'Will you be continuing your investigation today?'

Witherspoon made a face. 'I'm afraid I must. Duty before pleasure. I thought I'd pop around and have another chat with Shelby Locke.'

'Are you going to tell him you have witnesses that saw him going outside?' she asked.

'If I must. Naturally, I'd prefer the fellow tell me the truth straight out.' He sighed. 'But I've not much hope of that. He seems very much in love with Mrs Stanwick. I suspect he'll try and give her an alibi until the bitter end.'

'From what you've told me, Mr Locke does appear to be quite enamoured of the lady.' Mrs Jeffries reached for her teacup.

'I suppose being in love makes some men forget their principles,' he muttered. 'Understandable, really. But still, we can't have people dashing about and committing murder, can we?' The inspector cleared his throat. 'Er, Mrs Jeffries, I've a favour to ask.'

She looked up sharply. 'Of course, sir. What is it?'

'Well, you see, uh . . . I'm thinking about inviting Lady Cannonberry round for tea next Sunday afternoon.'

'What a splendid idea, sir.' She hoped they'd have this case solved by then.

'It seemed the least I could do,' he mumbled, his cheeks turning pink. 'After all, our evening at Miss Marlow's Jubilee Ball certainly didn't end very well. I was hoping you might write the invitation for me,' he said, giving his housekeeper a pleading look. 'I'm not very good at that sort of thing. And, if you'd be so kind as to plan the menu, I'd be ever so grateful.'

'I'd be delighted, sir.' She smiled broadly. 'Mrs Goodge and I will plan a splendid tea party for you and Lady Cannonberry. Just leave everything to me.'

As soon as the inspector and Constable Barnes had left, Mrs Jeffries hurried down to the kitchen.

Mrs Goodge looked up from the pan of bread she'd just pulled out of the oven. 'Is the inspector gone, then?'

'He and Constable Barnes are going to interview Shelby Locke this morning. Where is everyone else?'

'Wiggins and Hatchet took off right after breakfast to try and lay their hands on that boy.' She carefully eased the loaves onto a cooling rack. 'Betsy went upstairs to air out the linen cupboard, and Smythe's round back getting a bucket of coal.'

From the staircase, they heard the heavy thump of slow footsteps. Then a low moan.

'That'll be her nibs.' Mrs Goodge smiled diabolically. 'Too bad she's missed breakfast. I'll have to do up something special for her, won't I?'

'Mrs Goodge,' Mrs Jeffries whispered sharply. 'What are you up to?'

'Keepin' her nibs out of our hair,' she hissed back

208

just as Mrs Livingston-Graves shuffled slowly into the room.

'I want a pot of tea,' she croaked, glaring at them. Pale face a chalky white, thin hair straggling around her ears, and eyes bloodshot and ringed with purple, the woman looked like death warmed over. 'What are you two staring at?' she snapped. Then she groaned and leaned against the cabinet. 'I'm not well this morning.'

'Morning, Mrs Livingston-Graves,' the cook said cheerfully.

She winced and her hand flew to her temple. 'Morning,' she muttered.

'How are you feeling?' Mrs Jeffries asked softly.

'Would you like some fried bread for breakfast?' Mrs Goodge said loudly. 'I've just baked a fresh loaf, and I've got some really good bacon grease. Fresh, too. Cooked half a pound just this morning. You just sit yourself down and I'll fry you up a few slices in no time.'

'Oh, God.' Mrs Livingston-Graves put her hand to her mouth and fled the kitchen. 'I'll spend the rest of the day in my room,' she choked out as she hurried down the hall.

'Good one, Mrs Goodge,' Smythe said, strolling in from the back hall, a bucket of coal dangling from each hand. He chuckled as he walked over to the stove and put the buckets down. 'With the way 'er stomach's probably rumblin', just the thought of fried bread ought to keep Mrs Livingston-Graves 'anging over a chamber pot for the rest of the day.'

'Really, Mrs Goodge' – Mrs Jeffries tried hard

to be stern, but her eyes twinkled – 'that was most cruel.'

'No, it wasn't.' The cook grinned from ear to ear. 'We've got a lot to do today. I didn't want her nibs hanging about stickin' her nose in our business.'

'What did you do to Mrs Livingston-Graves?' Betsy asked as she dashed into the room. 'I just saw her on the stairs and she was positively green.'

'She's not well,' Mrs Jeffries replied. 'But that at least will serve to keep her out of our way today. Now, what are we all going to do?'

'Since I've aired them bloomin' linen cupboards,' Betsy said, picking up a teatowel and starting to dry the plates, 'I thought I'd slip back over to the Marlow house and see if I can find out anything else.'

'What are you going to do, Mrs Jeffries?' Smythe asked. He leaned against the doorway.

'Actually, I'm going to do some thinking,' she replied. 'There's something about this case that's been niggling me from the start. But I can't quite think what it is. Perhaps I should dust the drawing room. Mindless, repetitive activity frequently helps me to think better. Are you still planning on going to see what you can find out about Shelby Locke?'

The coachman shrugged. 'Might as well. I'm still not convinced he's innocent. Protectin' a woman you're in love with is a powerful motive for a man. And he's definitely crazy about Mrs Stanwick.'

Smythe fiddled with filling the coal bins until Mrs Jeffries, the feather duster neatly tucked under her arm, went upstairs. A moment later Mrs Goodge trotted off toward the cooling pantry, mumbling something about gooseberries.

He and Betsy were alone. He looked at her. She stood with her back to him, stacking dishes in the cupboard. Smythe silently took a long, deep breath and gathered his courage. He couldn't stand the way she'd been avoiding him since her outburst yesterday. It was as though she were shamed that he and the others had had a glimpse of her life, her past. At breakfast this morning she'd kept her head down, staring at her lap like it was a newspaper, and then bolted from the table the minute she'd finished one bloomin' cup of tea. She hadn't even tried to eat Mrs Goodge's homemade sausages. He wasn't havin' any of that.

What they shared together, all of 'em, was too precious. Betsy had no call to be embarrassed because she'd let something about herself slip out. And she should know them well enough to understand that there was nothin' in her past that would change the way he, or any of the others, felt about her. He was bloomin' tired of seein' her walk around with her eyes down and her shoulders hunched.

'Betsy,' he said softly. 'I'd like to talk to you, lass.'

'What about?' she asked, without turning around.

'About what 'appened last night.' He faltered, unsure of exactly what was the best way to say what he thought needed saying.

'I've already said I'm sorry for losin' my temper,' she said defensively.

He sighed. This wasn't going to be easy. 'Betsy, no one's lookin' for any apologies. I'm tryin' to tell ya we understand. I can tell you're still smartin' over it, and you've no need to. It's not like any of us 'asn't been . . . well, hard up a time or two in our lives.'

Slowly she turned and stared at him. 'It's nice of you to try and make me feel better, but I still feel a right fool. It were bloody obvious I was talkin' about myself.' She gave him a shaky smile. 'And it's embarrassing.'

'There's no shame in 'aving been poor,' he protested. 'You did the best you could. You 'ad to survive.'

She looked down at the floor. Blast and damn, he thought. I'm goin' about this all wrong. Maybe I shoulda kept my big mouth shut.

'So you don't think any less of me,' she murmured so quietly he almost didn't hear her.

He took a step closer. 'Not at all, lass. I'm just glad you're 'ere with us now.' He reached out a hand, intending to touch her shoulder, but he snatched it back quickly as they heard the pantry door crash against the hallway wall.

'I'm going to skin that boy alive when I get my hands on him!' Mrs Goodge cried as she charged into the kitchen. She stopped in surprise when she saw them. 'You two still here, then?'

'Who are you goin' to skin alive, Mrs Goodge?' Smythe asked, giving her a cocky grin.

'Wiggins, that's who! And when I'm finished with him, I might skin that ruddy Fred. They've been into them gooseberries again!'

★ ★ ★

'Mr Locke,' the inspector said politely. 'We'd like you to tell us again about your movements on the night of the ball.'

Locke arched an eyebrow. 'I've already told you. Rowena and I were together the whole time except for those few moments when I was in the library with Miss Marlow. For goodness' sake, do you want me to give you a blow-by-blow account of every step we took?'

'That would be most helpful, sir,' Barnes said politely.

'Don't be absurd!' Locke got up and began pacing the room. 'Is this inquisition necessary? Rowena's waiting for me in the drawing room. We're going out.'

The inspector sighed. He did so wish that people wouldn't persist in lying. It was so very demeaning. 'Mr Locke, we've had statements from several people who saw you leave the ballroom and go outside. Alone.'

Locke stopped in front of a balloon-back chair. 'Who told you that?'

'That isn't important. What is pertinent is that you weren't with Mrs Stanwick at the time of the murder and we can prove it.' Witherspoon stared him directly in the eye. 'Not only were you outside, but Mrs Stanwick was seen going upstairs after she'd had a rather heated argument with the murder victim. An argument, by the way, that was overheard by a witness.'

The colour drained out of Locke's face. For a moment he didn't say a word. 'Rowena didn't do it,' he finally said. 'I don't care what anyone says they saw or heard. She didn't like Hannah Greenwood but, for God's sake, she didn't kill her.'

'Mr Locke, why don't you sit down and tell us the truth?' the inspector suggested kindly. The man had gone so pale, Witherspoon was afraid he might faint. 'I'm sure we can clear this matter up very quickly once we have all the facts.'

'Facts?' He laughed harshly. 'What have facts to do with hatred?' Sighing wearily, he dropped into the chair. 'I'm not sure where to begin,' he said. 'I suppose everything began to go wrong when I asked Lucinda to come into the library with me. But you already know about that. What you don't know is that I wasn't discussing my missing notebook with Lucinda; I was telling her that I'd proposed to Rowena.' Locke closed his eyes briefly. 'I shouldn't have done it, you know. None of this would have happened if I hadn't left Rowena alone. That old witch couldn't have threatened her if she'd been with me.'

'By "old witch", I take it you're referring to Mrs Greenwood.' Witherspoon wanted everything crystal clear. Gracious, with these people, one never knew to whom they were referring unless one asked.

'Absolutely. And I don't care if she's dead,' Locke said angrily. 'She was an old witch. She couldn't wait to ruin Rowena's life.' He paused and brought himself under control. 'But that's not important now. I left Rowena alone in the ballroom, and I asked Miss Marlow to come into the library.'

'So you were in the library longer than you originally led us to believe?' Witherspoon asked.

'I'm afraid so,' he replied. 'You see, I didn't want to admit that I'd been away from Rowena for such a long period of time. I was actually talking to Miss Marlow for a good ten, perhaps fifteen minutes.'

'I take it Miss Marlow didn't take the news of your impending marriage very well,' the inspector suggested.

'No.' He shook his head. 'She was actually very kind about it. Wished me well and all that. But, dash it all, I was concerned about her, you see. I mean, she was saying all the right words, yet her expression was so very odd that I kept right on talking to her. I suppose it was guilt on my part – I did, at one time, have an understanding with Miss Marlow. Anyway, she finally insisted she had to get back to her guests, and we left the room.'

'So how did you come to be outside, sir?' Barnes asked.

'I went outside to get some fresh air.' Locke rose to his feet. 'Look at it from my point of view. I'd just behaved abominably to a lovely young woman, and she'd taken it with the best of grace. I was ashamed of myself. I wanted to get away where no one could see me and pull myself together.' He began pacing the room again. 'So I went down the hall, unbolted a side door and slipped outside.'

'How long were you out there?' Witherspoon asked.

'I didn't come back inside until after Mrs Greenwood was killed,' he said softly. 'After I'd been outside a few minutes, I tried to get back in, but someone had bolted the door on me. That side of the house leads off onto an alley, and the only way back in is to walk round to the front. It's a long walk, Inspector.'

'Where was Mrs Stanwick when you arrived back?'

'She was coming down the stairs.'

'And Mrs Greenwood was already dead.'

Locke nodded. 'But Rowena didn't kill her.'

'Did you see anyone else come down the stairs?' Witherspoon prodded. 'A number of people.' He flung his hands wide. 'They were all coming down to see what the commotion outside was about.'

Rowena Stanwick clutched Shelby Locke's hand. Her face was pale and her lovely eyes wide with fear. 'Shelby's telling the truth, Inspector. I saw him coming in the front door as I came down the stairs.'

'Do you admit you had an argument with Mrs Greenwood?' Witherspoon asked. 'And that she followed you upstairs?'

'Don't admit anything,' Locke told her. 'Don't say another word until we've talked to your solicitor.'

She shook her head. 'It's all right, Shelby. We don't need to send for Mr Borland yet.' She straightened her spine and looked at the two policemen sitting in front of her fireplace. 'We did have an argument. A vicious one. She was going to ruin me. She was going to tell everyone that her son, Douglas, had committed suicide because I'd refused to marry him.'

'Rowena, don't,' Locke pleaded.

'It's all right, darling,' she said, giving him a sad smile. 'I must tell the truth. I'm not afraid anymore.

Douglas Beecher didn't kill himself because of me. He had a terrible problem with alcohol. That's why I refused him. I'm not all that certain he committed suicide at all. When he was drunk, he did the most appalling things. Stepping in front of that train was most likely an accident. I'm sure of it.'

'But Mrs Greenwood was sure you were responsible,' Witherspoon said. 'And she threatened to tell the rest of the world – a scandal like that would have ruined you socially.'

'Yes,' she agreed, 'it would have. But I knew it wouldn't cost me the one thing that really mattered to me. Shelby's love.' She looked at him again.

'It hasn't,' he promised softly.

'So after the argument, you went upstairs,' the inspector prodded.

'Yes, I wanted to get away from her.' Rowena crossed her arms over her chest. 'She was half out of her mind that night. The things she said to me, it was unbelievable and very upsetting. When I realized I was losing control, I knew I had to get away from her. I went upstairs to the second floor.'

'Did you hear her behind you on the stairs?' Barnes asked.

'No. I'd no idea she was following me. All I wanted to do was to find a quiet place to calm down,' she explained. 'I was in tears and I didn't want Shelby to see me like that. So I hurried upstairs and popped into an empty bedroom. A few minutes later I splashed some cold water from the washbasin on my face and started down. By that time someone had murdered Mrs Greenwood. People were running about and shouting. I hurried downstairs to see what the commotion was, and that's when I saw Shelby coming in the front door.'

'Are you certain you went no further than the second floor?' Witherspoon asked. He wasn't sure what to make of her story. Dash it all, unless the lady was a superb actress, it sounded as though she were telling the truth.

'I'm certain.'

'Did anyone see you go into or come out of the bedroom?'

'No.' She smiled bitterly. 'Unfortunately. No one can verify my story. I was alone when I reached the top of the stairs. There was no one about. I didn't like Hannah Greenwood,' she said earnestly. 'But you've got to believe me, Inspector, I didn't kill the woman.'

Wiggins poked Hatchet in the side and pointed toward the row of tiny houses. 'Over there,' he whispered. 'There's someone movin' about in that passageway.'

Stealthily they scurried out from behind their hiding place behind a heavy wagon loaded with rubbish and dashed across the road. They heard the sound of feet again, in the narrow space between the last two houses. 'Go round the end,' Hatchet hissed, pointing toward the end of the road. 'Double back to the passageway. We can trap whoever's in there.'

'But what if it's not Jon? What'll we say?'

'Get on with it, Wiggins,' Hatchet snapped. Really, the lad was very good-hearted and all that, but sometimes he was a bit of a trial. 'If it's not Jon, then it's probably a cat and we won't have to say anything.'

Wiggins nodded and took off. Hatchet gave him what he hoped was enough time to complete the circuit before he moved to his end of the opening. The tiny space, barely wide enough for a broad-shouldered man to get through, was shrouded in deep shadows despite the afternoon sunlight.

Hatchet stepped inside. He heard a scrape, like a foot dragging against the ground. 'Jon,' he called out. 'If you're there, don't be afraid. We only want to talk to you. I promise you, no one's going to hurt you.'

There was no answer.

At the far end, he heard, rather than saw, Wiggins move into position. But the overhanging roof made the passage so dark he couldn't quite see. That, and the fact that his eyesight wasn't what it used to be. Squinting, he plunged farther inside.

Suddenly, he heard the hammering of footsteps as whoever it was made a run for it. Hatchet took off after them.

'Got you then, you little blighter!' Wiggins cried as a bundle of terrified boy exploded out of the passage and rammed into him hard enough to knock the wind out of him, but not hard enough to make him let go of the lad's arm.

Mrs Jeffries had dusted the furniture, polished the brass candlesticks on the mantel, and buffed the banister until it gleamed in the late afternoon sun, but she was no closer to a solution. This case was simply baffling. She had the horrible feeling that she was missing something but, for the life of her, she couldn't figure out what it was.

Placing her tin of Adam's furniture polish on the table, she sat down and stared blankly at the rows of copper pots hanging below the window.

Mrs Goodge had retired to her room to have a nap before dinner, and the rest of the staff was still out. She hoped they were having a better day than she was. She sighed and forced herself to go over everything one last time.

Hannah Greenwood had been viciously murdered by one of the other guests at the ball. There was no reason to believe a servant or an outsider had done the killing, because the victim was an isolated, lonely woman who didn't much care for people. She'd joined the circle only to have an opportunity to avenge her son's death.

Most of the members of the circle could account for their whereabouts at the time of the murder, so that let them out. Of the members that were left, the only ones that could have a reason to murder the victim were Dr Sloan and Rowena Stanwick. Unless, she reminded herself, you included Shelby Locke. But his motive would only be reasonable if he'd known that Mrs Greenwood planned on ruining Rowena Stanwick's reputation. And they had no evidence that he'd known anything of the kind. She made a mental note to talk to the inspector as soon as he came home.

Dr Sloan's motive was fairly weak. Or was it? He'd

confessed to being a plagiarist. Far less dangerous than confessing to murder. And, perhaps, far more clever.

Edgar Warburton. She made a face of distaste. Smythe had quietly told her the rest of the information he'd picked up about Warburton before breakfast this morning. She didn't much blame the coachman for not wanting to repeat what he'd heard in front of the rest of the household. Wiggins would have blushed to the roots of his hair. Warburton was obsessed with Rowena, enough so that he called other women by her name.

But if they believed Dulcie Willard, he did have an alibi for the time of the murder.

'Mrs Jeffries.'

Startled, she jerked her head around. 'Yes, Mrs Livingston-Graves. Is there something I can do for you?'

'Do you happen to have a stomach powder?' she asked, clutching her midsection. She staggered over to stand at the far end of the table. 'I'm a bit under the weather today.'

'I'm sorry you're not feeling better.' Trying to keep a straight face, Mrs Jeffries got up and went to the cupboard underneath the window. Rummaging around inside, she found a tin of Dinneford's Fluid Magnesia. 'I'm afraid this is the best I can do,' she said, holding it up.

Making a face, Mrs Livingston-Graves reached for the medicine. She suddenly looked up at the window and gasped. 'Oh, no, it's Mr Freeley. He's not supposed to be here until tomorrow. Oh, dear, I can't receive him now!'

221

Mrs Jeffries peeked around Mrs Livingston-Graves and saw the back of a man paying off a hansom driver. 'Would you like me to tell him you're indisposed?' she asked.

The man turned around.

'Thank God.' Mrs Livingston-Graves breathed a heartfelt sigh of relief. 'It's not Mr Freeley. But from the back, it certainly looked like him. I must get back to bed – I don't want to be ill tomorrow. Mr Freeley is escorting me to the Royal Procession.' Clutching the tin to her scrawny bosom, she hurried from the kitchen, muttering to herself with every step.

Mrs Jeffries shook her head. Considering the state their houseguest was in yesterday, it was a wonder the woman had any notion of what this Mr Freeley looked like.

At dinner that night the inspector told Mrs Jeffries about his meeting with Shelby Locke and Rowena Stanwick. 'So you see,' he finished, 'Mrs Stanwick does not have an alibi at all.'

'Neither does Mr Locke,' Mrs Jeffries pointed out.

'I'm afraid he does,' the inspector replied. 'After we talked to both of them, Barnes and I checked with the carriage and hansom drivers who were outside the Marlow house that night. One of the drivers remembers seeing him.'

'The driver is sure it was Shelby Locke?'

'Oh, yes, he knew Mr Locke on sight, you see. He'd driven Mr Locke and Mrs Stanwick to the ball earlier.' Witherspoon crumbled his napkin and tossed it next to his plate. 'He also drove them home that night. He said Mrs Stanwick was in an awful state.'

'Are you going to arrest her?' Mrs Jeffries asked. She held her breath.

'I'm afraid I may have to,' he replied softly. 'Though, I must admit, I tend to believe she's telling the truth. At the very least I'll have to bring her in tomorrow to answer some more questions.'

'But tomorrow's the Jubilee and the Royal Procession.'

'That makes no difference.' He smiled sadly. 'Nothing, not even a celebration of Her Majesty's ascension to the throne, is more important than justice.'

His words would have sounded pompous, but Mrs Jeffries knew he sincerely meant them. She sat back in her chair and tried to think. She could quite understand the inspector's reasoning, but something was bothering her. Something that was probably right in front of her but she couldn't see it. She glanced up and saw Betsy standing in the doorway of the dining room, waving frantically. 'Excuse me, sir,' she said, getting to her feet.

Betsy jerked her head toward the hall. 'Hatchet and Wiggins is back,' she hissed as soon as they were out of earshot. 'They've got Jon with them, and they want to speak to the inspector.'

'Goodness.' Mrs Jeffries frowned. 'That could cause all sorts of problems.'

'Hatchet's got it all figured out. He's goin' to send Jon round to the front door. Jon's goin' to claim he come to see the inspector 'cause he heard he was an honest copper. The boy won't let on he's talked to any of us,' she said quickly. 'Is that all right with you?'

'Fine,' Mrs Jeffries replied. 'Send the boy around. I'll get the inspector into the drawing room.'

Jon stared suspiciously at Witherspoon. He hoped them toffs wasn't havin' him on. If he ended up in Coldbath Fields or Newgate, he'd be right narked. Mind you, they'd done all right by him so far. Filled his belly with a hot meal before they begun askin' all their questions and that white-haired gent 'ad promised him work.

'Now, young man,' Witherspoon began. 'My housekeeper says you're here to see me about the murder of Mrs Greenwood. Is that correct?'

'That's right,' Jon replied. He'd been well coached on exactly what to say. 'I come here instead of goin' down to the station 'cause I heard you was a good copper. Not like some of them others. I don't like havin' anythin' to do with the police, not if I can 'elp it. But I've heard about you, and I reckoned this might be important.'

The inspector smiled at the boy. He was really quite flattered. Gracious, perhaps he was becoming a tad famous. 'Finding Mrs Greenwood's murderer is important,' he said. 'And you did right to come to me. But really, my boy, you've no reason to fear the police. We're here for your protection.'

Jon grinned. The bloke looked like he actually believed what he said.

'Now' – Witherspoon waved at the settee – 'do sit

down.' He waited until the boy had seated himself. 'What is it you want to tell me?'

'It's about Mrs Greenwood,' he began. 'About her gettin' herself done in. I were there that night.'

'There,' the inspector echoed, looking confused. 'Where?'

'At the Marlow house,' Jon explained. He hoped he didn't muck this up. This was goin' to be the tricky part. Tellin' the copper what he'd seen without tellin' him why he was hidin' up them stairs. 'You see, I worked for Mrs Greenwood. She always took me with her when she went out anywhere.'

'Why did she do that?' he asked curiously.

Jon shrugged. 'Who the bloody hell knows? I think she were half crazy. But I'm tellin' the truth. If'n you don't believe me, you can ask Mrs Hackshaw, that's her sister. She'll tell you.'

'I didn't say I didn't believe you,' the inspector said hastily. 'It's just that's a very odd thing to do.'

'I think she wanted company,' Jon said. 'Not that she ever talked that much. Anyways, like I was sayin', she took me with her all the time when she went out.'

'Did you accompany her to Dr Sloan's rooms on the day of the ball?' he asked.

'Yeah, I did.' Jon scratched his nose. 'Even for her, she were in a strange way that day. Kept mumblin' to herself about vengeance and justice and how she'd have 'em both. By the time she come out of the old gent's rooms, her eyes were all bright and shiny like, and she were laughin' her bloomin' head off. Scared me some, I can tell you.'

'Yes, I'm sure it did.'

'Like I said, she took me with her, even to that ruddy ball,' Jon continued. 'She got out of the carriage, then she told me to stay close 'cause she wouldn't be stayin' too long. Give me strict instructions to be in front of the house at half past ten.'

'Half past ten,' the inspector murmured.

'Right. Now it get's a bit borin', hangin' about on the streets, so I nipped round and slipped in the kitchen door.' He flushed in embarrassment and stared down at the carpet. 'Sometimes the cooks or one of the maids will slip me a bit of food, and well . . . I was hungry.'

'Of course you were, my boy,' Witherspoon said kindly. 'No one can fault you for wanting a bite to eat. Why, I've done that sort of thing myself when I was a lad of your age.'

Jon looked up sharply. He couldn't imagine this gentleman ever bein' cold or hungry. But maybe he was wrong. Maybe the bloke did understand. 'They was all busy in the kitchen; no one even noticed I were there.' He didn't add that he'd deliberately ducked behind a table and hotfooted it up the back stairs.

Jon cleared his throat to give himself a moment to think. He had to say this part just right. Nice bloke or not, this gent was still a copper. 'Anyways, like I said, I was right hungry. Mrs Greenwood were on the stingy side, there were never enough food round there, and all I'd had for me dinner was a bit of hard beef and bread.'

Witherspoon clucked his tongue. Really, the way

some people treated their servants. It was an absolute disgrace! 'I'm sure you were dreadfully hungry,' he said sympathetically.

He nodded. 'They was so busy in the kitchen, I didn't think they'd take kindly to me botherin' them for something to eat, so I nipped up the back stairs . . . I'd been there before, you see, and I was hopin' there might be some food in the pantry.'

'Yes, yes, I quite understand.'

'There was.' Jon grinned. 'And there was no one in there, either, so I helped meself to a couple of rolls and some ham, slapped 'em together like. Then I heard footsteps comin' and, well, I didn't want anyone to see me helpin' meself to the food, so I left and scampered up the back stairs to the second story. There's a nice little nook up there that's covered by a long curtain. I hid myself away and ate.'

'How long were you up there?'

Jon knew he was on thin ice here. He'd spent a good two hours upstairs. But he could hardly explain his activities to the police. 'Well,' he said hesitantly, 'I don't rightly know. There was lots of people comin' and goin'. And then a couple walked by, they was gigglin' and. . . . well, I think they was kissin'. They come right up to where I was hid. I was afraid they was going to open the curtain and see me. But at the last second someone called out to 'em and they left. But I knew I'd better not hang about where I was. So I waited till there was no one about and I nipped up to the next floor.'

'So now you're on the third floor,' Witherspoon stated, trying to keep everything straight in his mind.

'Right,' Jon said. 'I was tired by this time, so I tucked meself away in a corner behind the stairs and kept my eyes and ears open. It got tirin' after a while, even though I could see the floor below if I peeked over the side. I was there for a long time. Finally, when I thought it might be gettin' close to half past, I figured I'd better scarper. Mrs Greenwood would be madder than a skinned cat if I was late. I was just gettin' out of me hiding place when all of a sudden, here she comes up the stairs. For a minute I thought I'd been found out and she was up there to tear a strip off me. But she didn't even look at me, kept right on goin', a funny look on her face.'

'She continued up the stairs?' Witherspoon clarified. 'Is that correct?'

'That's right. I wondered where she were goin'. Wasn't nothing up there but the attic and a box room, but that's where she went all right. A minute or two later I heard more footsteps. By this time I'd come out from behind the staircase, and I didn't reckon I could make it back before whoever was comin' up those stairs saw me, so I flattened myself behind a set of curtains over the window at the end of the hall and prayed that whoever it was wouldn't see me feet.'

'And who did you see coming up the stairs?' the inspector asked quietly.

'A pretty lady in a blue dress. She were carrying a knife.'

CHAPTER ELEVEN

THE DAY OF the Jubilee dawned clear and beautiful. Mrs Jeffries smiled as she pulled open the drawing room curtains and let the sunshine fill the room. She still wasn't certain about this case; that tiny niggle at the back of her mind refused to go away.

And she didn't understand why. Jon's statement had made it quite clear that Rowena Stanwick was the killer. Why, even the inspector had remembered Mrs Stanwick's spectacular blue gown. She shook herself. Really, she must be getting old and fanciful. A smidgen of doubt hovering in the corner of one's mind was no substitute for facts.

And besides, she told herself, as she started for the kitchen, once Jon got a good look at Mrs Stanwick today, all her concerns would be laid to rest. The boy had no reason to lie.

She smiled again as she recalled the adroit manoeuvres of last night. Her staff had done her proud. Just as the inspector was wondering where to put Jon for the night, Hatchet, as planned, had shown up. Upon hearing of the inspector's dilemma, he'd immediately volunteered to take the lad home with him. As he'd said to Inspector Witherspoon, 'It wouldn't do for the defence counsel to find out the Crown's only eyewitness was living with the policeman who solved the case.'

Actually, Mrs Jeffries thought as she marched down the back stairs to the kitchen, she didn't see what difference it made where the boy stayed. But the inspector had seemed to think Hatchet was correct, and Jon had gone off quite happily.

In the kitchen Betsy and Mrs Goodge were sitting at the table, drinking tea.

'Is Smythe back yet?' Mrs Jeffries asked.

'Not yet,' Betsy replied. 'It might take him longer than usual. The streets are packed with people. You can barely move out there. All the main roads are closed because of the Royal Procession.' She frowned. 'I hope he doesn't have any trouble gettin' back. I won't really be able to enjoy myself today unless this case is solved.'

'Don't worry about Smythe,' Mrs Goodge said. 'He'll not have any problem gettin' through the mob. He knows this city like the back of his hand. He'll not need the main roads. The man knows every back street and mews from here to Liverpool Street.'

'I hope you're right, Mrs Goodge.' Mrs Jeffries cast a worried glance at the kitchen clock. 'Hatchet and Jon are due here in a few minutes.'

As it would be impossible for the inspector to find a hansom today, considering the number of people clogging the streets of the West End, Smythe had volunteered to bring round the inspector's carriage and drive him and Jon to Rowena Stanwick's home. Naturally, the inspector had protested, not wanting his coachman to have to work on a day the rest of London was celebrating. But Smythe had assured him he didn't mind in the least.

'Are they goin' to take Jon straight to Mrs Stanwick's house, then?' Betsy asked. 'To see if he can identify her?'

'That's the plan.'

'Mrs Jeffries!' Mrs Livingston-Graves's voice screeched down the stairs. 'Could you come up here, please?'

'Right away, Mrs Livingston-Graves.' Rolling her eyes, she got to her feet.

'She's got no call to be orderin' you about like that,' Betsy mumbled resentfully.

'At least she said please,' Mrs Goodge put in mildly.

'Not to worry,' the housekeeper replied cheerfully as she hurried toward the door. 'Her Mr Freeley should be here soon, and she'll be out of our way for the rest of the day.' She paused in the doorway. 'Let's hope that today she can recognize the man.'

Betsy and Mrs Goodge laughed.

'What took you so long?' Mrs Livingston-Graves whined as soon as Mrs Jeffries appeared at the top of the steps. 'Mr Freeley will be here any minute, and I can't get these silly buttons done up.' She lifted her arms, revealing the unbuttoned sleeves.

'Let me help you,' Mrs Jeffries said. Deftly she pushed the tiny black buttons through the grey fabric. 'There,' she said, 'you're all done. And I believe I hear footsteps coming up the front stairs now.'

'Answer the door, then,' Mrs Livingston-Graves ordered. She stepped back and smoothed her skirts.

There was a timid knock. Mrs Jeffries threw open the front door. Before her eyes stood a short, rabbitty-faced man in spectacles wearing a brown bowler hat, brown suit, and carrying an umbrella. 'Good morning. I'd like to see Mrs Livingston-Graves.' He smiled hesitantly.

'Please come in,' Mrs Jeffries said politely, 'and I'll announce you.' As Mrs Livingston-Graves had dashed into the drawing room, Mrs Jeffries had to go get her. 'Your escort is here,' she said formally.

Nose held high, Edwina Livingston-Graves waltzed into the hall. She stopped dead, her small eyes blinking in surprise. 'Mr Freeley?'

He smiled broadly. 'Edwina,' he said, 'how delightful to see you again. But I did ask you to call me Harold. My, don't you look lovely today.'

Mrs Jeffries wondered if he needed new spectacles. She also wondered exactly how much Mrs Livingston-Graves had had to drink before she made Mr Freeley's acquaintance.

Hatchet and Jon arrived a few minutes later. Mrs Jeffries had started up the stairs to get the inspector when Smythe burst into the room.

'Somethin' funny is goin' on at the Stanwick house,' he said without preamble. 'And I think the inspector ought to hear about it.'

'Hear about what?' Witherspoon asked as he strolled into the kitchen.

Smythe shot Mrs Jeffries a quick, hard look. 'Well,

sir. I were on my way back from the livery with the coach, and I had to pass by the Stanwick place. I saw the oddest thing — that Mr Locke were at her front door, arguin' with the maid.'

'You saw all this from the coach?' Witherspoon asked in confusion.

'No, sir,' he admitted, shooting another uncertain glance at the housekeeper. 'I, uh . . . uh . . .'

'Oh, it's all right, Smythe.' The inspector smiled. 'I know how you and the rest of the staff are always looking after my interests. It's quite all right for you to admit you stopped the coach and did a bit of snooping.'

Mrs Jeffries held her breath. Gracious, had the inspector cottoned on to what they'd been doing?

'That's right, sir,' Smythe replied. 'That's exactly what I did. A bit of snoopin', as you call it.' He took a deep breath and plunged ahead. 'I overheard the maid tellin' Mr Locke that Mrs Stanwick weren't at home. The maid said Mrs Stanwick had just left; she'd gotten a message sayin' there was an emergency meetin' of the Hyde Park Literary Circle.'

'Gracious!'

'Mr Locke got right angry. Said 'e was a member of the circle and 'e 'adn't 'ad any message.'

'Where was this meeting to take place?' Mrs Jeffries asked.

'At the Marlow house.'

Mrs Jeffries saw Betsy start in surprise.

'Oh, dear,' the inspector murmured. 'This does complicate matters.'

'What are they talkin' about, guv?' Jon said

to Hatchet. 'I thought I was goin' to identify the woman that come up them stairs,'

'That's right, boy,' Hatchet replied, throwing Mrs Jeffries a rather puzzled look. 'And so you will. But I do believe we may have to postpone that for an hour or two. At least until the inspector decides what he wants to do.'

'I say' – Witherspoon shook his head – 'this is getting muddled.' Dash it all, what should he do now? He couldn't go haring all over London looking for Rowena Stanwick. Goodness knows where the woman had gone. There was no point in sending a message to the Yard, either. With the mobs of people in town for the Jubilee, it would be pointless for the uniformed lads to even try spotting her at the train stations or the coach houses. Drat.

'All right,' Jon muttered. 'I don't mind waitin'.'

Betsy rose and went into the hall. Mrs Jeffries went after her. 'Mrs Jeffries,' the maid whispered. 'Something's wrong. Very wrong.'

'What do you mean?' Mrs Jeffries had great respect for the maid's intelligence and even greater respect for her instincts.

'There can't be any emergency meetin' at the Marlow house,' Betsy said earnestly. 'Rupert told me yesterday that Miss Marlow was givin' them all the day off. A woman like her don't have guests round unless there's a house full of servants to wait on 'em.'

'But why would Rowena Stanwick . . .' Mrs Jeffries suddenly stopped. A vision of Mrs Livingston-Graves standing in front of the kitchen window flashed into her mind. The last puzzle piece fell into place, 'Oh, Lord,' she exclaimed. 'We've got it all wrong.'

Turning, she dashed back into the kitchen. They all looked at her in surprise. 'Jon,' she said, 'what colour hair did the lady have, the one coming up the stairs with the knife?'

Jon, who was reaching for one of Mrs Goodge's currant buns, snatched his hand back when he heard his name. 'Huh?'

'I asked what colour the lady's hair was?'

'Brown,' he said promptly. 'She had brown hair.'

'But that can't be right,' Witherspoon exclaimed. 'Mrs Stanwick has fair hair.' He stared at Jon. 'Are you absolutely certain?'

Jon nodded and snatched up a bun. 'Course I am. I'd a told you last night, but no one asked.'

Smythe cracked the whip in the air and urged the horses down the narrow mews. Blast, they'd never make it to the Marlow house in time, and he had a bad feelin' about this one. Real bad.

'Do hurry, Smythe,' Witherspoon called from below.

'We're almost there!' he yelled back. He pulled the reins hard, guiding the animals round a sharp corner and onto the small road that connected with the mews behind the Marlow house.

Smythe set the brake and jumped down. 'This is as close as we can get,' he said, jerking open the door. 'There's too much traffic out front to get through, so we'll have to go round.'

Witherspoon, Hatchet and Wiggins, accompanied

by Fred, jumped out of the carriage. They raced down the road.

When they arrived at the front of the Marlow house, Witherspoon was breathless, Hatchet was red in the face, and Fred was barking his head off.

'Stay outside with Fred,' the inspector told the footman. 'Hatchet, you and Smythe come with me.'

Wiggins nodded and quieted the dog while the inspector banged the brass knocker hard against the wood. From inside they heard a scream.

'Egads!' Frantically Witherspoon tried the doorknob. It was locked.

Smythe shoved the inspector out of the way. 'Let me 'ave a go at it,' he said, bashing his shoulder against the door. He winced in pain, but the door didn't budge.

'This way,' Hatchet called. 'You'll never get through that door. It's solid mahogany.'

They whirled around and saw Hatchet shove a booted foot through the front window. From inside the screams started again. Fred started barking again.

Within seconds they'd kicked the glass out of the way and climbed inside. The screams were louder now, frantic.

Running, fearing the worst, the three men charged for the drawing room. Smythe had no trouble shouldering that door open as he hurtled himself into the room, the others right behind him.

He came to a screeching halt at what he saw. Behind him, Witherspoon and Hatchet froze.

Lucinda Marlow had a knife to Rowena Stanwick's throat.

'Don't come any closer,' she warned.

'Now, now, Miss Marlow,' the inspector said gently. 'We don't want anyone to get hurt, do we?'

Lucinda laughed and jerked her captive's head back farther. 'Of course we do, you stupid fool. That's why I've got a knife.'

Smythe looked helplessly at Hatchet. The inspector didn't dare take his eyes off that awful knife. He tried again, 'Miss Marlow—'

'Shut up,' she ordered, pushing the blade harder against her victim's throat. 'Just shut up and let me think.'

Rowena whimpered and, without moving, pleaded with her eyes for the inspector to save her. 'Please,' she moaned. 'Let me go.'

'I told you to be quiet,' Lucinda snapped. 'This is all your fault. You should have already been dead.' She yanked Rowena's head back farther and dug the blade in deeper against the woman's throat.

Rowena screamed.

Witherspoon didn't know what to do. He couldn't stand and watch a helpless woman be murdered before his eyes.

Suddenly Fred burst into the room, barking his head off.

Lucinda Marlow yelped in surprise and tightened her grip on Rowena's hair. Rowena screamed again. The confused dog, sensing that something was terribly wrong and not knowing what it was, lunged at the two women.

The knife went flying in the air as they fell backwards. Hatchet slammed his foot down on the blade seconds after it clattered on the floor. Smythe leapt across the settee and made a grab for Rowena Stanwick. The inspector, who'd never mishandled a female in his life, wished he were anywhere else but here, did his duty, and pounced on Lucinda Marlow. He didn't really have to do much, though. Fred had already taken care of her.

Sitting on her chest, he wagged his tail as he licked her face.

'Cor blimey,' Wiggins said from the doorway. 'I'm sorry about Fred, but he heard the screams and I couldn't hold him back. He thought somethin' was happenin' to the inspector.'

'How did you know it were Lucinda Marlow?' Mrs Goodge asked as soon as everyone but Witherspoon had returned. Poor Witherspoon had arrested Lucinda Marlow. He was going to spend the rest of Jubilee Day taking statements and filling out forms.

'I didn't know until Betsy mentioned that Miss Marlow had given her servants the day off.' Mrs Jeffries pushed the plate of cakes down the table to Jon.

'How did that make you realize what was goin' on?' Betsy asked. 'The inspector give us the day off.'

'Yes, but the inspector is a very rare sort of human being.' She picked up her teacup. 'As I said from the start, something about this case bothered me. Yesterday, when Mrs Livingston-Graves saw that man get out of the hansom cab, she thought it was Mr Freeley. As soon as he turned around, she realized her mistake.' She looked at Betsy. 'When you told

238

me that Lucinda Marlow had given everyone the day off, everything fell into place.'

'I still don't get it,' Wiggins mumbled.

'It's very simple,' Mrs Jeffries explained. 'So simple that none of us understood until it was too late. Hannah Greenwood was never the intended victim. She was murdered by mistake.'

'Mistake?' Smythe mumbled.

'Lucinda Marlow murdered the wrong woman. Rowena Stanwick told the inspector the truth,' Mrs Jeffries continued. 'She hadn't gone up that second flight of stairs. But Lucinda Marlow didn't know that – remember, she'd seen Rowena go upstairs, and that gave her the perfect opportunity. She followed her, went all the way to the balcony at the very top, shoved the knife in her back and toppled her over.'

'But she didn't kill Mrs Stanwick,' Smythe said.

'But she didn't know that until it was too late.' Mrs Jeffries smiled. 'All she saw was a slender blond woman in a blue dress going upstairs. Miss Marlow has very poor eyesight.'

'That's right!' Betsy exclaimed. 'Rupert told me she wears spectacles when there's no one about.'

'It's a wonder we figured it out at all.' Annoyed with herself for being so dense, Mrs Jeffries shook her head in disgust. 'It was so obvious from the start. From the moment we learned that Shelby Locke's poems had been stolen, we should have known.'

'Huh?' This from Mrs Goodge.

'Don't you see?' Mrs Jeffries explained. 'We've been looking at it backwards from the beginning. Mrs Greenwood was never the intended victim. All along, it was Rowena Stanwick. I think Miss Marlow started planning to murder Mrs Stanwick from the moment she realized she'd lost Shelby Locke forever.'

'But the murder weren't planned,' Smythe pointed out. 'Or if it were, it were right messy.'

'The actual crime itself wasn't planned,' Mrs Jeffries said, 'but I think from the moment Miss Marlow realized Locke was genuinely in love with Rowena Stanwick, she'd planned to kill her. Look at it this way. Locke told Miss Marlow of his intentions that night in the library. According to what Locke said, she took it very well – she should have, she'd had plenty of time to prepare herself. They leave the library, and she watches Shelby let himself out the door at the end of the hallway. Then, from her vantage point somewhere in the dining room, she sees Rowena stumble into the buffet table and go upstairs.'

'But wouldn't she have seen Mrs Greenwood following Mrs Stanwick?' Hatchet asked.

'No, you see, she wanted to make sure she had some time alone with Mrs Stanwick, and the one person liable to disturb them was Shelby Locke. So she hurried down the hall and rebolted the door. It was at this point that Mrs Greenwood started up the stairs. But Miss Marlow couldn't have seen that. She hurries back and starts up – but she doesn't realize that Mrs Stanwick has ducked into a bedroom on the second floor. All she sees is a blond-haired woman in a blue dress going up to the third floor.' She paused. 'Of course, you know the rest.'

'But how did she get downstairs so quick after she done the murder?' Wiggins asked.

'The back stairs,' Mrs Jeffries replied. 'Once the commotion started, all the servants had run outside to see what was going on. Miss Marlow had a clear run at it. She dashed down, rushed out onto the terrace, and it was at this point that she realized she killed the wrong woman.'

The inspector didn't get home until late that night. Betsy, Smythe, Wiggins and Jon had gone out with Hatchet to see the lights and decorations. After that the butler was treating them all to a late supper. No one had seen hide nor hair of Mrs Livingston-Graves, but Mrs Jeffries refused to worry about the woman or to say anything to the inspector. From the look of him, he'd had a very trying day.

Mrs Jeffries placed a cup of cocoa in front of him as he sat glumly at the kitchen table. 'There, sir. This ought to help revive your spirits.'

'Thank you, Mrs Jeffries, but I'm not sure anything can revive me.' He took a sip and closed his eyes briefly. 'She's quite mad, you know. She kept telling us over and over that she had to kill her.'

'Was it jealousy, sir?'

'No,' he replied. 'Some may call it that, but it was really madness.' He toyed with the handle of his mug. 'Do you know, I couldn't quite get her to understand that she'd killed the wrong person. That her first victim had been Mrs Greenwood and not Mrs Stanwick. But she wouldn't believe it; she kept insisting that Mrs Stanwick, Rowena, as she called her, wouldn't stay dead.'

'She sounds quite mad.'

'She is.' The inspector sighed. 'But I doubt she'll stand trial. Her solicitors are already working on her case. The family stepped in immediately, of course. They don't want any scandal. I finally asked her: I said, "Miss Marlow, surely you didn't think you'd get away with murder. You were bound to get caught." Do you know what she replied? She gave me this very bizarre smile, it was as though she could see right through me, and said, "Why should I think they'd catch me? They never did before."'

It was several days before the household settled back into its normal routine. Mrs Livingston-Graves had crept back to Upper Edmonton Gardens in the wee hours of Jubilee Day. She and Alphonse left for home the next morning. No one was sorry to see either of them go.

Mrs Jeffries and Mrs Goodge were in the kitchen making a provisions list when Betsy burst into the room. 'Look at this!' she cried, putting a bright gold coin on the table. 'Someone's left it on my pillow.'

'I got one, too,' the cook said.

'As did I,' Mrs Jeffries added. She picked up the coin. 'It's a Jubilee sovereign,' she explained, 'newly minted. See, here's the date, 1887. Someone wanted us to have a souvenir.'

'Did everyone get one?' Betsy asked.

'One what?' Wiggins asked as he and Smythe entered the room. Fred trotted along behind them.

'One of these.' Betsy showed him the coin.

'Found it on me pillow this mornin',' Wiggins answered.

'Me, too.' The coachman sat down next to Mrs Jeffries.

The teakettle began to whistle, and Betsy and Mrs Goodge made tea.

'I wonder who give these to us?' Betsy said. 'Do you think it was Mrs Livingston-Graves?'

'Not bloomin' likely,' Smythe replied.

Mrs Jeffries looked doubtful. 'I shouldn't think so, Betsy. Mrs Livingston-Graves didn't strike me as a particularly generous soul.'

'Maybe it was Hatchet,' the cook guessed. 'He's a right kind-hearted man. Look at the way he took Jon in and give him a position.'

'Wonder what Luty Belle will think of that.' Smythe grinned.

'We can ask her herself in a few moments,' Mrs Jeffries said, nodding her head toward the back door. 'That sounds like her coach pulling up now.'

A few moments later Luty Belle, loaded down with gaily wrapped packages and followed by a grinning Hatchet, charged into the kitchen of Upper Edmonton Gardens. 'I'm downright mad at the bunch of you!' she exclaimed, dumping the packages on the table. 'But seein' as I brung this stuff thousands of miles, I'll give it to you anyways.'

'Why, Luty, whatever is the matter?' Mrs Jeffries asked.

'Madam is rather annoyed that in her absence we investigated a murder,' Hatchet explained with a smirk.

'The minute my back's turned,' Luty grumbled, giving Betsy a quick hug, 'someone gets themselves murdered and I miss it!'

She cuffed a grinning Wiggins on the ear and patted Mrs Goodge on the hand. Smythe laughed and scooped the elderly American woman up in a bear hug. Luty snickered, caught herself having fun and sobered instantly. 'Put me down, you sneakin' varmint. I knows you all did it a purpose. Couldn't wait till I was gone so you could start havin' a good time.'

She glared at the smug smile on her butler's face. 'And you can wipe that gloat off yer face, Hatchet,' she called as Smythe released her and she swung into a chair next to Mrs Jeffries.

'I'm not gloating, Madam,' Hatchet replied.

Luty snorted. 'Stop lying, man. You'll grow warts on yer tongue. But enough of this. Now you all open them presents I brung you, and then you tell me every single thing. Just 'cause I weren't here don't mean I don't want to know everything.'

Laughing and chatting, they did as she ordered.

Mrs Jeffries opened her box first. 'Why, Luty, this is magnificent,' she said. 'How very kind of you.' She drew a pair of binoculars out of the box and held them up. 'And they'll be so very useful.'

'That's why I brung 'em for ya.' Luty chuckled. 'They's the best kind made, not like them piddly little opera glasses. Considerin' all the snoopin' you do on the inspector's cases, I figured they might come in handy. Bought myself a pair, too.'

Mrs Jeffries appeared stunned. 'I don't know what to say. These must have been dreadfully expensive . . .'

'Pish-posh,' Luty snapped. 'Just say thank you and leave it at that. Betsy, girl, you open yours now.'

Betsy tore the paper off the rather large box, popped open the lid and gasped. 'It's a travelling bag!' she cried, pulling the brown leather case out.

'Well, open it up,' Luty ordered.

Betsy sprung the catches. 'Look at this! It's got everythin' in it.' Carefully she drew out the removable centre. 'Ivory brushes, soap box, toothbrush box, glove stretchers – goodness Luty, it's got bloomin' everything in it. Oh, thank you, thank you so much.'

Luty acknowledged her thanks with a wave. 'Your turn, Mrs Goodge.'

The cook opened her package and let out a squeal. She held up a watch and shiny gold chain. 'It's a lady's watch and a Victoria chain. Oh, really, Luty, I shouldn't accept this . . .'

'Pish-posh,' Luty said again. 'What's the good of havin' money if I can't spend it on my friends? I bought that watch in New York, and you're danged well gonna enjoy it.'

'Can I open mine now?' Wiggins asked, clutching his package.

At Luty's nod he ripped open the box. 'Cor blimey!' he cried, drawing out a pair of shiny black boots. There was elaborate engraving on the leather.

'Those are cowboy boots,' Luty told him. 'And I had to guess about the size, so you'd best try 'em on.'

Smythe opened his last. He tossed the lid to one side and his eyes widened.

'Well, show us,' Betsy ordered as he continued to stare at the contents of the box.

Slowly, holding his breath, he drew out the gun and held it up.

'Don't worry,' Luty said, 'it's not loaded.'

'Blimey, Luty Belle,' he muttered with a wide smile, 'you sure know how to surprise a bloke.'

'It's a Colt .45,' Luty said chattily. 'I picked it up in Colorado. Thought you might like it. Hatchet said he'd be glad to teach you how to use it.'

'I know how to use it,' Smythe replied as he studied the weapon. 'But thanks for the offer.' He glanced up and faltered as he saw all of them staring at him.

'You know how to use that weapon?' Mrs Jeffries queried softly.

'Well,' he sputtered. 'Not very well. But I did use one a time or two when I was in Australia.'

'I didn't know you was ever in Australia,' Betsy said hastily. 'How come you never said anything?'

Smythe was quite sure he'd already said way too much. Mrs Jeffries had been giving him funny looks all morning. Maybe buyin' them sovereigns hadn't been such a good idea. But blast, he'd wanted them all to have a remembrance. And them sovereigns was worth a pretty penny, enough so that Betsy wouldn't ever have to feel destitute again. She'd have a little somethin' to hang on to if he weren't around to look after her.

'All right, now that you've had your presents,' Luty ordered, settling back in her chair, 'tell me all about this latest murder.'

Mrs Jeffries, after giving Smythe one last puzzled glance, did just that.

When she'd finished, Luty shook her head. 'Sounds like you all did a right fine job. Did the inspector ever find out what Lucinda Marlow meant, you know what I mean, when she claimed the police hadn't ever caught her before?'

Mrs Jeffries shook her head. 'No. Right after she made those statements, she . . . well, she stopped talking.'

'Faking bein' crazy?' Luty suggested.

'I don't think she's fakin',' Smythe put in. 'The woman's as mad as a march hare.'

'The inspector did tell me that they suspect Lucinda Marlow may have murdered her brother,' Mrs Jeffries explained. 'She was nursing him when he died. He spoke to the Marlow physician. The doctor admits he was surprised when the Marlow son died, because he'd been on the mend. Right before he'd become ill, he and Lucinda had had a terrible row over some young man. He'd ordered her not to see him again. Then he died. Lucinda did as she pleased. But whether she murdered her brother or not, no one will ever know.'

Luty shrugged. 'I reckon we won't. Still, I'm sorry I missed it.'

'You don't mind about Jon?' Betsy asked quickly. 'I mean, this is twice now you've had to take on more staff because of one of our cases.'

Once before, Luty had taken on a young girl and given her a position because of her involvement in one of the inspector's murder investigations.

'Essie Tuttle's worked out real well,' Luty replied.

Hatchet snorted.

'Course she drives Hatchet crazy,' the American cackled with glee. 'She does love talkin' about books and politics.'

'It was your idea that I teach Essie to read,' he complained. 'So you've only yourself to blame if the girl becomes an anarchist.'

'Fiddlesticks. She ain't no anarchist. Essie just likes a good argument.' She grinned wickedly. 'And Hatchet's her favourite target. He bein' such a fan of the established order and the monarchy. But as long as this Jon don't get a case of sticky fingers, we'll get by just fine. He seems a smart boy.'

'That's very good of you, Luty,' Mrs Jeffries said.

'Well, like I said, I'm right sorry to have missed everything,' Luty said. 'Course none of you are to blame. It's all her fault.'

'Whose? Hannah Greenwood, the victim?' Mrs Jeffries asked. 'But she didn't plan on getting murdered.'

'Who said anything about Hannah Greenwood!' Luty exclaimed. 'I'm talking about Queen Victoria. It was her danged Jubilee that sent me running for the hills. Well, never again. This is the last time I'm going to miss me a murder.'

This book is lovingly dedicated
to the memory of Doris Annie Arguile